The Secrets of Eastby End

ANNA JACOBS

The Secrets of Eastby End

Eastby End Saga Book Two

HODDER &
STOUGHTON

First published in Great Britain in 2025 by Hodder & Stoughton Limited
An Hachette UK company

The authorised representative in the EEA is Hachette Ireland, 8 Castlecourt
Centre, Dublin 15, D15 XTP3, Ireland (email: info@hbgi.ie)

1

A CIP catalogue record for this title is available from the British Library

Hardback ISBN 978 1 399 72997 0
Trade Paperback ISBN 978 1 399 72999 4
ebook ISBN 978 1 399 72998 7

Typeset in Plantin Light by Manipal Technologies Limited

Printed and bound in Great Britain by Clays Ltd, Elcograf S.p.A.

Hodder & Stoughton policy is to use papers that are natural, renewable and recyclable
products and made from wood grown in sustainable forests. The logging and
manufacturing processes are expected to conform to the environmental regulations of the
country of origin.

Hodder & Stoughton Limited
Carmelite House
50 Victoria Embankment
London EC4Y 0DZ

www.hodder.co.uk

The Secrets of Eastby End

I

1897

Joss Townley smiled at his wife and slipped his arm round her waist for a quick hug. 'We really do need to appoint a new nurse to Eastby End now, Rachel love.'

He patted her belly with his other hand, a proud smile on his face. 'The baby is starting to show now and people will be horrified if you continue working for much longer. Well, some of them are a bit shocked already that you've continued to work since we got married, and when they find out about the baby, they'll throw a fit.'

She rolled her eyes at that. 'Poor women have always continued to work after marriage because it was that or starve, and that includes when they're expecting. I'm a skilled nurse and my efforts were and are not only needed but can help save lives. What's more, I enjoy looking after people.'

'Well, I'd like you to be a bit more careful from now onwards, because of that young fellow you're carrying.'

'Or it might be a girl,' she threw back at him quickly.

He grinned because he'd known she'd say something like that. 'I don't mind which it is, really. But even you must admit that you're getting tired more quickly now and won't you find your job more difficult still as you grow bigger?'

She nodded, unable to hold back a sigh. 'Unfortunately, yes, I will and I don't intend to run myself ragged. But as we've already agreed, I am going to stay involved in some nursing work even after I've had the baby, not doing the visits to people's homes because I don't want to bring any infections back to my child, but helping to organise things at the clinic at least.'

'Well, Dr Coxton can't take over your duties and she has enough on her plate dealing with patients in Ollerthwaite, so can't do more in Eastby End. We need at least one more nurse to replace you and perhaps a second one as well.'

'But I can still help organise things, and I can read the medical journals, find out about new treatments and spread the word if it's relevant. There will be a variety of things I can do to help people, even if we have more than one child.'

'I always realised that you'd not give up completely – and why should you? I also bet myself that you'd be trying to help people in Eastby End particularly. Am I right?'

'Yes. I really care about improving things for those who live there. Parts of it are so run down and that could be improved with a little goodwill from people who own property there. Proper maintenance and decent housing can save lives, too, and especially women's lives because they have to care for their families as well as themselves. Their menfolk are mostly out earning a living.'

'What shall we do about Hanny when you stop work? She'll still need a job. Is there some way we can make sure the new district nurse accepts her as her assistant? She's a good worker.'

Rachel glanced sideways, watching him rather warily as she spoke. 'I've got a better idea. You keep telling me we're not short of money, so I'd like to offer to pay for Hanny to train properly as a nurse. She's so good with people who're sick or need some sort of help, and she's so eager to learn. What do you think?'

She waited, watching him frown in thought and as the silence continued, she said coaxingly, 'It won't cost a great deal. If she enrols at Bristol, she'll be able to live in the hospital dormitory while she's training and there's no charge for that, just the fees to pay the college for doing the course. I think we ought to provide some personal spending money for her, though.'

'Do you think she'll want to do all that training?'

'I've mentioned it to her and she's excited at the mere idea, can't seem to believe that she really can get such a chance, coming from a poor family. She's a really hard worker in anything she does, and I'm quite certain she'll do well on the course.'

'Then I'm happy for us to help her. But that means we'll have to find not only a new nurse but a new assistant as well, to go out and about visiting patients together. We've improved safety in the district and I intend to keep working on further improvements, but it's still not wise for a woman to go out on her own after dark round the centre of Eastby.'

He gave his wife a very solemn look. 'I shall be glad when you're no longer doing it, even with Hanny accompanying you, I must admit. I can't help worrying about your safety.'

She saw his eyes go to her belly as they often did and he smiled without realising he was doing it. He was so happy at the thought of becoming a father, as happy as she was to be bearing his child.

'And yet you've not stopped me from doing it.'

'I know how greatly you care about district nursing and how much good you've done with your visits to the poorer people in their homes. And as you're the first person to do such work in Eastby, it's you who's set it all up. I can't tell you how proud I am of what you've done, my darling. And fortunately, we know that you bear babies quite easily.'

Joss saw her look sad and pulled her into his arms. She had borne a baby while she was still a very young woman, following a rape by a man who lived nearby. She'd been very young and had had no family to help her raise the baby herself, and had moved away to live with a kind couple and allowed them to adopt her tiny daughter. The child would be what, twelve now? Nearly as old as she'd been when she fell pregnant.

He knew Rachel was looking forward to keeping this baby and bringing it up herself, and he was quite sure his wonderful wife would make a good, loving mother to their first child.

She put her arms round his neck and plonked kisses first on one cheek then the other. 'You're a wonderful husband, Joss Townley, and don't think I don't appreciate that. I love you to pieces.'

'I love you too. Some of the men round here think I should be more forceful with you and make you behave more meekly, like their wives do, and they don't hesitate to say so. But I don't happen to agree with them, so I tell them that you're an intelligent human being not a cabbage, and you're saving lives by what you do.'

'I'd not have married you in the first place if you hadn't been so modern in your outlook.'

They moved closer together for a few moments, clasping hands again briefly, after which they got on with their day.

Rachel didn't waste any time, but wrote to her friend and mentor at Bristol University about Hanny training as a nurse, and the need for a new district nurse to take her own place. Advertisements hadn't brought any replacements for her, probably because district nursing was a new area of work and there weren't many women experienced in it, certainly not enough of them to go round every town and village that wanted to hire one.

She walked along the street to the postbox to catch the last collection, blowing the letter a kiss as she dropped it in. Pearl Grayson was head of nursing and had been very kind to her when she was young. Any nurse trained under her supervision would be good at the job and easily find employment anywhere. And perhaps she might know someone who'd like to work in a small country town and would agree to come and work in Eastby End and live nearby in the shadow of the moors.

The Crossleys would take over supervising the new nurse and her helper as Rachel stepped away from the job to have her baby.

She hoped Hanny would come back to work in Ollindale once she'd qualified and gained a few years' experience. The two of them had become good friends when they worked together and she would miss her company.

In the meantime, the people who lived here needed another district nurse and surely by now the local town councillors had seen the good district nurses could do for the poorest citizens. It would make things so much better locally if they would agree to provide enough money to pay for two district nurses to cover the whole area properly.

The trouble was, some of the more old-fashioned councillors didn't like to see women going out and about to do their jobs like the men did. Some even refused to accept that such services were not only necessary but so useful that it was their duty to provide such services to their constituents.

She'd better discuss Hanny's future with her, though she was sure her assistant would jump at the chance of training properly as a nurse. And they'd need to work out how to find another suitable person as assistant for whoever took the job as the next district nurse. Perhaps Hanny would know someone who lived here who could take over her job.

However, even though she very much wanted this baby, Rachel would miss her work. She loved helping people, seeing their health improve, making sure their injuries were properly treated, seeing that babies were born safely.

2

On the morning of her husband's funeral there was a knock on the front door of the tiny two-up, two-down labourer's cottage in the quiet little village near Bristol. Livia's neighbour didn't wait for her to answer but opened it straight away as everyone did with their neighbours round here and peered inside. 'Ready, love?'

'Yes.' Livia checked her reflection in the speckled old mirror over the living-room fireplace and settled her black felt hat more firmly on her head. Then she took a deep breath and walked out to join both sets of neighbours who had been kind enough to wait and escort her to the church.

No fancy funerals for people round here but as always, friends and neighbours had rallied round to make sure Nigel had what they called 'a good send off'. He'd had no close relatives to take the necessary actions but Livia knew some of the men who lived nearby had already taken the rough pauper's coffin she'd been given and delivered it to the small church, using the hand cart belonging to the village shop.

Nigel would be waiting for her in the place where they'd been married five years ago. After the brief service she'd say a final goodbye to him and the coffin would be taken to be buried in the paupers' section of the council cemetery because she hadn't got the money to buy a plot in the churchyard. She'd decided not to go with it, couldn't bear the thought of that being her last memory of her dear, kind husband.

As she alternately sat and stood during the brief ceremony offered by the curate to those who were too poor for anything but charity funerals, she admitted to herself that it would be a huge relief to have all this fuss over and done with. But it was what people round here did, what Nigel himself would have expected, so she endured it and did as custom demanded.

One person was missing from the group of mourners, a former employer for whom she'd worked for five years before her marriage, and with whom she'd kept in touch ever since by monthly letters. They were also distant relatives, some sort of cousins, she wasn't quite sure of the exact connection, just knew that both sides acknowledged it.

She'd written to Pearl Grayson to invite her to the funeral, but perhaps her cousin was too busy today. She was an important person, head of the nurses' training school, and would have had to sacrifice nearly a whole day of her time and come by train from Bristol to attend.

After the ceremony was over and the coffin had been carried away, Livia stood at the church entrance and the few friends and neighbours attending shook her hand or kissed the air above her cheek as they left. They knew she couldn't afford to offer them any hospitality, not even a cup of tea each.

She walked home with her next-door neighbours, barely managing to hold back tears now. Only thirty-five Nigel had been, five years older than her supposed age, though she'd been pretending to be older than she was since the age of fourteen, so she was really only twenty-five now.

At last she was alone in the house she could no longer live in because it was needed for another farm labourer. She had only been allowed to stay there out of kindness by the farmer when Nigel grew really weak and unable to work at all.

The door knocker sounded as she was about to go upstairs to bring down the shabby suitcase containing her clothes and the few cherished personal possessions still left. She couldn't hold back a low groan. Who wanted her to do something now?

She nearly didn't answer it but that would be wrong, so she somehow summoned up the inner strength to walk across the front room and open the front door, which led out directly from one corner.

She found Pearl Grayson standing on the doorstep and only then did she lose control and burst into loud, sobbing tears because she knew she was no longer on her own.

Pearl put an arm round her and they walked through into the back room. 'My dear Livia, I'm so sorry I wasn't there for you at the funeral but the train was delayed by an accident at a level crossing. Fortunately more damage was done to the cart that got hit than to the people riding in it.'

She kept her arm round Livia's shoulders, occasionally hugging her slightly and waiting for her to calm down.

'Sorry to weep all over you . . . but it's been . . . difficult.'

'I'm sure it has. Hard enough to lose a loved one, desperately hard to have to nurse them for so long. Unfortunately I couldn't get away to help you today till later than I'd hoped and—'

Pearl stopped speaking to look round in shock as if she'd only just noticed that there wasn't any furniture in the room except for one scarred and battered upright chair and a small, wobbly table. Of course, she guessed what had happened.

'Have things been so bad that you've had to sell everything, Livia?'

'Yes. Dying slowly is rather expensive.'

'You should have asked me for help. Why didn't you?'

'I don't like to ask for charity.'

'I'd not count it as charity, it'd have been more accurate to call it helping a relative, don't you think? And I'd do that willingly, for your mother's sake as well as for your own.' She followed that with another of her lovely hugs, then studied the little gold pocket watch pinned to her bodice.

'It's a good thing I looked up train times for later today as well as for tomorrow. You're coming back with me this very afternoon, Livia Blake, and I won't take no for an answer. I have a spare bedroom and an idea for how to help you use your nursing skills to build an interesting new life.'

Relief shuddered through Livia. 'Are you sure? I don't want to be a nuisance. If you can just help me to find a job, I'll manage.'

'I'm very sure you can find employment quite easily. People always need nurses, but let's be practical about how we do this. First, we need to get you to Bristol, then we'll talk properly about another possibility. What else do you need to deal with here?'

'I only need to close my suitcase and bring it down from the bedroom, then say goodbye to the next-door neighbours, who've been very kind. They can take any furniture that's left. It isn't much, but they're very poor and will welcome anything.'

She gulped and only just managed to hold back more tears. 'I'm sorry but I've so little money left now that I can't even offer you a cup of tea.'

Pearl gave her a searching look. 'That doesn't matter. Did you have any breakfast?'

Livia pointed across to the stale end of a loaf standing on the windowsill, which was the only food she had left. 'A piece of bread and a drink of water. I wasn't hungry.' She'd didn't tell Pearl that she'd thrown half the slice of bread away, finding it difficult to swallow anything so dry and stale.

'No wonder you've lost so much weight, you poor love.'

Her gentle tone made more tears come into Livia's eyes. She smeared away the first few, but others escaped and then sobs followed them. She was glad to take the handkerchief Pearl held out and bury another set of sobs in it.

For the past few weeks, everything had been horribly difficult for her to deal with on her own, and poor Nigel's illness had seemed to go on for ever, a strain on him as well as her. Towards the end, he'd slept a lot, not seeming fully conscious, which had been a relief.

She'd coped and kept him clean at least. But she'd only managed to deal with his pain and medical needs by selling everything they owned, piece by piece.

Pearl glanced down again at the little fob watch hanging from her bodice. 'Is there someone who can fetch us a cab? I'll slip them sixpence to hurry. If we leave quickly we should be able to catch the early afternoon train back to Bristol. And isn't there a little refreshments kiosk at the station? Yes, I thought so. We'll get you something to eat there and you must force it down, if necessary. I don't want you fainting on me.'

Livia tried to speak calmly but she felt as if her own words were echoing from a long distance away. 'The lad next door will go for a cab but you don't need to pay him that much, Pearl. People would queue up to earn half that amount because there's not a lot of work round here and hasn't been for a while.'

'Will the lad share the money with his mother?'

'Oh, yes. He'll give it all to her. Like everyone else round here, that family is struggling to put bread on the table.'

'Then sixpence seems a fair payment to me and it's what I wish to offer.'

'You're always so kind to people.'

'I do my best to help others whenever I can, and once you've sorted out a new life for yourself I'm sure you will too, my dear girl. In the meantime let me take charge of your life for a while and give you time to recover. I can see that you're worn out.'

It was an effort even to nod, she felt so weary. 'Yes, I am rather tired. Thank you.'

They hugged again. Livia was so grateful for those hugs. Each one seemed to make her feel a little better.

She went next door and sent young Wilf off to earn the sixpence. She also told his mother she could have everything that was left in the house, like the stale loaf end, the few pieces of chipped crockery, the chair, the thin old flock mattress and the ragged blanket. She also asked her neighbour to return the keys to the rent man and apologise to him that she couldn't afford to pay the usual week's rent in lieu of notice.

Then she went upstairs for the last time and brought down the shabby suitcase, which was only heavy because it contained every single thing she still owned.

A few minutes later there was the sound of hooves and wheels from the end of the narrow street and the lad next door jumped down from a cab that had stopped there to wait for them. The two women walked quickly along to it and Pearl paid the lad his sixpence, which made both him and his mother beam.

As she got into the cab Livia waved and called goodbye and thank you to those of her neighbours waiting in their doorways to see her go. But once the cab set off she didn't look back again, not even once.

She wanted to leave all the pain behind her, leave everything except the memories of the few years of happy marriage before Nigel fell ill. How long ago those seemed now.

In Bristol they took a cab from the station straight to Pearl's flat, which was on the first floor of the college. It seemed like a palace to Livia after the mean little house she'd been living in for the past year. It had spacious rooms and windows, and seemed full of light and warmth.

Best of all, there was comfortable furniture, including a highly polished mahogany table with a vase in the middle and two armchairs you could sink right into, which she couldn't resist trying out straight away. Recently she'd had to manage without most of her furniture, which she'd sold piece by piece to buy food, and her life had been uncomfortable in every way, in body and in mind.

As they stood just inside the guest bedroom, Pearl said gently, 'You'll need a few days to rest and regain some of your old vim and vigour. Don't try to do or decide any-thing yet, dear, because you won't be thinking clearly till you've recovered your health.'

Livia didn't protest because she knew Pearl was right, and because she was so very weary.

It was wonderful to be at her cousin's home. She had books to read and keep her happily entertained for hours while Pearl was at work and enough food at every single meal, good food too. During the day she could stroll round a small park nearby whenever the weather permitted or simply walk along the local streets and stare at the well-kept houses.

And since her friend had an evening function to attend one night and often brought paperwork home to do, this restful period went on for the whole of the first week with early nights most of the time. That suited Livia perfectly because for the first few days she couldn't seem to get enough sleep.

On the Saturday, however, Pearl looked at her over the breakfast table as they finished their meal. 'You're looking a lot better. Are you ready to talk about the future now, dear?'

'Yes. And I'm more grateful than I can say that you've given me this quiet time to rest and recover. I can't thank you enough.'

'You've been no trouble, Livia dear. I only had to leave you to rest. You even cooked our tea the last three nights. I didn't realise you were such a good cook.'

'That task was exactly what I needed. I enjoy cooking, when I have the ingredients that is. But I'm ready to look for a job now.' It would still take a big effort to go back to work, but she mustn't depend on Pearl for too long. She had to learn to stand on her own feet again and that meant earning a living.

'Well, I can easily find you a job as a private nurse, Livia, or you can wait until a position comes vacant in a nearby hospital, but I have what I consider a better suggestion.'

'Oh? Tell me. If anyone knows what's going on in the nursing world and what's the best thing for me to do, it's you.'

'Why don't you enrol for the next course and become a district nurse? You're good with people, always have been, and I think you'd find that sort of work far more interesting than single-person private nursing, which can be lonely.'

As the idea sank in, Livia began to smile and nod. 'I've read about district nursing at the library and have a vague general idea of what's involved but I don't know much about the training district nurses receive or the actual details of what this new type of work involves. I've been a bit out of touch with the practicalities of modern nursing since I got married and had to give up work, I must admit. And out of touch with nearly everything since Nigel got really ill.'

Then her face fell. 'Oh, but how much does the course cost? I don't have any money left.'

Since she moved here she'd been able to catch up with some of what was going on in the nursing world by reading Pearl's old newspapers and journals. But her cousin used and referred to articles in back copies for her own job and for the lectures she gave, and kept those in her office at the college, so Livia hadn't been able to borrow all of them.

She realised her companion was waiting for her to pay attention.

'Are you all right?'

'Yes. Sorry, Pearl. My mind was just – wandering.'

'That's all right. You're bound to be upset by your loss. But you're starting to look better now and it's really important that we deal with this soon, so try to concentrate on what I tell you about our course. To get accepted on it, applicants need to have had two years' experience in hospital nursing, then have done other nursing work in the community as well, so you're easily eligible to apply for the six months' training. In fact, you pretended you were older and worked for about five years in all before your marriage, didn't you? And after your marriage you did part-time odds and ends for a while?'

'Yes.'

'Well, there you are. You're fully eligible. After the training has been completed, you will become a Queen's Nurse and will be able to start looking for an interesting job that will be better paid than usual for a woman. Some places will try to hire you and pay less, but fortunately the country is short of district nurses, so hold your ground on that and you'll get the wages you deserve.'

'That sounds . . . interesting.' Livia gestured with one hand for her companion to continue, listening intently now, because she really liked the sound of this sort of work and the wages she'd be earning. She never wanted to be penniless again or confined to one bedroom nursing a sick relative, even if he was her husband. Never, ever.

'Different parts of the country are setting up their own District Nursing Associations to organise the work, but most smaller towns or country districts are contenting themselves with becoming affiliated to a larger association. In other words, things are starting to come together all over the country. A job like that would, I'm sure, suit you nicely.' She waited, a questioning look on her face, but was already sure of what her younger friend would say from the expression on her face.

'I'd love to do some more training, Pearl, absolutely love it. I've always enjoyed learning new things but I'll be the first to admit that I'm rather out of touch with the latest developments in nursing and medicine generally. You know how quickly things can change.'

'I'm sure you'd enjoy this course and I have a brochure for you that explains and lists the details of what's involved in the training. Once you've completed the course, however, the job itself is so new that no one has fully fixed ideas of how things should be done. And to make things more difficult, there is country versus town work, so places can have extremely different nursing needs.'

'Yes, that makes sense. Go on.'

'The district nurses usually work alone or in pairs in their own areas, especially in the smaller country towns, and they do whatever seems necessary in their own circumstances, as well as the usual basics like keeping an eye on babies, young children and pregnant women.'

Pearl could see that Livia was still listening intently and looked like a different woman from the tired pale creature who had walked slowly and wearily into the flat just over a week ago.

'We who have not married have found it easier to keep up to date, I'm sure. However, when it's a question of going out into the community to care for sick people and perhaps organise small clinics, some of the new types of job can be different from ours too, so even we can't keep up with everything, I admit. You will perhaps know of needs that I'm not aware of, yes, and of different ways to deal with them too. If so, I'd be pleased to learn about your discoveries.'

She smiled. 'If I were starting out now, I think I'd try to become a district nurse.'

'I like the sound of it, I must admit. And actually, it'd be good to have a little more freedom in my work. Some of the male doctors I've had to deal with before I left nursing to get married—' She broke off and rolled her eyes. 'Well, you know how unrealistic they can be about both nurses and women patients.'

'I certainly do. Luckily I'm not in a position where I have to do as such old-fashioned creatures try to tell me.'

After a nod of agreement with that statement from Livia she continued talking. 'There is a definite teaching element in the job, that I do know, a need to spread the word about the simple methods people can adopt to stop themselves and their children from getting ill as often.'

'Yes, I can see that being useful.'

'It's usually women who care for the daily needs of their families, so they'll be the main ones able to prevent them from getting sick as often too, and they're the most important people to teach these facts to.'

'I'd enjoy that aspect.'

Pearl paused again, then admitted, 'We can't aim at enforcing Nightingale standards of cleanliness in the poorer homes, of course, much as we'd like to, but we can help improve the way households are run and make them a lot cleaner, which can make a surprising difference to families' general health.'

'So the job will mostly involve dealing with women and children, I'd guess.'

'Yes, and remember, as you'll be mainly working on your own, you'll be much freer to do things in whatever way you see as relevant to each individual situation, apart from dealing with the urgent matters like vaccinations, of course.'

She waited a moment for that to sink in, then prompted, 'What do you think?'

'I think it sounds far more interesting than private nursing but how would I pay for the cost of the course? Not to mention my daily expenses and rent while I'm studying?' She could feel her cheeks heating up. 'I've hardly any money left, Pearl, only the few coins in my purse. I was saving that to pay my train fare to Bristol and intended to ask your help to find work, only you came for me, thank goodness.'

'It was my pleasure to do that. You're a very good trained nurse and the world needs more of those.'

'I missed my work when I married, especially when we didn't have any children, however hard we tried.' She'd been surprised because he'd been such a healthy looking man and she had always considered herself a normal, healthy woman. And anyway, she'd had one child, hadn't she, so she was definitely fertile.

'There are scholarships available to pay the fees,' Pearl went on, 'and I'll help you to apply for one of those. If you're not successful, I'll help you financially myself.'

'I couldn't ask you to do that!'

She held up one hand to stop Livia's protest. 'It'd be my pleasure and privilege to do that for a cousin.'

'Second cousin, sort of, not really a close relative at all.'

'You're cousin enough for me and you're also my dear Beryl's daughter. And I'd be doing it for the many poor folk who're sick whom you'd be able to help more by working out in the community than by being shut away in a hospital.'

How generous Pearl was, so often thinking of others' needs! Livia swallowed hard and began to feel a trickle of hope run through her that things might work out even better than she'd hoped.

Much as she'd loved Nigel, she'd missed professional nursing desperately. After she married, she'd fully expected to be busy bearing and raising children, but when she'd not become pregnant, she'd found herself with time on her hands.

She'd wept about not having a child to love many a time in the dark hours of the night or while her husband was at work and she was scrubbing a floor. And since she knew the fault wasn't hers, she'd also known that she'd never be able to bear child.

She realised Pearl was speaking again and straightened up, forcing herself to pay better attention.

'The women studying on the course are expected to live in at the hospital for at least part of the time so that they can learn more about other aspects by helping attend night calls, which all seem to happen at once or not at all. They go out on those with experienced district nurses, of course.'

She smiled wryly. 'There's a dormitory for the students, and food and other daily necessities are paid for by the college in return for help in any way needed with the actual nursing. That would make things easier for you financially, so you'd only be dependent on me for part of the time.'

'It'd certainly help. You don't mind?'

'Of course I don't.'

She stared at her elegant cousin and admitted, 'I'm rather short of decent clothes these days. I shall need some more clothes.'

'Well, I can help with uniforms and a few nicer clothes. You're not the only person struggling financially, so I've taken a leaf out of my cousin Flora's book, or rather her husband's, and have gathered together a store of decent second-hand garments. You can take your pick of them if you don't mind wearing other people's cast-offs. They're all clean, I promise you.'

'I'd not mind at all. In fact, I'd be hugely grateful.' Livia stared down at her own worn clothes as all this sank in, ashamed of how shabby they were. She was grateful when Pearl didn't hurry her to make a decision because she didn't like to dive into a situation without thinking it through. Even agreeing to let Nigel court her had taken weeks to come to terms with. But in the end love for him had won her over. He'd been such a dear, kind man.

This current decision didn't take her very long, however. 'Thank you. I think you're right, Pearl, and I'd greatly enjoy the training as well as the work itself.'

'I knew you would agree. It's because I think you'd be well suited to this new sort of nursing that I made the suggestion in the first place. And you'll let me buy you a few personal necessities as well as giving you some things from my stores before you start, won't you?'

She raised one hand to stop the protest that was clearly hovering on her cousin's lips. 'And don't you dare try to stop me buying you a few new things or I'll summon up your mother's ghost to haunt you and she'll go on doing that until you do agree to accept them.'

They both chuckled at that, not because either of them believed her mother could come back to haunt her, but because Beryl had been known for being extremely stubborn when she felt something to be right.

Livia gave her companion a rather tearful smile. 'I can't tell you how grateful I am for this, Pearl. Thank you for suggesting it and I promise to pay you back by helping a lot of poorer people to gain better health for themselves and their families.'

'Good. That's such a worthwhile aim. And as it happens your timing is good. There's a course starting at the beginning of next month. In the meantime you can recover your own health completely, and read my old nursing journals and other publications to bring you more up to date. I'll bring some of the ones I think contain particularly good articles home for you. Now, let's get on with our day. You and I have some clothes to select.'

She didn't tell Livia that during the following couple of weeks she had to pull a lot of strings to get her protégée a place on the next course but she managed it. Beryl would have been proud of her.

And during the next few months Pearl had the great pleasure of hearing nothing but praise from the tutors about the young widow's progress. A 'born nurse' was the phrase used by many of the people training her.

3

Many miles away from Bristol on the outskirts of central London, Ellis Quinn came home from his office mid-morning and stood for a moment as the cab drove away, staring along the street of tall grey houses and equally grey pavements. He'd be glad to leave here.

He let himself into his home, turning down the maid's offer of a pot of tea.

'Could I please have a word with you, sir?'

'Can it wait half an hour, Sally? I've had an exhausting morning winding my business up and would like to sit down quietly for a while.'

She looked unhappy at that but he turned away before she could insist on explaining about whatever domestic problem there was today for him to solve. She didn't get on well with his son's new tutor and that was causing trouble at times.

He felt he desperately needed a little time to reorient his thoughts after taking the huge step of moving out of business and related activities, so he walked briskly along the hall into the room at the rear and shut the door firmly behind him. He leaned back against it, looking round and feeling relieved that he wouldn't need to use this room so much from now on for what had seemed like endless hours of tedious paperwork.

His uncle had always insisted that some of the jobs couldn't wait until the next day. That man had been a slave driver, getting the most work he could out of his employees, including his own nephew, and indeed asking far too much of them at times.

Ellis looked round the dark room with its outlook to the side of the house and the next house's wall of old, stained bricks. He was delighted that he'd soon be moving not only from this house with its unhappy memories of his wife's illness and death, and its dreary outlook on the world, but moving right away from London.

The past week had been horrendously busy and he'd had to work until midnight and then start again early the next day a couple of times to get all the paperwork completed in time for the date he'd set for moving out of that office. But he'd accomplished what he'd been longing to do: he had sold his late uncle's business interests, every single one of them, and handed them over to their new owners with great relief.

He'd never wanted to work with his uncle, but his family had insisted he did when he'd been too young to go against them. From now on, someone else could worry about sales and profits, accounts and staff. The lists of problems had seemed endless at times, and it seemed as though as soon as you solved one, another took its place. Not a comfortable way to live.

After his uncle's sudden death, he'd also inherited not only the group of businesses in which he had worked since he left Oxford University but also a considerable number of profitable stocks and shares. He had been surprised at how much money his uncle had left him, including financial interests that he'd kept outside the business and not a word said about them to his nephew.

They'd made a wonderful difference to Ellis's life and future plans, and now he had more money than he would need without working those gruelling hours to earn more for his uncle. This made him very happy. He wasn't lazy but money had been Arthur Quinn's god, not his. What's more, Ellis intended to use some of this money to help others, which would have given his selfish penny-pinching uncle a fit.

He went into the next room and sat down in the big armchair in the bay window, letting silence fold round him like a warm embrace. He'd lived here very quietly since his wife died and hadn't often joined in social activities with their former friends. He had only wanted to make sure his son was cared for and healthy, and to keep his uncle satisfied at work. And, of course, to save as much money as he could in order one day to escape working for a tyrant.

After he sold this house, he was going to move somewhere quiet and green in the country. It'd be good for Gil and for himself too. He'd have a studio, not an office. He'd see whether he still had any ability to paint and sketch. He hadn't been able to enjoy this hobby since his wife's death because it had been such a shock to lose her so young. It had turned his whole life upside down and dampened down any creativity he might once have considered he possessed.

He was nervous of trying to enjoy painting again. He passed any leisure time reading, only occasionally visiting museums and art galleries. He hoped that the activities he had once enjoyed and which had been so long neglected, would come to life for him again.

To crown this terrible time, just after his uncle's heart problem took a turn for the worse, Gil's tutor had suddenly left after he'd been paid his quarter day wages. He hadn't given any notice, had only left a brief letter saying he'd gone to join some cousins in Australia and was sorry for any inconvenience caused but didn't want to lose this sudden opportunity.

Ellis had hastily found another tutor to look after and teach his lad, making it a temporary appointment. After all, it would be no use enrolling Gil in a local school when they were about to leave the area. He would send his son to school when they found somewhere to live, however, and make sure they settled somewhere with a good school nearby. He didn't want to keep Gil at home with a tutor, as his uncle had insisted on doing. It was more than time his son interacted regularly with other lads.

Ellis had felt for a while that his son needed to get out of the house more and simply enjoy playing with other children. Only he hadn't dared go against his uncle's wishes, because the old man had displayed some very chancy behaviour towards the end of his life and had even threatened to cut Ellis off without a penny at one stage.

An action like that, after all these years of working hard for his uncle, would have ruined Ellis's long-term plans. He had money saved, but not enough yet to live comfortably.

Gil waited on the landing outside the schoolroom for his tutor to join him. It was taking Mr Chater a long time to get ready and he was fed up of waiting for him.

He didn't like the man who'd suddenly come to look after him, didn't like their slow walks along grey pavements, which were the only outings now allowed.

Was that the sound of drawers being opened and shut from inside the schoolroom? He pushed the door a little wider and peered in, horrified to see the tutor carrying out his threat and throwing Gil's treasures into the waste-paper basket. The shelf they'd stood on was completely empty now and he was also throwing away the things from the top drawer.

That might not be a very good sketch that Gil had drawn of his mother but it still helped him remember what she'd looked like. And her gloves, which had just been tossed away, still smelled faintly of her perfume. When no one was around he sometimes pressed them to his cheek.

Horrified, he waited till his tutor's back was turned, pushed the door a little wider and tiptoed into the room. He took the man by surprise, snatching the waste-paper basket from the chair it was standing on, then turning and running out of the room before Mr Chater could stop him.

He clattered down the stairs at top speed, ignoring the shouts to come back this minute. He didn't go out of the front door, but ran down to the lower floor at the back of the house and into the kitchen, where he thrust the waste-paper basket at Sally, begging her to hide it. She'd hidden some of his other treasures that the new tutor had tried to throw away as punishments for not obeying his stupid rules, and she nodded now, gesturing to the back door.

He ran out of the house and used the side gate to get into the street, intending to cross it and take refuge in the park for a while. This was totally against his father's strict orders never to go out on his own, especially on a Friday, which was market day when the street was busy with carts and pony traps, and the footpaths were full of pedestrians, all going past their house to get to and from the market. There were even a few motor cars driving along the street nowadays.

One heavily loaded cart was just turning into the end of the street and was causing others to yell or sound their horns because the two horses pulling it were moving much more slowly than the other vehicles, whether horse drawn or motor driven.

To make the crush of traffic worse, now that the legal speed limit in towns had been raised to fourteen miles per hour, drivers of motor vehicles were able to go much faster than they had before, and many did, whether that suited the other traffic or not. Gil had seen the motor cars spinning along but had never ridden in one himself or even got close to one. He'd love to try doing that.

His tutor didn't allow him to read newspapers but he'd heard the servants talking about what they'd read about road speeds. Like a lot of people, they thought this new limit to be dangerously fast. Lives were apparently being lost as a result because pedestrians simply weren't used to allowing for vehicles to be going so fast when they tried to cross the road. There were reports of fatal accidents in the newspapers nearly every day.

He was forbidden to cross the road on his own and anyway, it was dangerous, so he made sure to stay on the pavement, but he also kept an eye on what was going on in the street itself as well as what his tutor was doing.

A motor car was trying to pass the big cart and had needed to slow down to a mere walking pace because the cart driver wouldn't get out of the way, no matter how much the young gentleman driving behind him yelled and gesticulated and tooted his horn.

Gil watched with great interest, grinning as the driver eventually managed to get past and start to speed up again, then resumed his conversation with the elegant young lady sitting beside him with an adoring expression on her face.

The lad suddenly gasped as he realised his tutor had moved along the pavement and was getting too close. He tried to move faster, weaving his way through the crowd of pedestrians, terrified of being caught and thumped again.

Once again the driver of the motor car began to show off what his vehicle could do by speeding up to overtake another horse and cart, then swerving across its path in order to get closer to the footpath. Gil ignored it, more concerned to get away from Mr Chater, who was getting much too close for comfort.

He was having trouble getting past people chatting as they walked. None of them seemed to notice him, let alone move to allow him to pass. He needed to cross the road, even if it was forbidden, and go into the park to get away. He'd be able to run much faster than his tutor there. He'd sneak back when his father came home from the office and beg him to send this tutor away, or at least to stop the beatings.

Only one man noticed Gil, a tall young workman who had been striding along the outer edge of the pavement with a bag of tools slung over one shoulder. He smiled as he saw the lad trying in vain to find a way past a particularly slow pair of older women who were not only chatting earnestly, but carrying big shopping baskets that jutted out to the very edge of the pavement.

As Gil got close to the road itself, the tall workman realised suddenly how little attention the driver of the motor car was paying to the traffic, his eyes on the young woman beside him, and how close the lad was getting to the edge of the pavement. He yelled at the top of his voice, 'Hoy! You, boy! Stop moving! Stop this minute!'

But before Gil could do that some loose kerbstones at the edge of the pavement suddenly shifted beneath one of his feet and he staggered so awkwardly he began to fall. He let out an involuntary cry of panic, windmilling his arms in a desperate attempt to regain his balance.

The young workman dropped the bag of tools but had to move into the gutter himself to grab the boy's sleeve and yank him back on to the pavement out of the way of the motor car.

Unfortunately, the boy struggled so desperately to get away and continue his headlong flight that his rescuer was now the one thrown off balance and the loose kerbstones tipped even further sideways under his greater weight. He tumbled helplessly off the edge of the kerb into the roadway and fell sideways towards the car. It was he who now let out a yell of panic.

The driver was laughing about something with his passenger and was slow to react but there was a chorus of shouts and yells from passers-by. One man grabbed the rescuer's jacket but it was jerked out of his hand again. Fortunately his intervention deflected the young workman who was thrown against the side of the moving vehicle rather than down in front of it.

He bounced off the motor car and fell helplessly but ended up sprawling on the edge of the pavement rather than under the wheels of the vehicle.

Its driver had suddenly become aware of him but too late to completely avoid hitting him. He pulled up a little beyond the sprawling man, changed gear into neutral and put on his handbrake. Then he jumped down and joined the crowd of pedestrians staring down at the still figure sprawled on the edge of the pavement.

'I say! Is he all right?' he asked the man next to him.

'No, he damned well isn't!' the man yelled. 'Don't you have eyes in your head to see that for yourself? You're a menace to the public, drivers like you are, not keeping your eyes on the road and going too fast for safety.'

The boy was now standing motionless, mouth wide open, staring in horror at the man who'd saved him but was now lying unconscious at his feet.

An older woman grabbed the lad's coat collar and shook him hard, shouting, 'See the trouble you've caused not looking where you're going, you wicked child!'

The tutor was now standing on the bottom step of the five steps that led up to the front door of the house. The sight of the figure sprawled motionless on the pavement had brought him to an abrupt halt as well.

Then he suddenly moved forward and grabbed the boy's shoulder, dragging him back as he asked a bystander, 'Is that chap dead?'

'If he isn't, it's no thanks to this boy and the poor chap was lucky to be thrown away from the car not under it, very lucky indeed.'

The old woman yelled to those around her, 'Don't just stand there gaping like idiots, someone send for a doctor.'

But no one moved.

★ ★ ★

The first shouts had drawn Ellis's attention and he stood
up and stared out of the sitting-room window at the
group of people. To his horror he saw that a lad was
starting to fall forward towards the moving vehicle and
that it was his son. He let out a groan of relief as a
stranger yanked Gil back from danger.

Then he could only watch in helpless horror as the
brave rescuer was the one who was thrown on to the
roadway by the kerb giving way and hit by a car, luckily
going slowly. Jerking suddenly into awareness of the need
to help them, he rushed outside.

He yelled, 'Keep tight hold of Gil!' to the tutor as he
passed him, then pushed quickly through the group of
watchers to kneel beside the unconscious man.

'This young man just saved that foolish lad's life,' a
woman standing nearby told him loudly.

'He's a hero, this chap is,' another one called.

'Looks like he may be a dead hero,' an older man leaning on a walking stick added, almost with relish. 'Never
seen anything like it, I haven't. Them motor cars should
be banned in towns, not allowed to drive along streets full
of people. And what's more, if you ask me it's dangerous
to go that fast anywhere, however carefully you drive. It's
not natural, that isn't.'

But no one did ask him or even pay much attention to
what he was saying at the moment because all eyes were
on the unconscious man. As the newcomer felt the man's
pulse, another woman asked, 'Is he dead, sir?'

'No, he isn't, thank goodness.' He turned round to look
towards his son and saw the tutor clout him round the
ears, and when Gil yelped and struggled to get away he
got another thump, and a painfully hard one too from

what Ellis could see and from the even louder cry of pain that Gil let out. This was clearly audible even from where his father was kneeling.

That made him angry because what good did thumping a child do? And in any case, he'd told the man when he hired him not to hit his son. He didn't believe in grown men beating children, and Gil was not only shorter than Chater but was at that ultra-thin stage lads go through sometimes when growing fast.

His attention was drawn back to the injured man as he groaned and his eyes flickered open. But he seemed not to have regained full consciousness yet and they closed again. There was a cut on his forehead which was bleeding profusely.

When Ellis looked for the well-dressed young man who'd been driving he saw that he was back in his car. Before anyone could stop him, he set off down the street, again driving too fast but this time in order to get away, judging from the anxious way he looked back over his shoulder towards the figure on the ground.

'That's a deep cut on the chap's forehead,' a woman said loudly.

'Someone ought to have stopped that dangerous lunatic, only you won't be able to catch him now,' the old man called loudly.

Ellis looked down again and stayed where he was, because someone had to take charge of the chaos. And since the man had been injured saving his son from harm, he felt responsible.

'Can someone please carry this man into my house?' he called out. 'It'll need two people bigger and stronger than me. And is that his bag of tools? Can that be brought inside, too, please?'

As two men moved to pick up the man, Ellis added, 'And can someone fetch a doctor, please? Dr Featherby's surgery is just along the main road to the right at the end of this street.'

A tall young fellow called, 'I know where it is. Shall I tell him to come to your house, sir?'

'Yes, please. Ask him to come as quickly as he can. Tell him I'll pay.'

As the youth started running along the street, Ellis saw that the men had picked up the injured man. 'Bring him into my house.' He glared across at the tutor now standing at the top of the outer stairs and saw Chater shake poor Gil like a rat.

'I'll take this one back to the schoolroom, shall I, sir?'

'Yes. But do not hit him again.' Assuming he'd do as ordered, Ellis turned back to the injured man. 'This way!' The two men began to carry the semi-conscious man slowly towards the house.

'Big chap, isn't he?' one of them puffed.

Ellis frowned at the two rescuers, who seemed to be struggling with their load. 'Careful how you go. You don't want to bang his head against the doorpost.'

A woman who'd been standing on tiptoe trying to see what was going on, now saw an opportunity to find out what happened next. She nudged her friend to help her pick up the heavy canvas bag of tools and they followed the others inside, each holding a handle. They waited just inside the entrance hall, however, hesitating to go further into a gentleman's residence without permission.

'Please be quick,' Ellis urged the two men, who had paused for a moment to ease their burden into a more comfortable position.

'Can't go any faster, sir. He's a big chap,' one of the men said. He nodded to his friend and they set off again, continuing to make their way slowly across the hall into the room indicated.

'I'm very grateful for your help,' Ellis told them. 'Set him down there, if you please. Gently!'

'Yes, sir.' They lowered their burden on to the sofa.

He'd been fumbling in his pocket and now held out some coins. 'Thank you very much for your help. We'll manage now.'

'Thank you, sir. Happy to be of assistance.' They glanced at the coins and one nudged the other with a beaming smile as they left the house.

A burly older man dressed in the dark, formal clothes of a butler came from the rear of the hall and said quietly, 'Let me help you straighten him out, sir. We'll put a cushion under his head, shall we? We don't want that cut dripping on to the upholstery. Or do you want to have him carried below stairs?'

'No, thank you, Partling. We'd better leave him here, I think. We don't want to try to haul him down into the kitchen area. Moving him might make his injuries worse.'

The man groaned and moved his head again, opening and shutting his eyes as if he was trying to see more clearly where he was.

'I think he's coming to, thank goodness,' Ellis muttered, then noticed the two women still standing in the hall holding the bag of tools between them, gaping across at the now semi-conscious man inside the room.

'Thank you, ladies. Very thoughtful. Put that bag down next to the hall table, if you please. Give them a tip, will you, please, Partling? I've run out of change.'

The butler fumbled in his pocket then handed each one a half-crown piece and the two women left, beaming just as broadly as the male helpers had done.

Ellis glanced round but the tutor and his son were nowhere to be seen and had presumably gone up to the schoolroom on the second floor.

The housekeeper came to join the group in the front room. 'Is there anything I can do to help, sir?'

'Do either of you know anything about dealing with injuries?'

Both his senior servants gave quick shakes of the head.

'Then move further back and leave the way clear for someone who does know to get through to him. There should be a doctor on the way.'

Fortunately, medical help arrived shortly afterwards, and the doctor didn't wait to be admitted to the house but walked into the hall and paused in the doorway of the room he'd heard voices coming from to say, 'I'm Dr Featherby, sir. A young chap said there had been an accident here and I was needed urgently.'

'Yes, you are. I'm Ellis Quinn. Very glad to see you. Thank you for coming so quickly. This chap was just injured by a motor car while saving my son from getting run over by it. He's got a bad gash on his forehead and I'm not sure about the rest of him. Can you please check him completely and do whatever's necessary to help him? I'll pay whatever it costs.'

The doctor had already hurried across to the man on the sofa and begun checking him. He didn't look round but tossed words out, 'What exactly happened to make him fall?'

'There was a loose kerbstone and it tipped up when he trod on the edge of it. He was dragging my son back from the road and it caused him to fall instead of Gil. Sadly, he was knocked sideways by a passing motor car but at least he wasn't thrown under the wheels and run over.'

'Do you know his name, Mr Quinn?'

'Um, no. I'm afraid not. I'd never seen him until today but I'm extremely grateful to him for saving my son, which is why I want to help him in return.'

By that time, the stranger had opened his eyes fully and was looking round, but he still didn't say anything. He moved his head, groaned and tried to touch his forehead.

The doctor pulled his hand gently away and said, 'You've hurt your forehead, sir, and it's bleeding. Don't touch it. I'm a doctor, so let me check your injury and do what's necessary.' He asked a few questions and examined the man for other problems, then moved back a little. 'I think the gash on the forehead and concussion are the main problems. He's been lucky. What did the driver of the car say?'

'He checked that the man was still alive then drove off.'

'Leaving someone else to deal with it. That's shameful. Very good of you to help him.'

'Well, my son did cause the accident so I was glad to help, but I shall complain to the local council about the uneven kerb, believe me.'

He turned back to the stranger and saw with relief that he was now beginning to look more alert and to answer the doctor's questions sensibly. However, he was speaking rather jerkily as if it was still an effort to pull his thoughts together coherently.

There was no sign now of that damned temporary tutor and Gil, but the man had better not have thumped his son again. Ellis sighed but didn't like to leave the injured man yet to check on the boy. He needed to find someone who was more lively physically to keep an eye on his son, and more lively mentally too. Well, he'd have time soon to see to that properly.

Dr Featherby was studying his patient carefully. 'Could you please tell us your name, sir?'

'Logan James.' The injured man tried to sit up but he must still have been dizzy because he only managed to stay upright by leaning sideways against the back of the sofa. He raised one hand to his forehead again, trying to rub it as if it hurt then closing his eyes for a moment. Once again the doctor pulled his hand away from the injury.

'Don't touch that cut, sir. It needs washing and a dressing putting on it, after which you must keep it clean and take things easy to give it time to heal.'

Having finished his examination the doctor moved away and gestured to Mr Quinn to join him. He said in a low voice, 'He's definitely got concussion and I'd like to wash that cut on his forehead carefully in warm water and put a dressing on it. We don't want it getting infected.'

The man on the sofa joined in, speaking with a marked northern accent. 'I'll be all right, doctor. I have a hard head. But could you please give me a few minutes longer to pull myself together, sir? I'm still feeling dizzy when I try to move about.'

'Take as long as you need. I'm grateful to you for saving my son from injury.' Quinn strode over to the bell pull and rang it. When a maid appeared, he said, 'Bring the doctor a bowl of hot water and some soap, please, Sally.'

'Also some clean rags plus a towel or tea towel,' the doctor added.

She glanced at her master who nodded approval of this.

The butler came back just then from seeing the helpers off the premises. 'I've spoken to some of the bystanders, sir, and they said there were no markings of any kind on the car, so we don't know who the chap was or where he's gone.'

'Damn the fellow!' the doctor said. 'He should take responsibility for his own mistakes. And as I've said many times, the government should insist on all vehicle owners putting some sort of identification mark on their motor cars. I've had one or two patients hurt in accidents caused by damned motor vehicles and nothing could be done about apprehending the drivers.'

'The politicians are talking about doing something to give them identification marks, I believe, sir.'

'Well, they're not doing it fast enough.'

No one spoke after that until the maid brought the things the doctor had asked for. He attended to the patient's cut quickly and efficiently, before covering it with a bandage.

'Head wounds bleed a lot but this one won't be serious as long as it's kept clean and allowed to heal without being bumped about again,' he told Ellis, after which he turned back to his patient. 'The bandage can come off tomorrow if you can keep it clean without one. You should come to my rooms in a couple of days for it to be checked, Mr James. I'm just past the end of this street.'

'Thanks anyway but I'll be all right,' the man said. 'I can keep it clean myself.'

'You should do as the doctor advises,' Ellis told him.

The man flushed slightly and asked, 'And how much will that cost?'

Ellis gave him a sharp glance. 'Nothing. I'll be paying all the doctor's fees. You saved my son's life, so I'm more than happy to do that and I'm deeply grateful to you.'

'Thank you. However, I've got a job to do in two days' time, so even if you do pay the doctor for that visit as well, I'll still lose my wages if I have to come back to this part of town. I'll not only lose my pay but worse still, the chance of further jobs from this chap.'

'What do you do for a living?'

'I'm a carpenter. Cabinetmaker too when I get the chance but I don't know enough people down here in London to have the contacts for getting the more skilled types of job, which would bring in the most money.' He sighed. 'I'm thinking of giving up trying to find work down here in the south and going back home to the north again. Eh, I miss the moors, I do that. I'm sick of the sight of grey streets an' tall houses blocking out the sun.'

He stopped talking and leaned back, clearly fighting another wave of dizziness, and the doctor turned to Mr Quinn and said in a low voice, 'He really should lie down for a while and take things easy for the rest of the day. He looks to be dizzy still.'

'I'll make sure he's cared for properly and I'll pay you whatever that costs so don't stint on your treatment of him.'

'Well, time is the best doctor for him from now on. The main thing you could do to help him would be if you could stop him going back to manual labour for a few days, because he might get the cut dirty and infected. Anyway, concussion can play sneaky tricks on people, catch them out again after they think they're better.'

'I'll make sure he follows your advice and rests properly,' Quinn said firmly.

'I doubt he'll be in any condition to work at a normal speed today and possibly not tomorrow either, even if he tries his hardest, poor chap. I've seen it in vehicle accidents before: the metallic frames of motor cars can inflict a lot of damage on soft human bodies.'

Just then the man tried once again to stand up and failed, and the doctor whispered, 'See what I mean. He should give himself time to rest and recover.'

The man seemed to catch what he was saying and looked at Ellis. 'Sorry, sir. I'm afraid I shall be forced to rest a little longer.'

'You're welcome to do that, Mr James. You're not in anyone's way here,' Ellis told him. 'Just let me show the doctor out then if you're up to it, you and I will discuss the practicalities of your situation and how I can help you in return for the huge favour you did for me by saving my son.'

'Well, the main practical help I need at the moment is to rest here for a while before I try to get on with my day's work. So if I'm not in anyone's way, I'll do that and try not to disturb anyone.'

'I meant precisely what I just said: rest here for as long as you feel the need. You won't be disturbing me, or anyone else either. Now, I have to show the doctor out. I won't be long, then we can chat if you're up to it.'

'But the lad's all right?'

'Yes. He's fine.'

'Thank goodness.' He closed his eyes again.

4

When Ellis had escorted the doctor to the front door and watched him stride off down the street, he went quietly back into the sitting room. His unexpected guest was lying down again, with his head on the arm of the sofa, his eyes closed and the fingers of one hand splayed against the uninjured side of his forehead as if it were aching.

Logan must have heard him come in, however, because he opened his eyes and immediately tried to struggle into a sitting position. 'I need to get going. I have a job waiting for me.'

Ellis went across to help him sit up properly and said frankly, 'You're not well enough yet to move about the house let alone go out and do any more work today, Logan. When you're able to move properly you should go home and rest.'

His guest looked wearily across at him. 'I've no home to go to, just lodgings, Mr Quinn, and the ones I moved to recently haven't turned out well. Lodgers aren't allowed into the house after breakfast until teatime so I'll have to find a park with seats and sit there until then.'

'Good heavens! That's not what I call good service from your landlady.'

'I agree. It can be very uncomfortable too on rainy days at weekends, though she does allow us back inside in the afternoons then, as long as we're quiet. I'm going to need another place to lodge if I decide to stay in the south any longer.'

'Are you thinking of going back north?'

His voice softened. 'Yes, I am. My heart is there, I must admit. It's not only the people I miss but my valley and the moors around it as well.'

'I've seen photos of the moors and always wanted to go walking across them but have never managed to find time for a holiday there, or anywhere else lately, come to that.'

For some reason he found the man's intelligent expression as he listened to Ellis speak encouraged other confidences, so he continued talking. 'A few years ago I set myself to earn a fortune so that I would feel secure, which I hadn't been as a child and youth. And I've been working for my uncle for most of my early adult life, a man who didn't believe in taking holidays.'

'And have you earned your fortune now, sir?'

'Yes, I have. And my uncle's just died, so my inheritance from him has added to it, for which I'm very grateful to him.'

There was a brief silence, then he said, 'How about I pay your wages for the next few days so that you can rest properly? And at the same time we can surely find you better lodgings than those.'

Logan looked surprised. 'I can't ask you to do that!'

'You didn't ask. I offered because you were injured saving my son. Any father would be grateful to you for that, so please don't hesitate to accept my offer.'

They stared at one another and gave slight nods at the same time as if they both approved of what they saw.

'I couldn't let any lad get hurt, could I, Mr Quinn? Folk are going stupid over driving round in motor cars, but people walking along the streets don't seem to realise how fast they can move, so they don't always judge when to cross a road safely, even if they do notice that a car is approaching. Some don't seem to notice even that, maybe because of bad eyesight, though how they can miss the noise of the car engines, I don't understand.'

'I agree. I live here and I've seen several near or minor accidents in the street.' He gestured to his house, whose ground floor was raised above street level. 'I was watching my son from the front room today. He was a prime example of not understanding the situation. Well, he was too desperate to get away from his tutor to even think of slowing down and checking first for oncoming traffic.'

'He's a child. They're like that, focus on what they want to do, which isn't always what they should be doing.'

'You're right, but I'll say it again: I'm very grateful indeed that you didn't let him get injured or killed. He's a disobedient brat but he's my brat and his mother is dead, which makes him doubly precious to me.'

Logan smiled and nodded. 'I have nieces and nephews I'm very fond of, so I can understand your feelings. I was glad to be able to prevent him from getting hurt.'

Ellis pulled a small chair across and sat down near the injured man so that he wasn't standing over him, which might seem intimidating. Well, he hoped his companion felt more comfortable chatting like this because he'd taken a liking to the genuine warmth of the man's slow smiles and the intelligent look on his face, apart from feeling deep gratitude to him. 'Is Logan your surname or your first name?'

'First name. But it does puzzle some people because it's unusual. I'm Logan Higson James, but I usually ignore the Higson.' He grinned. 'Ugly, that name is.'

'I don't blame you. I'm Ellis Dobson Quinn, but I usually ignore the Dobson, which I don't like.' They exchanged further smiles. 'Why did our parents give us such ugly middle names, do you think?'

'Ours both end in -son, which presumably means son of, and that's been done to please elderly uncles and aunts from other branches of our families, probably.'

'Yes. That's what I think, too. I wish my parents hadn't bothered. I don't like the Dobsons. They're distant relatives and the further away they stay the better, as far as I'm concerned. Which part of the north do you come from?'

'Lancashire. I've been working in London for a few months, and I've done a lot of looking for work because there's not as much to be found as folk said. I didn't expect it to be so difficult to make a living here, I must admit.'

'Your way of speaking sounds a bit different from the accents of some people from Manchester that I know.' And this chap hadn't been eating very well, Ellis would guess by the gaunt look of his face. Perhaps that was something he could help with straight away, if the man's pride would let him accept a meal or two, that was.

'I speak differently because I'm from the far north of the county not the south. Ollindale is a small Pennine valley and the accent can be different in two places only ten miles apart in Lancashire sometimes.' He sighed and murmured, 'Eh, it's a beautiful place, my valley is, well most of it is, anyway. I miss it far more than I'd expected to.'

'What's the nearest town or is it just a village?'

Logan looked at him in surprise. 'My home is near a place called Eastby End, which used to be a village in its own right but has now been swallowed up by the only town in the valley, which is called Ollerthwaite. I doubt you'll have heard of the valley, let alone the various places in it. Maybe you'll have heard of Lancaster, the nearest big town to us?'

'I haven't heard of Ollindale, I must admit, but yes, I have heard of the county town. Is the countryside near your home pretty? Is that why you're missing it so much?'

'Some of it's pretty. Well, I think it is. But I miss the people I know too, especially my mother and sisters. And when you live close to the countryside there's always something new to see outside, whatever the season. I miss that variety. London streets are mostly just, well, grey, whatever the time of year. Or so it seems to me. Except for the parks, of course. There are some really nice parks, I will admit. I must have visited most of the ones near here in my hunt to fill my soul with greenery.'

He let out a sad little sound. 'Eh, I can see my home in my mind's eye this very minute if I want to. The flowers in Ollindale are pretty in spring and summer, though pretty isn't a good word to describe the nearby moors, and now we're towards the end of spring, they'll be, well, striking I'd call them, majestic even in parts. When you're up there and look out across them, they seem to stretch for miles.'

'That sounds beautiful.'

'It can be but honesty compels me to confess, Mr Quinn, that some parts of the town itself aren't as pleasant to live in these days as they used to be. The council has let the streets and other amenities run down badly in places and some of the owners of the small businesses in Eastby don't seem to care if they inflict damage on the areas and buildings near their premises, not as long as whatever they're doing there makes money for them.'

'That sort of attitude crops up everywhere, I'm afraid. I've never visited the far north of England, I must admit, though I've wanted to. I've seen most other parts of my own country. Tell me more about those moors you love so much. Are they anything like the Chilterns, for instance? I've enjoyed occasional walks on the lower slopes of those.'

'No. Not really. I've only seen pictures of the Chilterns in magazines, mind. Some folk call the moors "the tops", because they're higher land, but they aren't all that high. I mean, they're not really steep or jagged like the Swiss mountains, which I've also seen photos of in magazines, though when you go up on the tops there are occasionally steeper parts. Even up on these parts there are usually paths and you can stride out across the rolling, bumpy terrain, which stretches for miles.'

He paused, smiling as if seeing the moors and said softly, 'Doing that takes your eyes a long way ahead and your thoughts seem to go with them. I've solved many a problem by taking it for a walk across the tops.'

Ellis waited a moment or two and when his companion didn't continue, prompted, 'I like the sound of that. Go on. Please tell me more.'

'The paths up there have been used for centuries. Just think of that. Centuries. The pack horses used them to come across from Yorkshire carrying loads of goods when the Tudors were on the throne, and then they carried other goods back again. The trains do the carrying nowadays but they spew out dirty smoke across the countryside as they pass through it, which is a shame.'

He shook his head, looking sad, his deep love for his home showing clearly to his companion and making him wish he had somewhere to live that made him feel like that.

'You're very eloquent, really good with words, Logan. You make me want to go and see these moors of yours for myself.'

'Folk do come to visit in the summer, more hikers each year and we're getting a few people in motor cars too. They usually spend some money, which helps the local shopkeepers. Eh, I need to go back. Talking to you has made me realise how much I've missed my home, far more than I expected to. Even the strangers who bump into you in London don't make you feel at all welcome here. They make no attempt to say good morning when they pass you in the street, don't even seem to notice that you're a living creature, not just another lamp post.'

After another pause, he went on, 'Parts of London are as bad as the worst parts of Eastby. I didn't expect that when I came down here, I must admit. I mean, London is our country's capital city, isn't it? It all ought to be beautiful.'

'It is in parts.'

'But the beautiful parts can be quite far from one another and hard to reach, as well as crowded with sightseers when you do get there.'

When Logan fell silent, Ellis prompted, 'What brought you here then, if you love your home so much?'

'I came because I love it so much. Talk about a fool! I wanted to try to earn more money than I'm able to back there. Folk said you could do that if you worked hard in the south. Only it isn't true. Or perhaps I'm not pushy enough.'

Ellis asked quietly. 'Have you been going hungry often here?'

Logan gave him a sharp look as if surprised he'd guessed that, then shrugged. 'Not often. I can usually earn enough to feed myself something cheap and simple, but I don't seem to be good at making bigger amounts of money, either back home or down here.'

'What do you need the extra money for?'

'I'd like to set up a proper business of my own and make beautiful things out of wood, not just build shelves and simple stuff, only I'd need bigger premises and better tools.'

Logan's eyes were on his dreams now and it suddenly occurred to Ellis that he could do with a few more specific dreams of his own. He envied the other man that. 'Go on.'

'I'm a good cabinetmaker, really good if I say so myself, and I'm a good carver, too. I used to love doing the fancy parts of furniture. But the master I'd done my apprenticeship with died suddenly a few years ago and his son sold the business to a fellow who already had a son trained up to follow him, so I lost my job.'

He rolled his eyes. 'And then they went bust because they weren't all that good at making beautiful pieces of furniture, so people went elsewhere to get their work done or to buy new pieces more cheaply. Now, well, I mostly do general carpentry, repairs and such, any job I can manage on my own to earn a bit of money.'

'It seems a pity to waste your skills.'

'Aye, well, there you are. That's life. Hits you on the head when you're not expecting it.'

After another pause, he added, 'As for Eastby, my dad said it used to be a pretty village, but I've never seen any part of it looking pretty since I grew up. It's a slum in the central area these days, though there are still some nicer streets on the outskirts and some decent houses on the slopes going up to the moors. That's where some of the better-off folk still live. I love Ollindale. The valley is . . . well, home. That word says it all, doesn't it?'

'Even if it's so bad you call parts of it a slum?'

'Aye. That's only in the central part of Eastby, mind, and it could be improved if anyone with money to spare organised things properly. There are two or three businessmen who've started getting together and are trying to find ways to improve things, but though they've made some progress, it's been slow and they're not acting urgently about it because they don't want to spend a lot. And anyway, there are other folk trying to stop them doing even that.'

Ellis was startled. 'Stopping them making improvements! Why would they do that? Who are these people?'

'They're the ones whose businesses make the most money often by making the most mess in the process. Unfortunately they have enough money to pay others to cause problems that slow the improvements down. When someone complained to the council last year, some of the councillors said openly that prettying things up would make employing people and running businesses far more expensive. They even claimed that they'd not be able to employ as many workers if they had to provide better-looking houses and streets.'

'That's not true from what I've seen of the world!'

After a short pause Logan said softly in the tone of one sharing a secret, 'No, it isn't. I'd like to help the decent chaps who're trying to change it, which was another reason why I wanted to earn more money, so that I could afford to do something worthwhile for my home town. I've wanted to for years, because I love the whole valley, but because of my dad dying suddenly while my sisters were still children, I had to help support them, which meant I had to wait till they'd all grown up and got married so that I was no longer needed. It wasn't until then that I had any money or even free time of my own.'

He smiled fondly as he added, 'I know I'm a bit partial, but they're lovely lasses even if I do say so myself, so I was glad to be able to help them.'

'I envy you. I don't have any brothers or sisters. Go on. Tell me more about this Eastby place.'

'What's to tell? It could be made nice again, it really could, but no one's going to take the whole job on. It's in a pretty situation, you see, lying in a valley that I always think is like a cradle for people to shelter in at the edge of the moors. It wraps itself round you. But in some parts children go hungry or people have to live in houses that have leaking roofs and ill-fitting windows.'

'Repairs don't cost as much as building new houses would.'

'I know. And most ordinary folk round there are decent souls, given the chance, but there are a few I could tell you about who . . . Well, let's not go into that now. You're never going to meet them and I find it upsetting when there's nothing I can do about them. Sadly, I shall be going back empty-handed.' He bit off further words, breathing deeply and looking upset.

This was a caring man, Ellis thought and said gently, 'Unfortunately there are places that are lawless and people who are greedy everywhere in the world, not just your valley.'

'Yes, but there's no need to leave places in as bad a condition as the centre of Eastby is nowadays. It wasn't always like that and it wouldn't take much effort to repair the worst parts. They've brought in an extra policeman, which is helping to reduce crime, but what can one man on patrol do? People should be able to go out safely after dark and walk along their own street to visit a neighbour or a relative of an evening, don't you think?'

His voice had sounded angry again as he said that but he stopped and took another deep breath before continuing more calmly, 'Sorry to go on about it, sir.'

'I did ask so I wanted to know. Besides, it's your home and you clearly love the place, faults and all.'

'Aye. I do. I didn't know how much till I came down to London. I've been really homesick here. That's the exact way to describe how I feel: sick for a sight of my home. I even dream I'm back there.'

'I envy you that.'

'You envy me?'

'Yes. I don't have anywhere that I feel I can call home because my family moved around so often when I was a child. And since I turned fourteen, my uncle has kept me firmly tied to London, working in his businesses. He only let me marry Emily because she brought me a nice little dowry and he thought she and I would give his business an heir or two for the next generation.'

Ellis smiled reminiscently. 'I encouraged him to think that but I married Emily because I loved her. She was a kind, gentle person, so unlike my uncle it was wonderful to go home to her. And we did give the family one heir, at least.' He frowned, shaking his head. 'But I wouldn't want Gil to have as limited a way of life as I've had to put up with, which is part of the reason I've worked so hard to become independent and comfortably off.'

He stared blindly into the distance for a few moments, then went on. 'I don't have any brothers or sisters, and my wife died having another child so we seem to be a very sparse family. It's a strange word to use for people but it's how we've been, sparsely scattered around the world. I'd wanted several children but Emily was very sickly carrying the second one, and when she died I didn't have the heart to start a marriage all over again, whatever my uncle said. It can take a lot of effort at times, dealing with a marriage.'

'I've never tried it,' Logan said, 'but I want very much to get married one day, like my sisters are. They've wed decent, loving chaps, thank goodness. If I ever meet someone I can love and I have a steady job, I'd get married like a shot. I'd not want to do it without the love and without enough money to live on in a modest way. I love my nieces and nephews but it's not the same, is it? I've seen how people look at their own children and envied them.'

'Well, nieces and nephews are better than having no close relatives at all, surely?' Ellis asked.

A shrug was his only answer.

'I bet you'll make a good father one day, Logan, better than I've been so far. I'm hoping to make up for that from now on.'

'I'll do my best to be a good father if I'm lucky enough to have the chance,' Logan said. 'And maybe some of us will even manage to improve things in Eastby End, too, even if not as much as we'd like. You have to try to make the world a better place than you found it, don't you?'

Ellis looked at him thoughtfully. This man didn't talk like someone who worked with his hands, judging by the wide range of words and ideas he brought up. He didn't have the accent of an educated chap when he spoke, though. 'Did you learn about that sort of thing at school?'

Logan laughed rather harshly. 'Our village school wasn't up to much except for keeping kids out of mischief till they're old enough to go out and get jobs, and it still isn't. Any old jobs will do, it doesn't matter what as long as the workers put bread on their own tables and help make their masters rich. The old headmaster who's been in charge of the school for years definitely doesn't try to expand his pupils' mental horizons. It's shameful how old-fashioned he is about schooling the kids, especially the girls. He barely teaches the lasses to spell and add up. He has them helping his wife in the house whenever she gets too busy.'

'Then how did you get your education? You clearly know quite a lot about the world and you discuss it in an educated way. Is all that from reading books and newspapers?'

Logan smiled. 'Partly. We have a small branch library in the better part of Eastby. It's an offshoot of the bigger library in Ollerthwaite and they keep threatening to close it down, but I pray they won't. I've been borrowing books from it for years because reading is a cheap form of entertainment. Miss Litton, the librarian there, is wonderful and she's helped me a lot over the years, ever since she found out how much I love reading and learning.'

He was silent for a moment, clearly remembering something pleasant. 'Sometimes, if the library was quiet, she and I used to simply sit and chat. I came to realise that she sometimes planted ideas in my mind that gave me a lot more to think about. And I'm not the only one she's helped over the years.'

'She sounds to care about her job, which is surely not just books but spreading the knowledge they contain around to as many people as possible.'

'She does care greatly. She's even lent me some of her own books. And she's really kind to anyone in need as well, has helped quite a few families through bad patches, slipping food to the children when they were going hungry.'

'You've been lucky to have had someone like her to help you, Logan. I wish my Gil had had tutors who inspired him to learn.'

'I was very lucky but unfortunately she's getting really old now and I have to wonder who will take her place and help those who really want to learn more about our world if anything happens to her. Or whether they'll be left to flounder along through life on a bare three Rs by a librarian who cares about tidy books more than tidy minds.'

After a few moments of silence, he moved his head from side to side and said, 'I think I'm less dizzy now, sir. I should leave you in peace instead of bending your ears nattering on about where I live and our old librarian. You'll have more important things to think about than that, I'm sure.'

He tried again to stand up and this time made it but didn't start moving. He stood swaying slightly, then suddenly reached out to grab the high back of a nearby dining chair. 'Sorry. I'm not as steady on my feet as I thought I would be by now.'

Ellis moved to support him, even though Logan was much taller. He was surprised at how muscular the arm he was holding felt in spite of the man's present general weakness. 'Perhaps you shouldn't try to leave yet. Please sit down again, Logan, and give your body long enough to recover properly.'

'I don't want to take up your time, sir. If someone could help me and make sure I don't fall, I could maybe go and sit in a corner of your kitchen for a while. I'd appreciate that. You must be a busy man to have a lovely big house like this one.'

'Actually, I'd rather you stay here. You're not in my way and I'm enjoying chatting to you and learning more about the north of my own country. I'm ashamed at how little I know about Lancashire, even though my grandmother came from the north.'

'Well, I must admit that I've found what you've said very interesting too and I thank you for sparing the time to chat to me.'

'It's been a pleasure.'

Logan gave Ellis a rather shy smile. 'Oh. Well, that's all right then. As long as I'm not holding you up.'

'You're not. And what's more, I have plenty of time to spare at the moment and I'll tell you why. It's because I've just sold or withdrawn from most of my various businesses. I've made enough money over the past decade or so to keep me in comfort for the rest of my life. No, more than comfort, luxury because of what my uncle left me recently. So I can please myself about how I spend my time from now on, and it won't be making more money that I don't need. And actually, what pleases me at the moment is chatting to you. I'm really enjoying your company.'

'Thank you.'

A steamroller chugged slowly past in the street just then, going so slowly the horrible noise seemed to echo round them for a good while. They both winced and fell silent till it had faded away into the distance.

'Dratted things,' Ellis murmured. 'You can see why I want to move away from here.'

'Yes, I can. And that was a nasty, uncomfortable sort of noise, as well as an uncomfortably loud one.' Logan frowned in the direction of the window, past which vehicles of all sorts had been passing intermittently the whole time they'd been chatting. 'Doesn't the noise from the street drive you mad living here?'

'I used to work in a room at the side of the house, where it didn't seem as bad. It's only when I spend time at the front that I realise how very nasty the noise in this street is. I'm definitely going to move away as soon as I can. I'd already decided that.'

'You're lucky to have the freedom to do what you want.'

'I do still have a couple of major problems before I can leave, though.' He shook his head as if annoyed about them.

'What are they, if you don't mind me asking?'

'I need to work out exactly where to live and how to spend my time. I can't just sit around doing nothing for the rest of my life. I'd like to do something genuinely useful for other people, especially those who are less fortunate than me in life. I hope that doesn't sound too arrogant. I don't want to just dole out occasional gifts but to help them find or set up ways of earning their living that suit them and bring in money regularly.'

'That would be very worthwhile indeed. Don't you intend to do some leisure activity for yourself, something you enjoy?'

'Of course. I'm not one to sit round idly, that I am quite sure of. I've always enjoyed sketching and painting, which I've had to sneak time for until now, but I'm not sure it'll be enough. I'm starting to understand why Gil gets so restless.'

'Yes, your son needs something worthwhile to fill his time with. All lads do.'

'I found out he'd been set to copy passages from books. Well, doing that occasionally may give you good handwriting, but it can be tedious sitting around doing such things all day, especially for someone who is bursting with energy as he obviously is. Yes, and who's intelligent, too.'

He sighed and was silent for another few moments then gave Logan a very direct look. 'I've got as far with my plans as deciding to move out of the city to the country, but I've been trying in vain to work out exactly where would suit me best.'

'I'm sure you'll work something out.'

'All I'm certain of at the moment is that I don't want to be close to London. As you say, it's crowded and grey, and the buildings are spreading further out all the time. In fact, as I walk round the streets, I sometimes think of a poem – I think it's by Robert Browning – in which the line "A common greyness silvers everything" occurs. It's so apt for describing London most of the time, and on a dull, stormy day even the word "silvers" sounds too bright for what I see around me.'

'I like that line. I shall remember it from now on, and look up the poem in one of the books in the library in Eastby after I get settled again there.' He hesitated then asked, 'You're sure you don't mind me staying a bit longer?'

'Very sure. I'm actually finding it useful to chat to you about the north. When you answer my questions about that part of the country, it fills in some big gaps in my knowledge. You've no need to hurry away for my sake, believe me.'

'Thank you. And if I may be so bold, I can tell you one thing for sure: you'll have to find somewhere that suits your son as well unless you want him to continue getting into trouble. You've only to look at his face to see he's bursting with unspent energy. And . . . ' He hesitated, then said, 'I don't like the looks of that new tutor.'

'No. You're right. But this tutor is only temporary and now that I've seen him thumping my son after I told him not to, I'm going to dismiss him.'

The door was flung open and the maid came in without her master calling her. 'Sir, I want to give you my notice, and urgently.'

'What? What's so urgent about it?'

'That man is hurting Gil again. I can't bear to listen to him being hurt. He's a good little lad given half the chance.'

Ellis stood up hastily. 'I've just told him not to hit my son again.'

'There are ways of hurting children without hitting them. If I hadn't hidden Gil's photos and sketches, he'd have destroyed them, even the ones of the boy's mother.'

'What? Surely not?'

'He threatened to. I heard him. And Gil has left some of his treasures with me. He daren't even keep them in his room to look at. Can I give them to you to look after when I leave?'

She glanced up as a faint sound could be heard from the schoolroom two floors up.

Ellis moved across to the door. 'You've no need to leave. I'll go up to the nursery straight away and sack that man. Don't go away, Logan. I've got other things I want to talk to you about.'

But Logan stood up. 'I think I should come with you. I'm taller than you and I look stronger than I feel so you'll be safer dismissing a man with me nearby. You are going to dismiss him, aren't you, from the look on your face?'

'Yes, I am. But surely he wouldn't attack his employer?'

'He's a bully. He's got that look to him. And if he gets angry at being dismissed, he may not care what he does. How could you not spot that attitude when you were hiring him?'

'My uncle had just died suddenly. Things were in a right old muddle to sort out. And the old tutor left without giving notice. This man has always been polite to me.'

'Well, when he realises you're going to fire him, he'll not hold back. I doubt he'll know how weak I'm feeling by looking at me. He'll just see us as two against one, and me taller than him, likely.'

Sally gave Logan an approving look then turned back to her master. 'He's right about that man, Mr Quinn. If you sack him, I'll stay. I'll go and fetch the gardener as well, shall I? Harris is a big chap, too. Luckily it's his day to work here.'

'Good. You do that, Sally.' He turned back to Logan. 'Has the dizziness passed enough for you to do this or shall we wait for the gardener?'

'I'm feeling better all the time. Don't wait.'

But Ellis hesitated, because Logan was clearly still a little dizzy. 'I don't want you getting hurt, either.'

'I'll manage. I can't abide people who hurt children deliberately. They sometimes take such pleasure in doing it that things can go very wrong indeed. You lead the way.'

They'd moved into the hall and both froze briefly and exchanged glances as they heard a faint cry of distress.

'I'm not waiting a second longer,' Ellis said grimly and started running up the stairs, followed more slowly by Logan, who was trying to hide the fact that he was still slightly dizzy, though not nearly as bad as he had been.

As Ellis entered the schoolroom, he saw the tutor holding Gil with one hand and slashing at him with a cane with the other hand. He rushed across the room and took Chater by surprise, snatching the cane from him and hurling it across the room. 'Stop that at once!'

Logan entered the room and the cane just missed him, hitting the door frame beside him and falling to the floor.

He picked it up and broke it in half, using his foot to help him.

'You'll have me to tackle as well, you damned bully, not just a little lad!' Ellis yelled at the tutor.

After his first yell of shock the tutor got angry. 'And I'll do that too. Your spoiled brat needs teaching to obey orders from those teaching him.'

He had his fists raised as if he was about to punch Ellis when the gardener arrived, strode across to stand beside his master and asked, 'What's the matter with him, sir?'

'Get out of my way, Harris, damn you!' the tutor yelled. But he didn't try to hit the gardener, just stood and glared at them all.

'I found out that Chater's been ill-treating my son and I've fired him,' Ellis said quickly to the gardener. 'I want him out of the house as quickly as possible, and not allowed to come back.'

'Good riddance to that one, I say. He don't fit in with the rest of us an' we none of us like the way he treats the lad.'

Gil was behind his tutor and had pressed himself against the wall in one corner as if desperate to keep out of his way. One of his cheeks was bright red, which further angered his father.

Chater let his clenched fist fall. 'I have a right to chastise him when he misbehaves. All tutors do that, sir. Let me tell you what he did.'

'Doesn't matter what he did. I told you not to hit him,' Ellis said slowly and loudly. 'And you were hitting him hard. You're fired, Chater. Pack your things and get out of my house within the hour.'

'Shall I keep an eye on him while he does that?' Logan asked.

Ellis was about to say yes, but realised Logan was still looking pale. 'No, I'll let Harris help me see him off the premises. You take Gil downstairs and get him some hot milk.'

Chater glared at them and stormed off to his bedroom, slamming the door in their faces.

The two men exchanged glances of surprise when they heard the key turn in the door.

'I can do my own packing without your help!' Chater yelled from inside the room.

'He'll have stolen something,' Harris said. He had a spade in his hand. 'Shall I break the door open, sir?'

Ellis hesitated then stepped back. 'Yes, please. Can you do it quickly?'

'Oh, yes. Stand further away, please.'

Logan lingered to make sure he wasn't needed. If nothing else, it'd look better for another person to be there.

Harris had the lock smashed within a minute or so and after he'd flung the door wide open, he moved towards the occupant of the room, holding the spade in front of him like a weapon.

The suitcase was lying open and as Chater tried to close it, the gardener batted his hand away with the end of the spade.

'Take a look under them socks, sir.'

Ellis stared in shock at the glint of metal just visible under them.

Harris continued to hold the weapon at the ready and Ellis moved forward, snatching the socks aside to reveal several small silver ornaments nestled beneath them.

'Make sure he doesn't get away,' he said to Harris and picked up a candlestick to use as a weapon himself if necessary. Then he spoke to Logan who was still standing by the door. 'Can you go down to the kitchen please and ask Sally to fetch a policeman. There's usually one in the square.'

'It'll be my pleasure, sir.'

Chater tried to make a dash for the door, but Harris used his spade to trip him up.

Logan ran down the stairs and the other servants listened, then smiled and there were more mutters of 'Good riddance!'

Sally ran out to fetch the policeman and Logan went back up in case they had trouble with Chater. He wasn't staying away from what was going on until the man was out of the house. He didn't want a decent chap like Ellis Quinn getting hurt.

5

Once the police had taken Chater away, Ellis left Gil with Sally and asked her to bring him and Logan a snack and a pot of tea. He thanked the gardener and slipped him 'a bonus for your extra work' then went to sit with Logan.

'Do you think it'd be a good idea to take Gil with me when I leave London, Logan? I don't have a tutor for him and I don't want to risk another hasty appointment of one, just in case there's a problem.'

'If you don't mind me saying so, I think it'd be a good idea to give Gil a taste of freedom, and that would include freedom from a tutor trying to give him lessons. He'll be able to run around out of doors in the country-side with other lads, and it should do him good to associate with them as well as to use up some of that energy. Where exactly are you thinking of going?'

'I'm not sure. I need somewhere with good outdoor spaces for him to play out in, instead of roads where he can run in front of cars. Even the countryside near London has busy roads cutting through it, so maybe I'll have to move further north than I'd initially planned.

He shuddered at the memory of that moment of intense fear when he'd thought Gil was going to be knocked down and killed, and then his further sudden fear of the former tutor hurting his son. 'Perhaps I ought to bring him in here with us now to keep an eye on him?'

Logan gave a wry smile. 'Can you leave him with one of the servants?'

'Sally would probably calm him down better than you or I could . . . age often are.'

He nodded as if approving that thought.

'Yes. And he seems to trust her.'

Logan smiled again. 'He doesn't know you very well yet, but he will, if you give him even half a chance.'

'I hope so. But I hope my son will never do anything as foolish as running blindly away from someone again.'

'Kids can be careless, wherever they are. They rarely stop to think at that age if they're upset. My mother always jokes that it's a wonder so many of them manage to survive to grow into adults.'

Ellis rolled his eyes. 'I think you're right about one thing: I'm sure it helps to let them be active and run about, using up that energy. I'm sure you can definitely do that more and do it safely too in places like Ollindale than in big smoky cities like London.'

Logan smiled reminiscently. 'I think the countryside is better for grown-ups like you and me, as well. The air up on the moors always feels really bracing, as if it's doing you good.'

He'd caught Ellis's attention again. 'What exactly might a lad like my Gil find to do in Ollerthwaite?'

'On summer evenings or at weekends, the children still at school all seem to run wild with their friends on the moors.'

'And what about playmates. He's a clever lad and will need friends to match.'

Logan looked at him, head on one side, thinking this through. 'Well, I think there are some grand kids around, judging by the friends my young nephews and nieces bring home, so he could easily get to know several decent kids in a place like Ollerthwaite. But though they may have good brains, they won't be from posh families.'

'Who cares about that? And what about the schools?'

'The primary school's headmaster is old-fashioned and I reckon the kids who go there would do better in life if they had the chance of more rigorous schooling and interesting modern things to learn about. '

Ellis looked thoughtful. 'That might be one of the things I can look into if I settle there. Where do the clever children there get their secondary education?'

'There's a boys' grammar school, and they'll soon be appointing a new headmaster when the old one retires. And the primary head teacher is retiring this summer. They've interviewed folk already and appointed a woman this time, and one with more modern attitudes to girls and their place in the world too.'

He gave one of the soft chuckles that Ellis found very attractive. 'That caused a big fuss from some of the old fogies, I can tell you. But she has very good references from people you could trust so it's a done deal.'

'What's the grammar school like?'

'It's two schools: girls and boys, both small. But there aren't a lot of local families who can afford to have their kids stay on for full secondary schooling, because they need their wages.'

'Aren't there grants to help the poorer families keep their children at school?' Ellis asked.

'Yes, but they cover school fees and uniforms not money to keep the children fed.'

'I could easily set up a couple of grants, one to the boys' grammar and one for the girls".'

Logan looked at him in surprise. 'The trouble is, the girls' grammar is even more old-fashioned than the boys' school.'

'All the more reason to help it along a little.'

'You'd do that? But you don't live there and don't know the town at all.'

'I'm looking for ways to put some of the money I inherited from my uncle to good use.'

There was silence and Logan sighed and stared blindly into space, or perhaps into his memories. He seemed to realise suddenly that Ellis was watching him. 'Sorry. I was just remembering – I don't think I told you that we have a lake near our town, did I? Jubilee Lake, it's called. It's only a small one, mostly man-made by clearing some swampy land, but it's really pretty now that's been done. Some people volunteered to put a path all the way round it and that was recently completed. Now, even old folk and women with prams can go for walks.'

'Gil would go mad at the sight of a lake.'

'And he'd find other kids to play with there. They make paper boats to sail at one end of the lake – we fenced off a shallow part for the children to paddle in, didn't want any of them drowning. And heaven help any child who tries to play in the deeper stretches of water. Everyone in town has made a point of keeping an eye on that, even the old fogies. That's one thing we're all agreed on. A little lass drowned a few years ago, you see. That upset everyone.'

'You make your valley sound like a good place to live.'

'I think it is, not only good but the very best as far as I'm concerned. Does your lad have any school friends to play with round here?'

'Unfortunately not. Most of the people I know are older, so their children are too. They go to universities now rather than schools.'

The words escaped Logan before he could stop them. 'Eh, poor kid. Your Gil must be that lonely.'

'I suppose he is. I never thought about it so clearly before. Talking to you is good for me.'

Ellis looked as if he was thinking deeply so Logan didn't interrupt him but looked round the room as he waited for the conversation to start up again. There were shelves of books and he was itching to go and look at their titles. Imagine owning all those books. That was being rich, as far as he was concerned.

When he looked up again, he saw that Ellis was now staring at him, waiting for him to come out of his reverie. It was unusual how comfortable they both were with silences as well as with chatting.

'Are there any big comfortable houses for sale in Ollindale, do you think? You've talked about slums in the Eastby End part of town. I'd not want to live too close to that sort of place. What are the better areas like?'

Logan was amazed that his companion had jumped along so quickly with his thinking without even seeing the valley of Ollindale. He couldn't keep the sharpness out of his voice when he replied, though. 'Few people want to live in or near the slums; they just have to take what they can afford, and live as near as possible to where they work so that they can get there easily on foot. It wouldn't take much to give them better places to live in. They'd not expect palaces.'

He glanced towards the clock on the mantelpiece, frowning and wondering whether he'd upset his host by this sort of comment and might now be told to leave. Then he'd have to walk the streets because it wasn't time for him to be let into his lodgings yet. He was feeling better now, at least, not dizzy, and clear in his mind.

But Ellis's next question was the exact opposite of what he'd been dreading to hear.

'Can you stay here for the rest of the day answering my questions, Logan, and telling me more about the north of England? I'll pay you a fair day's wage for doing that and feed you, of course. What you've said so far has made me feel I'd like to know more about it, quite a lot more.'

'You sound as if you mean that.'

'I do.'

'It isn't just a pretend job you're offering me? It'd really help you if I stayed?'

'You've helped me already, Logan, by focusing my thoughts on specifics. I can see now that I'd been thinking too broadly and not getting down to a proper search of the different areas.'

'You were working hard.'

'Well, that part of my life is over now. I'm about to move on – when I figure where to, that is.' He glanced towards the clock on the mantelpiece. 'Look, it's midday. I'm going to ask Cook for a bowl of hearty soup and some sandwiches. She always seems able to produce one if I'm at home unexpectedly and feeling hungry. You'll share a quick snack with me, won't you?'

Logan looked even more surprised at this offer. 'Yes, please. That'd be, um, nice.'

'After we've had a bite to eat, you can tell me more about this valley of yours, as well as giving me further details about the countryside in that whole area if you can. What sort of farming is practised, for instance? What sort of businesses are there for people to work in?'

'I'm happy to do that.'

'I like the sound of Ollindale, I'll see if I like it even half as much as you do.'

'But if you're looking for somewhere to live, surely you'll be more interested in the south? You already know people near here and you'll know no one in the north.'

'I've been working so hard for years, thanks to my uncle, that I don't have any close friends. The man I was closest to went to Australia when we were in our late twenties.'

He sighed and added softly, 'I've realised recently that it's mostly business acquaintances I meet up with. I've no real friends.'

Another silence fell, then he added, 'Last year a long-time acquaintance who was only a few years older than me dropped dead suddenly. That made me think about my own private life and a more peaceful future and when my uncle died, I started divesting myself of my businesses. But I couldn't seem to work out any definite plans for the future, apart from wanting to find somewhere more pleasant to live and raise my son.'

He let out a low laugh. 'And there's another thing I haven't told you: my grandmother came from Lancashire originally, not as far north as you but near Manchester. Only she married a southerner and spent her time with his family, rarely going back to the north, so we lost touch with that branch. I have very fond memories of her.'

'Where exactly did your grandmother come from?'

'Just outside Blackpool, a little place called Cleveleys.'

'I visited it on my way south,' Logan said. 'I'd not like to live there. Salty breezes and sandy beaches are all very well, but I love greenery: trees, long walks in the countryside or across the moors, that sort of thing.'

'You've never been attracted to marriage?'

He shrugged. 'Attracted to women occasionally, yes. I'm a normal man about that. But not attracted enough to want to get married to any of them.'

He stared into the distance and added softly, 'When my third sister married, I felt I'd earned the right to see more of my own country, something I'd always wanted to do. And as I told you, I also came to the south because folk said you could earn more money here. But I travelled here slowly, hitching lifts and walking, doing odd jobs. I stopped off to see a few places I'd read about on the way, like the Peak District and Oxford.'

He shrugged. 'Then I got to London and began to look for work. Only I haven't been able to find a steady job down here and well, I'm missing the north.'

There was silence for longer this time, as Ellis continued to stare at him, brow wrinkled in thought, as if trying to understand his very soul. So Logan didn't hesitate to study him in return. This had been quite a long discussion and about very personal things, not something other men he knew often shared information about. And yet he had felt quite comfortable chatting to a near stranger in this way. Indeed, he felt that if there hadn't been such great differences between them socially, they might have become good friends.

When Ellis spoke again, he said, 'You're looking a lot better now.'

'I'm feeling a lot better.'

'I'm guessing that you were hungry, weren't you?'

Logan shrugged.

What his companion said next surprised him. 'How about you escort me to the north and show me this Ollindale valley of yours? I want to see more of my own country and I find you easy to get on with. And you know about some things I'd not been aware of. I've enjoyed learning something.'

He paused, waiting patiently for an answer.

Logan looked at him, then nodded and said, 'All right.'

'Good. I shall look forward to my travels with you.'

6

One afternoon during the final week of her district nursing course, Livia went out on an urgent call to tend a young woman who had apparently been badly injured.

She went with Edna, the older nurse-tutor with whom she'd been working for her final stint of the practical side of the course, though she was so close to finishing her studies that she would have felt quite confident taking this call on her own.

It felt richly rewarding to be able to help people in this way by going out to see them. Pearl had been right. She was well suited to this kind of work and she enjoyed doing it.

They went into a very shabby, three-storey terraced house, which was divided into a lot of small single rooms, and she couldn't help wrinkling her nose in disgust at the sour smell of the entrance hall.

No one had answered their knock on the half-open front door, but when Edna called out, a scruffy old woman peered out of one of the doors on the ground floor, seemed to know who they were there to see and directed them down some narrow stairs into the basement.

There another older woman let them into a rather dimly lit room. This felt stuffy because the only external opening was into a light and air well, at the top of which was a metal grill set into the pavement. Every now and then someone outside would walk across this, causing a faint clanking sound. There was no external window in any of the other walls and the corridor was stuffy and also sour smelling.

Edna took charge, something they often had to do. 'Can you light a candle, please?'

'Just for a little while,' the woman said grudgingly. 'Candles cost money, you know, missus.'

'I'm miss, not married. And of course I know that candles have to be paid for but if I'm to examine and treat this injured woman, I shall need to see her injuries more clearly.'

'Well, get on with treating her quickly then because I've got work to do and so has she.'

Livia had seen a lot of accidents but was horrified at the sight of the battered face and belt-buckle marks on the arms of the young woman lying on a narrow bed. This was no accident. Someone had beaten this poor woman. The callous way the older woman spoke about her injured companion, then scowled at her as if she had done something wrong, utterly disgusted Livia.

'What's your name, dear,' Edna asked the injured woman gently.

'Janie.'

The older one folded her arms and stayed where she was. 'Never mind chatting. See to her wounds, then she can go home and cook her man's tea.'

'What on earth happened to her?' Edna asked.

Livia had been instructed many times during the training not to show her feelings about what she saw and not to get emotionally involved with patients and their problems. She always found that difficult and even more so today. It was obvious that this was no accident: someone had struck this woman, who was obviously twenty at most, with a belt and punched her too, and they'd hurt her badly.

'How did this happen?' Edna asked gently as she turned the bloodied face of the patient towards her. The woman moaned, tears coming into her eyes. Much of the blood was clotted so the beating must have taken place several hours ago.

'Her fellow came home drunk last night and she didn't have his meal ready, so he gave her a thumping,' the older woman said.

'Is that right?' Edna asked the patient.

'Billy hadn't left me any money to buy food. But he'd been to the pub and spent money there on booze. Only, he never listens to reason when he's drunk. He wouldn't let any of the neighbours help me after he'd hurt me, said I deserved to suffer. Then he pulled his mattress across the door and went to sleep there, so I couldn't get away till after he'd left for work this morning. He kicked me before he left and threatened to kill me if I tried to get away, and – and he said there'd better be a meal ready when he got back. Only how can I do that when he's still not given me any money?'

She began sobbing wildly. 'I can't stay with him, Tess, I just can't. I didn't want to go out with him in the first place because he had a reputation for being violent, but you pushed me into it. And he's worse to live with than I'd expected, far worse. He likes hurting me.'

'He'd be better if you fed him more often.'

'How am I supposed to do that if he doesn't leave me any money for food?'

'Put some on tick at the corner shop. If you tell them who it's for they won't dare refuse to serve you something.'

'I'd never be able to pay it back and he won't even try. Can I stay here till I'm well enough to run away? He doesn't usually hit me when your Sid is around.'

'No, you certainly can't. I don't want anything to do with him in this mood. He's changed for the worse lately.'

'But Tess—'

'I have no room for you here once the others come home from work, and no food to spare either. If you're with him, at least you'll be eating.'

More sobbing greeted this. 'I'd rather die than go back to Billy.'

The two nurses gave Tess disgusted looks but she only scowled at them and said, 'Get on with it quickly, will you? That candle's going to burn right down at this rate.'

Edna said, 'I'll need some clean water, then, to deal with these cuts and grazes properly.'

Tess folded her arms and scowled at them. 'There's a pump at the end of the street. We don't have any running water here and I'm not fetching any for her. And don't you two look at me like that. If she stays here, that chap will come after me and my family as well once he gets home, especially if he finds her gone. He's turned into a vicious sod lately, that Billy Doyle has, and why he ever set his mind on having her, I don't know.'

'You surely don't intend to send her back to him!'

'She'll do better with him if she keeps her mouth shut. She always was a cheeky piece. Answers you back as soon as look at you, she does. No man will put up with that.'

The poor young woman didn't look to have any cheekiness left in her now, Livia thought sadly.

Edna nudged her with one elbow. 'Will you fetch me some water please?'

'Yes, of course.' She took out the container they carried with them in the medical bag. It was much smaller than a bucket, but she could see the bucket belonging to Tess and it was so dirty she'd not use water from it to clean an injury, or for anything else, either.

As she hurried along to the end of the street, anger was seething through Livia at anyone treating another human being like that. And she felt worried too. Would the injured woman really be forced to go back to such a man? The poor creature would be risking her life if she did.

When the wounds had been cleaned, Tess said, 'You'd better go home now, Janie.'

'I daren't. It takes longer than this for him to calm down again. Please let me stay.'

She saw the other woman shake her head and begged again in an even more wobbly voice, 'One night. Please! I'll keep out of sight and tell Billy tomorrow if he sees me trying to get away that I hid in the church porch. And I won't ask you for anything to eat.'

Tears welled in the older woman's eyes but she still shook her head and repeated, 'I daren't. You know I daren't.'

Livia tugged Edna's sleeve and whispered, 'We can't let her go back to the man who did this.'

'What else can we do?' her companion whispered. 'We're always told not to get involved in domestic disputes beyond patching up the injuries.'

Livia took a few deep breaths and tried to stay detached, but as Tess tugged Janie off the bed and pushed her towards the door, the young woman began sobbing. The thought of the danger the poor thing might be facing upset Livia so much she whispered, 'I'm going to take her home with me, Edna.'

'You can't do that. What will Miss Grayson say? Anyway, it's her home, not yours either. You're only staying there. So you can't just take other people to stay there.'

'I don't know what she'll say and it makes no difference. If that man beats this poor lass again, he could kill her – no, he *will* kill her. We all read in the paper about that other chap killing his wife only last month. He wasn't charged with murder, either, just causing death by accident.'

She waited and when Edna said nothing, only shook her head again, refusing to get involved, Livia said, 'If we don't help this woman, she'll be in danger from the minute she walks through the door to his room. I couldn't live with my conscience if she were killed, Edna, I just couldn't.'

'I shall have to report you to your supervisor if you do this, Livia.'

'Go ahead and report me. We're trained to save lives and I'm not going to let her go back to that brute. Whatever they tell us in our training, I just couldn't leave her to a fate like that. Anyway, Miss Grayson will help me to hide this poor woman until we can find her somewhere else to live. I'm sure she will.'

'I doubt it. It's against all the rules.' Edna hesitated, then stared at the patient again and said in a whisper, 'But I've never seen a beating as bad as this one. If Miss Grayson lets her stay for a day or two and she stays hidden, I suppose it'll give Janie a bit longer to recover before she goes back to him, if nothing else. Or she may even manage to get away.'

Livia didn't say it, but she was already determined to get Janie permanently away from a bullying brute as bad as that. The saying that leopards didn't change their spots came to mind and he would be the same. He already had an increasingly bad reputation. He must have been hitting poor Janie for a while, judging by the faded bruises and scars on the poor young woman's body.

Surely, with Miss Grayson's help, she'd be able to find a way for that poor lass to escape? She had to, couldn't live with herself if she didn't.

'Well, are you going to leave me in peace?' Tess suddenly demanded.

Sobbing, Janie tried to tidy her clothes but Livia put an arm round her and said, 'If you want, I'll try to get you away from that man permanently.'

She clutched Livia's hand. 'You really will? Oh, yes please help me! But how?'

'I'm not sure yet but I'll do my best.' She flung her own nurse's cloak round the poor woman's thin shoulders to cover up the torn and blood-stained garments.

Tess only stood and watched, arms folded across her scrawny chest.

Livia said sharply, 'I hope you're not going to tell him who's taken her away?'

There was silence, then Tess said, 'No. Not as long as you get out quickly now before he comes back from work. But be warned. If he does find out who helped her, he'll come after you too.'

'Surely not?'

'He can't abide anyone getting the better of him.'

Edna threw her another warning look but Livia didn't care. She was utterly determined to save this poor battered creature. Wasn't that what her life was about, helping people who'd been hurt to recover? And the worse they were hurt, the more effort you made. You just did.

'Can you try to walk as normally as possible once we're outside until we're away from this street, Janie? Try not to limp even if it hurts more to move that way,' she whispered as she helped the young woman to follow the older nurse up the cellar steps towards the entrance hall of the building. 'We don't want people to notice you at all, if we can help it.'

She had a sudden thought. 'Is there a back way out of this house?'

'Yes, miss. Through that door.' Janie pointed towards the rear of the hall.

'We'll go out that way, then.'

'I'll do my best to walk normally once we're outside, I promise. I'm grateful to you, miss. I was going to throw myself into the reservoir if Tess wouldn't help me. I couldn't bear the thought of that horrible man even touching me again. And you might as well be dead as beaten nearly every day. I'm not his wife and he couldn't marry me because he's already got a wife. The police know that and so does everyone else round here.'

'What happened to his wife?'

'She ran away and he hasn't been able to find her to force her to come back. He gets furious about that some-times when he's had a few drinks and swears he'll find her and kill her one day.'

'I'm not surprised she ran away if you're an example of how he treats women. We'll try to make sure you get away too. We'll look for somewhere to send you where he won't even think of looking for you.'

Livia tried not to show it but she was already worrying about whether Miss Grayson would help her get this poor woman away from here. She didn't know what she'd do if her kind cousin didn't help because she was still short of money herself. She couldn't have afforded train fares for this woman to go anywhere far enough away from him and she still had her own future to think about as well.

She helped Janie right herself as she stumbled and wished they could walk faster or could afford to call a cab. She was never going to let herself get so broke again. Never, ever. Once she started working as a district nurse, she'd earn a better weekly wage than most women did and she'd save something every single week, even if it was only twopence.

That made her feel sad because it reminded her of her late husband and Nigel's expenses when he was ill. It hadn't been her own fault that she'd run out of money. Only, how could she not have done everything possible to save her husband and later, when they knew he couldn't be saved, to buy laudanum to ease his pain?

Nigel hadn't been at all like the brute who'd hurt Janie. He'd never once threatened to hit Livia or been anything but gentle with her in bed and elsewhere. And they'd wept together over their lack of children. She banished that thought. You couldn't change the past, just had to cope with whatever the future brought you.

When they got back to the college, Edna said, 'I'll leave it to you to ask Miss Grayson's help.'

'All right.'

She tried not to show her disgust at Edna's refusal to help as she watched the older woman walk away. As a nurse she too was supposed to help people.

'Are you going to get into trouble for helping me,' Janie asked suddenly.

'I don't think so. It's not up to Edna to decide about whether I should be helping you or not; it's up to Miss Grayson, who's a distant cousin of mine and a very kind person.'

Well, Livia hoped she wouldn't be in trouble. Surely Pearl would be as horrified as she was at the sight of Janie's injuries. There were marks on her arms and body that must have come from former attacks, only just healed, some of them.

She decided to take Janie into the residential part of the college by the rear entrance, because the poor young woman looked so ragged and filthy people would remember her. To Livia's relief, they met no one on the way in and she led her companion quickly up the narrow back stairs that led mainly to the principal's large flat, relieved that no one else had come in and seen them because they were moving so slowly again. She had to support Janie and help her up the last few stairs because the poor thing was exhausted and finding it more and more difficult to move at all.

At the kitchen entrance to the flat, Livia took a deep breath and prayed that she'd find the help she needed here, then she opened the door and called, 'It's me and I've brought someone who needs help.'

As she guided her injured companion inside, the living-room door opened and Pearl came hurrying through into the kitchen. She took one look at Janie and gasped in horror.

'Bring her in. Whatever's happened to her? Sit here, dear.'

Janie sank down on a kitchen chair with a groan she tried and failed to muffle, then closed her eyes, her whole body so limp it wasn't immediately obvious whether she was still fully conscious.

Livia explained quietly what little she knew about the injured woman while Pearl kept an eye on her. Janie didn't attempt to join in at all and after a while she put her crossed arms on the table and rested her head on them.

'Did you say she'd been living with Billy Doyle?' Pearl whispered.

'Yes.'

'Oh dear! You wouldn't have heard of him but he's well known in the district as a thug, and he may come after you as well when he finds out that you're the one who helped her get away from him.'

'Oh dear. Someone else told me that. And I suppose my bringing her here means that he'll come after you as well, though we used the back entrance and didn't meet anyone on the way in. I'm so sorry. I didn't intend to bring trouble down on you as well.'

The silence seemed to go on for a long time then Pearl said, 'I have to admit I'd have done the same. You were right to get her away from him. You've probably saved her life. And I'd never refuse to help someone in such a distressed state.'

'I did hope for that.' Relief shuddered through Livia and she sagged back against the nearest wall.

Pearl patted her arm. 'I don't know how we'll manage to help her escape from him permanently but we'll find a way. Clearly we'll have to get her as far away as possible from here to keep her safe, though. We don't want to risk anyone who knows them both seeing her and telling him.'

She turned back to study Janie, then moved to stand closer and lay one hand on her shoulder. This made her visitor jerk away, as if expecting to be thumped.

'No one's going to hurt you, Janie. And you're welcome to take refuge here till we can get you away.'

'Oh! Oh, thank you, miss. I'll try not to be a nuisance.'

'Let's start by getting you bathed and into some clean clothes. A nice warm bath will be very soothing and help your injuries heal more quickly.'

Janie roused enough to say in tones of wonderment, 'You're still going to help me? Even though you know who did this?'

'Yes, of course. What's your second name?'

'Clayton. I'm Janie Clayton.' She began to weep in what was obviously sheer relief.

Both Pearl and Livia had tears of sympathy welling in their own eyes too as they helped her to the bathroom and out of the torn, stained clothes because this revealed more signs of abuse to shock them.

'A man like him should be put in prison and never let out again,' Pearl said in a low, angry voice.

'I can't think of anything bad enough for him,' Livia said fiercely.

When they'd got Janie bathed and wearing a faded pink flannel nightie from Pearl's store of second-hand clothes, they gave her a glass of warm milk then left her to sleep.

'Sleep will do her more good than anything at the moment,' Pearl said quietly. 'We can guess she feels safe here from the way she fell asleep so quickly, so we've made a good start to helping her.'

When the two of them were back in the kitchen, Livia couldn't help asking, 'You're truly not angry with me for bringing her here, Cousin Pearl?'

'No, of course not. I couldn't have left her to his mercy either. Billy Doyle is notorious for his violence and word is that he's getting worse. I've rarely seen a beating this bad, though, and I shall, of course, report it to the police. I doubt they'll do much, however, except warn him not to do it again. As if a mere warning will make any difference to him!'

She didn't attempt to put on the kettle but stood still a few moments, looking angry, then said, 'What to do about your situation long term is going to need some careful consideration. We shall need not only to keep her safe but you as well now.'

'Me? You're the second person to say that. Why would I need keeping safe? And what about you?'

'You'll have upset Doyle by helping her get away and so will I. But I have the protection of some very important men and he knows better than to upset them. This won't be the first time I've had to deal with a dangerous man, you see. Sadly, however, it's highly likely he'll come after both you and Janie, to get his revenge.'

'Why can't the police stop him?'

'They aren't always as helpful as they could be when it comes to women who've been beaten by their menfolk. Besides, Billy will no doubt get friends to swear he was with them at the time it happened. He's done that more than once before.'

'And the police believed him? Surely not!' She had little experience of this sort of thing.

'I'm afraid they had no choice but to accept his alibi, since he's always had so-called witnesses.'

'Oh, dear. And I've brought her to your flat so this Billy person might go after you as well this time if he really is getting worse.'

'I don't think so. I've lived here a long time and I have friends not only in high places but in significant positions in poorer places too. But the police will have no one breathing down their necks and making sure they keep you safe. What's more, you're going to be going out into the world very soon and will be on your own once you start a permanent job. I'm afraid he may see you as someone he can go after if he's careful how he does it, even if he has to wait a while. Give me a few moments to think about what to do, dear.'

Livia sat waiting, feeling worried and not sure whether to stay with her cousin. Had she brought danger on Pearl as well as herself? But how could she not have tried to help Janie?

Pearl went across to fill the kettle with water and put it on her modern gas stove, then lit the gas and stood looking thoughtful. By the time the water had boiled and the pot of tea was brewing, she was nodding slowly and staring into space as if she'd thought of something.

When she'd put the tea things on the table, she looked across at Livia. 'Come and sit down, dear. We need to talk. I'll pour us a cup of tea first but we'll wait to have something more substantial to eat until after our little chat, if you don't mind.'

After they'd both had a few comforting sips of tea, Pearl said, 'You'll soon be moving away from Bristol to wherever you get a job. I think you'd now be best taking one as far away as you can get from here because of that man.'

She let that sink in for a moment, then went on, 'It's fortunate in one way that you don't have family expecting you to settle near them, so your job can be anywhere. You've already told me you don't mind where you go. Do you still feel the same?' She cocked her head on one side, waiting.

'Yes.'

'Well, I know of a place that is desperate to hire a district nurse and the people organising things in the area aren't having an easy time finding one.'

'Is there a reason for that?'

'Yes. It's because it's a small place in a quiet valley in the far north of Lancashire and because it's also rather a rough area.'

That sounded rather ominous. 'What happened to their last district nurse?' Livia asked.

'She got married to a local man and has settled there happily. She's continued working but she's expecting a child now so she won't be able to do that for much longer.' She smiled and added, 'The good thing about the area is that no one made her stop work when she got married because her husband is proud of her medical skills, and the town needed her. People value what she's done for them very highly. There are a lot of good people there who want it to continue as well as a few of the usual fools and villains we get everywhere.'

'The authorities there must have a more modern approach to women than most, then,' Livia commented.

'Yes, they do. Would you be prepared to work in such a distant place?'

'Of course I would. People are very similar wherever you work.' And she wasn't sure of having another baby, was she, because although she'd love one, she wasn't sure she'd get married again. So she'd be able to continue working for many years.

'What about Janie?' Pearl went on. 'Would you take her with you and help her to get a job once she's recovered. If she helps you whenever she can till then and you find her to be a good worker, references from the district nurse should impress people and lead her to some sort of steady domestic work.'

Livia was about to ask about their travelling expenses when Pearl added, 'I know you're short of money, dear, so I can also give you some for your and Janie's travelling expenses from a local charity and I'll add a bit extra from me to cover other expenses till you're earning properly and Janie can earn a living again. How does that sound?'

'Very generous. Not surprising, though, because you saved me before when I had nowhere else to turn and now it looks as though you're about to do it again. The world would be a far better place if there were more people like you in it.'

Pearl smiled at her and held out one hand to clasp hers. 'Thank you for that lovely compliment. It's good when one's efforts are appreciated.'

'I'm still worried that helping us will put you in danger, though,' Livia said.

'Even that horrible man won't dare go after me. Truly.'

'I hope you're right.'

'I am. I have some very important friends, as I said.'

Pearl seemed so serenely certain of her own safety that Livia relaxed a little. 'Where exactly in Lancashire is this place that needs a district nurse?'

'It's in a small Pennine valley just outside the town of Ollerthwaite. The part that needs the district nurse is called Eastby End. You won't have heard of either of those places, I'm sure.'

'No, I haven't. But that doesn't matter. I have nowhere I can call home now and no close relatives so I'm free to go where I choose.' She managed to keep her expression calm as she said that, at least she hoped she had, though it was a constant source of pain that she had no family to turn to and she couldn't help envying those who had.

She didn't hesitate. 'If that's the price I pay for helping Janie, then I'm happy to pay it. Will they want to meet me first to see what I'm like before they appoint me?'

'Heavens, no. It's much too far away to do an interview. Besides, they'll take my word for it that you're capable, efficient and pleasant to deal with – which you are. Don't blush, it's true. They have trouble attracting extra skilled workers of any sort to go there, because most people prefer to live in places which are located closer to their families or where they already know people. Once the folk in Ollindale get to know and respect a person, they can be incredibly friendly and loyal, though. As I told you, Rachel has now settled there permanently.'

'That does sound promising.'

'It is. But we have to get you there first. We'll need to arrange a secret departure for the two of you as soon as Janie is fit to travel, with no destination that a certain person can trace.'

'Can you do that? Keep it secret when and where we go?'

'I think so. With the help of some friends of mine and an extra train journey for you two.'

'What do you mean?'

'We'll send you to London first and I'll get a friend to buy you tickets in advance so that you don't have to queue to buy them when you leave here.'

'How will I pay them for that?'

'You won't have to. He likes to help people in trouble and can easily afford to do this for you two. He won't meet you but he'll get the tickets to me.'

'Please tell him thank you from me then.'

'Of course.'

'I don't think Janie will have enough possessions to fill one suitcase, though, let alone a trunk. And I'll only have enough because of my books and mementos.'

'I'll find some more clothes and underclothing for her and for you.'

'You continue to be kind to us in so many ways, Pearl. I can't thank you enough, for myself and for poor Janie too.'

'You can thank me most by helping others who're in trouble once you're past this difficult stage. One day I'm sure you'll be settled somewhere, with enough time and money to spare to do that.'

Livia nodded and they were both silent for a few moments, gazing at one another warmly.

It was Pearl who broke the silence. 'Now, let's get back to planning your escape, which will be the first step on your new path: you'll set off very early one morning with just a small travelling bag each, and catch the first train to London, the one they call the milk train because it takes the fresh milk to market.'

'That will be an enormous help.'

'My friend will have obtained tickets for you by then so that you don't have to queue for them, which would give more chance of you being noticed. If you sneak out of here before it's light, I'm hoping people won't even see you going so they won't be able to connect you to me at all. When you get to the station, stay in the shadows till the train arrives.'

'That sounds like an excellent plan.'

'When you get to London you'll need to cross the city to another railway station to catch a train to the north-west, and if you change your clothes in the ladies' waiting room before you do that, you'll look different from when you arrive at the first London station, just in case someone from round here is making the same train changes.'

'You're a cunning woman.'

She smiled. 'Years of practice. Now, you'll need to buy your tickets to Ollindale at that second London station and I'll provide you with the money to do that.'

Livia nodded again as she took this in.

'You'll be exhausted by the time you get there but it'll be worth it.'

'How clever you are!'

Let's hope it'll be clever enough to fool that horrible bully, Pearl thought, but didn't say that. She could only do her best and pray that it would be enough. And she doubted that even Billy Doyle would bother to follow the two women to somewhere so far away, even if he did find out where they were, which he probably wouldn't.

She wondered sometimes why a few people seemed to have been born wicked, as he had. Life seemed to her so much easier if you made the effort to get on well with your fellow human beings, easier for you as well as for them. Why could these bullies not see that? She had never been able to understand their view of the world.

7

Logan stared at Ellis in amazement. 'Say that again. I'm not sure I heard you correctly.'

'I suggested we visit Ollindale and you show me round. I especially want to walk on those moors you love so much. I've never done it before and that sort of countryside always sounds gloriously free from human clutter to me. I've sighed longingly over photos of it but been unable to go there.'

'It does have a – a sense of soaring freedom. That's the only way I can describe it. But there are moors in other parts of the country, in places easier for you to reach from here, too. Why would you go all the way to Ollindale, which is probably one of the sets of moors furthest away from here?'

'Because I need to start looking seriously for somewhere new to live, a place that will suit both me and my son. And, I must admit that it's at least partly because you sound so enthusiastic about the area of the country you call home. I'd like to see it at least, but where I settle permanently remains to be decided, of course. At the moment I'm just – bearing in mind what sort of place I'd like to live in. If I start in the north, I can work my way south and I'm sure I'll eventually find a place to live in.'

He waited and Logan shrugged. 'I'm happy to do it. I've nothing better planned.'

'I'll pay you to help me, of course. That will only be fair. So it'll be – what? – a week's work for you at least, give or take.'

Logan immediately looked happier. 'Really? I wish I could afford to do it for nothing but I have to ask how much you will be paying.'

Ellis named a sum and added, 'You'll get your keep as well while you're helping me, and of course I'll see to all our travel expenses.'

His expression brightened still further. 'That'd be . . . very generous.'

'Yes, maybe, but you'll be working long hours to earn it, because every evening I shall want to talk over what we've seen and done during the day, and I'll probably ask a lot of questions about the north in general and Lancashire in particular. The things I ask may sound stupid to you, because I know so little about ordinary life in the north at the moment.'

'That doesn't matter.'

He gave Logan another of his warm smiles. 'I warn you, I'm famous for asking more questions than other people.'

'I don't mind answering a million questions or working long hours. Besides, it sounds a far more interesting job than I usually have to take on.'

'Good. I like that attitude.'

'You might not like this comment, though. We'll both have to make sure that lad is kept entertained while we're travelling or he'll get into mischief.' He waited for his companion's response, almost holding his breath. Had he upset him? Would the offer of a job be withdrawn?

Ellis appeared to be mildly surprised at the question but not at all annoyed by it. 'We should be all right with two of us.'

He paused to let that sink in, then added with a smile, 'My gran used to say that lads of that age were heedless of everything but themselves, and leap about like frogs in a bucket.'

'Well, that certainly describes how my Gil can behave, as we saw today.'

'Yes, he needs a firm hand on the reins as well as love and kindness.'

'Yes. I can see that now. I do care about my son and I definitely don't want to make another mistake.'

Ellis was speaking slowly, with pauses, as if some of this had only occurred to him for the first time, Logan thought. He'd clearly learned a lot from his uncle but was a very intelligent man in his own right, must be to have made his fortune by such a young age, compared to others who dealt in finances. If he now turned his intelligence on dealing with his son, things should go a lot better and both father and son benefit from the new state of affairs.

'Then if you and I both keep an eye on him, I'm sure he'll be a lot happier. It's not just a question of caring for a lad's body properly but caring for his mind and well, his emotions too, don't you think? I've seen the way Gil watches you and as far as I can tell, you seem to be one person whose authority he truly respects. He certainly pays attention to what you tell him, because he truly cares about you. And if you're with him, you'll be able to look after him properly.'

He let that thought hang in the air without further comment and waited as Ellis stared. It gradually became obvious that some of the seeds Logan had been trying to plant were taking root during that silence.

Words suddenly burst out. 'Well, we've agreed to take him with us, haven't we?'

'I'm glad. Your son will learn a lot from travelling round the country with you and you'll not have to worry about whether he's safe or not. You'll also get to know him far better. If you don't mind me saying so, you don't seem to know him as well as a father should, however greatly you care about his welfare and safety, because you haven't spent much time with him. And he doesn't know you much better? Though he wants to.'

Again, he waited to let that sink in, but though silence was his answer, the expression on Ellis's face said a lot about his reaction to the whole situation, regret being one of the main ones.

Logan felt fairly certain he'd not ruined his own chances of this tempting job, but he had felt obliged to point out the lad's needs as he felt it was the right thing to do morally. And anyway, where children were concerned he usually knew instinctively what to do, as he'd proved in the past. Unfortunately for his present need of a job, he always felt compelled to do his best, his very best, whatever it cost him, for every single child in need whom he encountered, rich or poor. And there were other needs than money, equally important ones too, like the need for affection.

'I'm sure Gil will respond well to more attention from his father,' Logan went on softly. 'He seems to be desperately lonely as well as bored by the life he's been forced to lead.'

He watched and saw Ellis nod as if accepting this, so he continued trying to give him some hints. 'Bringing up a lad as lively and clever as Gil, you have to take care or he can head towards trouble, as you've seen today. In my experience, the most intelligent children are far more hungry for stimulation than others, but whether they're clever or not, all children need to make friends and play with others. I don't think he's been allowed to do even that, has he?'

He kept a wary eye on Ellis, who was still frowning at him, or was the other man frowning at his own thoughts about the situation? Either way, Logan didn't mind letting another few moments of silence tick past and he hoped the ideas he'd planted were sinking in, for the lad's sake.

Eventually the other man said slowly, 'Even if we do take Gil with us, I shan't know how to care for him and will need help with that. I'm talking about the practical details of daily life now, like what clothes to wear each day, getting him washed and when to change his clothes. Then there's the need to obtain clean clothes for him – all sorts of details.'

Logan couldn't hold back a chuckle. 'We'll manage just fine. It's not hard to care for lads of that age. He's old enough to sort out his own clothes when he has to choose what to wear. And if he misses the odd bath or two while we're travelling, what does that matter? I can show you both how to organise most of the necessary little daily tasks. They aren't hard. Then you'll know how to do them with him on your own in future.'

He waited yet again before adding softly, 'He's your only son. I'm sure you'll enjoy getting to know him better.'

He still wasn't sure whether he'd said too much or not, but from the look on Ellis's face, these ideas were making him look thoughtful not angry. In fact, Logan was feeling increasingly hopeful of helping the lad.

He'd noticed before that people with what seemed to him a lot of money often used it to get others to look after their children. So what was the point of having those children in the first place? Just to have someone to pass their money to one day? He couldn't help smiling at that thought. He'd not have that problem because he didn't seem very good at doing more than merely scraping a bare living. Until recently, he'd needed every penny of the money he'd earned to care for his family.

When he thought he'd given Ellis enough time for his advice about Gil to sink in, he let the topic drop and turned back to sorting out the arrangements for their journey. 'I know of a comfortable new hotel in Ollerthwaite where we could all three stay while I show you round the valley. The landlady will get our clothes washed for us and help with any other little jobs that crop up if necessary, I'm sure. She's very efficient and pleasant with it.'

'That sounds good.'

'It is. And the lad can sleep in the same bedroom as me if you don't want him to share with you. I'm used to sharing rooms with others. He shouldn't be left on his own at night in a strange place, though. Children can get nervous, even those of your son's age, though the lads especially try to hide it. But ten isn't all that old.'

Ellis stared at him then a smile slowly crinkled his face. 'You seem certain it'd be good for Gil to come with us and you do sound as though you know how to care for children, even though you're not married, so

I'll take your advice. But remember, I'll need your help with him.'

'I will. I have quite a few young nieces and nephews, and I helped my mother to raise my sisters after our father died, so I know quite a bit about looking after kids, believe me.'

Something else occurred to him. 'Once we're there I can introduce your Gil to my family. I have a few nephews of roughly the same age and I'm sure they'll take him under their wings if I explain to them what his life has been like until now. And the older ones will make sure he stays safe. They're used to keeping an eye on the younger children. If they're the oldest in a big family, they learn to do that while they're quite young.'

'You seem to know how to deal with all the personal details that may arise.'

'I've had a fair bit of practice at both travelling and looking after children. And I bet your Gil will enjoy not only meeting other kids but going outside to play with them in the evenings once school lets go of them.' He grinned. 'He'll enjoy actually being allowed to get dirty, instead of always being told to sit still and stay clean.'

Ellis chuckled. 'What lad wouldn't? You know, you're very perceptive and efficient too, I'm sure. In fact, you keep surprising me, Logan.'

'Do I? I'm good with children, if I say so myself, so I won't let your son come to any harm that's avoidable, I promise you. I find children of that age particularly interesting, they're taking in so much about the world and learning to do things independently. They're also trying to sort out their own views of other people and the world – well, they are if given half a chance.'

He heard his own voice grow pleading. 'Most of all, though, I think your son is desperate for more of your attention. He watches you a lot when he doesn't think you're looking at him.'

'Does he really?'

'Oh, yes. He'd love to sleep in your bedroom and imitate the ways you do things generally. How do you think children learn about the world?'

Another minute or two of silent thought greeted this then Ellis said, 'Very well. You do sound to know about this sort of thing. I'll try it. I'd be very happy to, actually. I really would like to get to know Gil better and now would be the perfect time, especially if we can move away from London and find somewhere more peaceful to live.'

'I definitely prefer living in smaller towns and villages. I've enjoyed seeing some parts of London, especially famous monuments and churches, but I haven't enjoyed the way of life here.'

'Well, then. Could we be ready to set off tomorrow morning, all three of us, do you think, Logan?'

'We can try. But if we're doing that, I'll need to get my own things together from my lodgings as well as sorting out Gil's clothes here.' He could feel himself flushing in embarassment as he added, 'I can't collect my possessions from the lodgings until I'm allowed back into the house. Though I don't have a lot of clothes, I'm afraid, so I hope you won't be ashamed to be seen with me.'

Ellis looked at him and shook his head. 'I'd forgotten about you not being allowed back into the house during the day. That's utterly ridiculous. If you're paying for a room there, you should be able to use it any time you wish, as long as you pay your rent properly. People don't always know what they may need during the day or when they'll need it. And I still can't believe the trouble you have when it's raining if you've finished work early.'

'I manage, though it does get a bit chilly, I will admit. I'd have had to make better arrangements come winter.'

'That's not at all satisfactory.' Ellis stared at Logan and changed the subject abruptly. 'You're looking a lot better now than when you were brought in here. Are you feeling better?'

'Yes, definitely. You can't beat having something to eat, followed by a peaceful sit down and rest.' He felt anxious so said it straight out, 'Have you changed your mind about me travelling with you? Do you want me to leave your house?'

'Heavens, no. On the contrary, I'm looking forward to spending more time with you and continuing to chat about the north and the world in general. I asked because I was wondering whether you're well enough to come with me to collect your possessions straight away? Then you can sleep here tonight and we can all leave together early tomorrow morning.'

'I'll be ready to do that as soon as I'm allowed into the lodgings.'

'We'll do it straight away.'

'But—'

'Leave that to me. We'll go to your lodgings in a cab. Sit in the park, indeed! You'll catch your death of cold sitting around chilly places in this weather.'

'I'm afraid the landlady won't open to us until six o'clock.'

'She will to me. I'll deal with her if she tries to prevent you from collecting your own possessions. I doubt she's legally allowed to do that.'

'I shall enjoy watching you handle her.' Logan couldn't help smiling at the mere thought of it. How good it would be to see Mrs Totterby dealt with firmly by someone who had the power, status and confidence to succeed. For all his affable manner, there was something about Ellis Quinn that said he was not a man to be trifled with, and he had that aura of calm confidence that richer men often seemed to display as they dealt with the world.

'Why have you put up with it, Logan? Why didn't you find somewhere else to lodge?'

'I wanted somewhere that was both cheap and clean, and I have to grant Mrs Totterby that at least: she keeps everything immaculately clean. So I've put up with her sharp ways and stupid little rules. There are plenty of cheap lodgings to be had but not many of them are as clean as hers. And I knew I'd not be staying more than a few months, if that, so I'd be away before winter.'

He let out another of his sudden chuckles and Quinn smiled back at him involuntarily. 'What's amusing you now?'

'I don't know which that woman hates most, her lodgers or dirt.'

That brought a grin to the other man's face as well. 'Leave her to me. She'll probably hate me as well by the time I've got you back your possessions. You're sure you've recovered enough to be capable of doing this?'

'Yes. I really am feeling a lot better. There's nothing like good food for putting heart into you.'

As they got ready to leave, Ellis said in a low voice, 'I don't think we should tell Gil that he'll be going on this trip with us until after we get back from your lodgings, in case he gets too excited and misbehaves.'

'Yes, I agree. You're certainly right about one thing: he will get excited. Very excited. Any lad would.'

8

When they arrived at Mrs Totterby's house, Ellis asked the cab driver to wait. Logan tried to take him round to the side entrance but he said firmly, 'I don't use tradesmen's entrances, thank you very much. And it's even more important this time to make the right sort of impression on this woman if your account of her ways is anything to go by.'

When she opened the front door to them, the landlady immediately began berating Logan for trying to come into the house the front way, and before it was time for her to open the door to the lodgers, too. She gave Ellis a scornful look then frowned and studied him again much more closely, before turning back to her lodger. 'My rules haven't changed: no strangers allowed inside my house.'

'I need to—'

'You must stay out till teatime, as usual, Mr James, and as you know very well, your friend is not allowed to come into the house at all since he isn't one of my lodgers.'

Logan kept his foot in the door so that she couldn't close it on them and she scowled down at it. 'You can jolly well take your foot away, too. It won't make me let you in and if you try to force your way in I'll yell for help and the neighbours will come running, and I daresay the police too.'

He took a deep breath and said loudly as she tried again to close the door on them. 'I'm here to tell you that I'm moving out, Mrs Totterby, because I'm leaving London. And that's why I've come here now. I need to collect all my things straight away.'

'Not at this time of day, you don't. And if you're leaving, I shall need to check that room carefully before you take anything away.'

Ellis's pleasant expression changed from a near smile into a frown at the way she spoke and he turned to Logan. 'I think you should go and find a policeman straight away to stop this woman going into your room and interfering with your possessions. For all we know she may be planning to steal some of them now that she knows you're leaving town.'

'I'd never steal anything!' she protested, but she'd turned pink and looked more than a little flustered now.

That made him feel sure that he'd guessed correctly, based on tales he'd heard of rapacious landladies. 'Then why can't my friend get his own possessions back straight away? And why do you need to keep him away from the room in the daytime anyway?'

'I like to make sure my house is clean. If I let lodgers come and go all day, they tramp in dirt and who knows what? I don't like to see my nice clean floors messed up till they have to be. And when people leave suddenly, without any warning, they steal things if they can.' She jabbed one forefinger in Logan's direction. 'So don't think you can get away with anything of mine.'

Ellis took over. 'We're only intending to go in and out once, madam, and I guarantee that we won't be stealing anything. And we'll wipe our feet carefully before we come inside, naturally. But given how unwelcoming you are to people, we shan't be recommending your lodging house to anyone. Indeed, I'm surprised any lodgers stay long at all, given the way you treat them.'

She was staring at him with an absolutely furious expression now, not trying to hide her feelings, but he didn't give her time to speak, simply carried on and finished what he wanted to say. 'I'm definitely coming in with my friend, so kindly move back and stop blocking the entrance.'

She hesitated and studied him suspiciously. But something about his posh accent and appearance seemed to win the day for him, so she stepped to one side, scowling. But after shutting the door, she pushed in front of him and began to follow Logan up the stairs.

When Ellis started to move up after them, she turned to bar his way, holding up one hand palm outwards as a sign to stop following them any further.

'Please remain in the hall while you're waiting for your friend, sir. You have no reason to come anywhere near the lodgers' bedrooms and you're certainly not going inside any of them.'

'I'll only be coming into one bedroom and that's my friend's. He may need a witness if you decide to claim he's taken something that wasn't his. Or he may only need help carrying his things downstairs, which I shall be more than happy to do, and the sooner the better, given your unhelpful attitude.'

She'd flushed so bright a red when he mentioned stealing items again that he was now certain that's what she'd intended to do. She had that look to her, that of a person prepared to cheat and swindle anyone they considered to be in a weaker position.

He continued to stare at her thoughtfully. Yes, she was definitely a person hungry for money, who didn't care how it was acquired. He had learned about that sort of person the hard way when he was first starting out in business, and with his uncle's help he had learned how to recognise that cavalier attitude towards the world and guard against people playing dirty tricks on others.

She hesitated then let out a little huff and turned to follow her lodger again, running up the last few stairs to catch up with him. This time she didn't try to stop Ellis going inside the bedroom with them.

It didn't take Logan long to empty his three drawers on to the bed, then stuff his things into two large canvas drawstring bags of the sort sailors often carried. Every single thing was visible as it was put in and he packed as quickly as he could, keen to get away from this woman and her nasty ways.

'These bags don't look very smart, I'm afraid,' he said apologetically to Ellis as he picked one of them up and slung it over his shoulder, 'but they've been far more convenient than suitcases whenever I've needed to carry things around during my travels.'

Ellis took the other one out of his hand. 'It's a good idea in the circumstances. I'll carry this one for you, shall I? Wait for me on the landing.'

He turned back to the landlady. 'Please check the rest of this room now, to make sure nothing is missing or broken.'

She scowled at him as she made a show of opening and closing the drawers and wardrobe doors, then shrugged and led the way down the stairs.

At the bottom she let Ellis pass her to get to the front door but barred the way to stop Logan following him down the last few stairs. 'You'll need to pay me another week's rent in lieu of notice before you leave, Mr James. That's the rule.'

He looked at her in shock. 'I've already paid you for two more nights that I won't be spending here. That should be more than enough notice. And you never said anything when I moved in about paying an extra week's rent if I needed to leave suddenly.'

Ellis turned back and came to stand as close to the landlady as he could get. 'If this wasn't part of the rental agreement, madam, you can't suddenly impose an extra charge on a tenant, not legally anyway.'

Mrs Totterby folded her arms, still not attempting to get out of Logan's way and let him finish going down the stairs and leave the house.

Ellis asked her in a very soft voice, 'Do I need to bring in legal help on this, madam? I have a cab driver waiting outside and can send him to fetch my lawyer, who will come here straight away to deal with you, because I'm a very good customer of his.'

She gaped at him. 'Lawyer? Why should you need a lawyer?'

'Because you're trying to cheat my friend by claiming a payment from him that wasn't agreed on at the beginning of his tenancy. And who knows what other tricks you may be planning. Yes, I think a lawyer is definitely called for.'

She gasped at this, then tried to outstare him and snapped, 'It was agreed verbally.'

'My friend says differently, and I believe him, so we'll have to ask my lawyer to judge the rights and wrongs of it, and prosecute you, if necessary.'

She let out a nasty little growl of sound then stepped back, glaring at first one man then the other. 'I hope you're satisfied to be preventing a poor widow woman from getting her rightful amount of money due, Mr Whatever You're Called.'

'I'm not preventing him from doing anything that's lawful in his dealings with you but my lawyer will sue you on his behalf if it turns out you're trying to trick Mr James into overpaying you.'

'Sue me?' She let out a squeak of sound at this, managing to sound both angry and afraid at the same time. 'What for? It's you as is cheating me out of what I'm rightfully owed.'

'I've never cheated anyone in my life,' Ellis said loudly and slowly. 'Never. Can you place your hand on a Bible and say the same thing?'

She gasped and flushed an ugly darker red. He suddenly wondered if she was a heavy drinker, because he'd seen men in public houses who were boozers and developed that particular shade of complexion when they got angry.

'Well?' he prompted.

'Get out of my house and don't come back!' she screeched suddenly, pushing past him to shove the front door wider open. 'Get out!'

The scowl she gave them both as they passed her would have fitted the expression 'if looks could kill' perfectly, Logan thought as they walked away from the house towards the cab, which had moved a little further along the street. And yet she had seemed quite pleasant when he rented the room from her.

He stopped for a moment as they got into the cab. 'Thank you, Ellis. Your intervention prevented her from taking the last of my money.'

'You're confident about children's needs, my friend. I'm confident when it comes to financial dealings and spotting people who're trying to cheat others.' He clapped Logan on the shoulders. 'So you're completely free of her now.'

'Which is a real relief, I can tell you.' He grimaced. 'She's still got a couple of my handkerchiefs from when she last did my washing, though she denies ever seeing them.'

'You should have said.'

'It wasn't worth the extra trouble and they vanished two weeks ago. Anyway, how could I have proved it? She'd just have said they were never in the wash in the first place.'

'Hmm. I suppose you're right. It isn't worth it. Though it goes against the grain with me to let anyone cheat me or my friends, even in small ways. Let's get back into the cab now, Logan.'

He smiled at the driver and apologised for keeping him waiting for so long, then asked him to take them to a nearby shopping bazaar. 'I'll pay for your time to wait for us outside it and we'll leave my friend's bags with you so you'll know we're not trying to cheat you.'

'I'd not think that of you, sir. I've had a lot of practice at recognising cheats and you're not one.'

It surprised Logan how well Ellis seemed to get on with everyone, whatever their level in society. He didn't think he'd ever met anyone quite like him.

As the cab set off, his companion laid one hand on his arm to stop him moving along the pavement. We're going to do a little shopping now because I think you'll need a few more items of clothing for our trip, my friend.

And as you'll be needing them because of working for me, I'll be the one who pays for them.'

Logan flushed in embarrassment. 'I can't keep accepting gifts from you.'

'We can keep accepting help from one another as needed, surely? And you've helped me greatly with my son. Besides I feel that you and I are destined to become good friends from now onwards as we care for young Gil together.' His smile was warm and not at all patronising. 'Don't you agree?'

You couldn't argue with that smile, Logan thought. Charm. That's what this chap had in abundance, and genuine charm not false smiles. Besides, he didn't want to argue. It'd feel good to be decently dressed again. 'Yes, I do agree. I had begun to hope we could become genuine friends.'

'But you still took the risk of speaking out on behalf of my son.'

He shrugged. 'It didn't take much to make you understand the situation. I shall accept your help with more clothes and be grateful to you for them. And I'll give you good value for your money, I promise.'

'I'm quite sure you will.'

It had surprised Logan at first that he'd felt the possibility of a friendship between them, well a sort of friendship perhaps, since Ellis was from what was usually considered to be a much superior background to his. Only, the other man had been the one to cross the usual social barriers first and if he hadn't felt at ease with him, Logan wouldn't have dared venture to speak out about young Gil.

Even then he'd considered it a big risk, which could have ended his chance of this job. Only it hadn't. It had brought them closer together instead.

He stole another quick glance sideways. This man was like no one he'd ever met before and he not only felt at ease with him but rather envious too. It must be wonderful to be rich enough to pass through life with such confidence about dealing with your fellow human beings. And also wonderful to be able to help other people get their lives in order again whenever you saw a real need and a deserving person.

He smiled as it suddenly occurred to him to wonder how the people of Ollindale would react to such an unusual man. Logan was looking forward very much to finding out, but above all looking forward to getting home again to the north, he admitted to himself. He hadn't felt to fit in here in London, and more than one of the locals had mocked his northern accent.

Well, he'd learned a lot about the ways of the wider world here during his travels, so it had been well worth coming but he'd had enough of it now. More than enough.

They didn't spend long in the bazaar and Logan let Ellis dictate what to buy, though he had to bite back protests as the brown paper packages of clothes and underclothes mounted up and were eventually carried out to the cab for them by two shop assistants, who accepted tips from his companion with obvious delight at the amounts given.

Ellis winked at him when he noticed him watching the interaction.

Logan came away from the shopping trip with more items of clothing than he'd ever owned at one time before in his whole life, and garments that were of far better quality than what he usually wore, too. He was torn between pleasure and shame about having these items bought for him.

He'd had to buy one or two pieces of clothing to replace things damaged or worn out since he came to London, but had got them second-hand from pawnshops.

He doubted Ellis had ever even been into a pawnshop. He hoped he'd never have to do so again. They seemed to reek of misery.

There was no sign of young Gil when they got back to the house and Ellis asked his quiet, elderly butler to have their parcels and his friend's luggage taken up to a guest bedroom. 'Mr James will be using this room whenever he stays with us from now onwards. But today it'll only be for one night because we're leaving early tomorrow morning to spend a few days in Lancashire. We'll be taking my son with us as well, so I shan't bother to look for another tutor.'

'Very good, sir. I'm sure Sally will be happy to help you with Gil tonight and tomorrow morning, if needed.'

Ellis nodded and started to move away then turned to add, 'Can you check the early train times up to Lancashire and then on to Ollerthwaite for me, please?'

'Of course, sir. Ollerthwaite, you said?'

'Yes.'

The name of the town seemed to puzzle the butler so Logan stepped in, quickly explaining where it was and about its small branch railway line.

'Thank you for that helpful information, sir,' the butler said with a regal inclination of the head.

He could teach the queen how to deal with people, that one could, Logan thought, managing not to smile at the thought that he was far more majestic than his master.

Ellis took over again. 'In addition, could you please have some suitcases brought down from the attics for both of us and also for Master Gil?'

'Yes, sir. How long will you be away for? I shall need to tell Cook to change our orders with various tradesmen, you see.'

'About a week. I'm not sure exactly. I'll let you know if it's going to be longer than that. You can give the servants some extra time off while we're away and of course take some yourself. I'll leave how you arrange that to you. You'll know the situation and the people better than I would.'

'Yes, sir. They'll be very pleased.'

'Good. Now, where's my son? I haven't told him about our little holiday yet.'

'He's up in the schoolroom waiting for you, sir.'

Logan wasn't surprised that the butler's smiling responses showed he genuinely approved of the man he served. You could tell somehow.

'Right.' Ellis turned back and studied Logan. 'You're looking weary now, my friend. I should probably have let you rest and not taken you shopping till tomorrow. But when I'm looking forward to doing something, I tend to grow impatient to start it at once.'

He hesitated then added, 'I'd like us to set off early tomorrow morning but if you don't think you'll be up to a long train journey yet, say so now and we can postpone it for a day or two.'

'I'll be perfectly OK for travelling tomorrow, I'm sure.' He smiled. 'I shall have no trouble recovering quickly if you continue to feed me so well.'

'That's good.'

'Um, doesn't your son ever come running down to greet you when you get back?' Logan asked.

'Sometimes. But not when he knows he's in trouble.'

Logan didn't say what he really thought of that and Ellis gave him what he was beginning to think of as another of those searching, thoughtful looks.

'What do you think I should do? Go up and speak to him in the nursery or send for him to come down here?'

'What do you want to do? Where will you feel more comfortable chatting to him?'

Ellis smiled and rang the bell again.

The butler's face was as expressionless as ever.

'Could you please ask my son to join us here and then bring in a tea tray for three, with a glass of milk for him. We're all hungry and need something that will keep us going till a hearty tea, again for all three of us to eat together. Maybe a piece of Cook's excellent fruit cake now? It's about time Gil came out of the nursery for his meals, don't you think?'

'Indeed I do, sir. It will teach him his manners nicely.' The butler inclined his head and walked out again.

Ellis gestured to a chair next to the hearth and flung himself down in the one on the opposite side.

Logan was glad to sit down again even though he was feeling better generally. You couldn't beat good hearty food for setting your body to rights, and he hadn't been eating properly for a while.

When the door opened and the boy peeped in, he looked anxious and didn't come far into the room.

Ellis beckoned to him. 'Come and join us, Gil. You know Mr James, don't you?'

'Yes, Father. I'm pleased to see you again, Mr James.'

'Sit down, Gil. I hope you're hungry because I've just ordered tea and cake for us all,' Ellis said.

The lad sat on another chair, looking at his father uncertainly. 'Am I not in trouble, then?'

'Not unless you've done something else wrong while we've been out.'

'No, I haven't. Well, I don't think I have. I'm not always sure whether I'm doing something wrong or not, because some things don't feel wrong, whatever my tutor says.'

'You haven't done anything wrong that I know of. What I want to know at the moment is how hungry you are? And if you'd like a piece of this cake.'

The boy's face brightened. 'I'm very hungry. I usually am. Can I really eat some of your food?'

Logan didn't like the sound of that. Why should the lad feel there was one sort of food for him and another for his father? It clearly puzzled Ellis too.

'Of course you can. Why do you call it my food? Don't you eat the same food as I do?'

'No. Mr Chater used to say that boys need plain food, so I get a lot of bread and butter, and they didn't even allow me to put jam on it. And there's boiled cabbage and stewed fruit ordered every day, too. I'm fed up of those though I do like fruit, especially apples, but they're nicer fresh than stewed.'

'I agree. What's more, I think you're big enough now to eat the same sort of food as I do, and even to ask for some of your own favourites, so I'll tell Cook. Is that all right?'

Ellis got a beaming smile and several vigorous nods and a loud 'Oh yes! Yes, please!' as his answer.

So he asked an even more important question next. 'Would you like to come away with me and Mr James for a few days? We're taking ourselves off for a little holiday up north?'

'Really? Go away with you?'

'Yes, really.'

'Is Mr Chater coming with us?'

'No. He's left and he won't be coming back.'

'Oh, good. I didn't dare believe that he'd really gone until you said it. He can be very sneaky.'

'As you won't be doing any lessons while we're away, we'll wait to look for another tutor.'

That brought a beaming smile then, 'What about Mavis?'

'We'll manage without a maid. You're old enough to dress and undress yourself now, surely?'

The lad stared at his father, still clearly trying to come to terms with all these changes, before saying, 'Yes, I can look after myself perfectly well, and I hate the way she fusses with my clothes. But who's going to look after the dirty clothes or choose what I should wear? I'm no good at sorting that out each day or folding the clothes neatly after they've been washed to make them fit into drawers. Things seem to get themselves all tangled up and when I pull one thing out, another falls out with it. And if I mislay anything, I get in big trouble.'

'Well, neither your tutor nor the nursery maid is coming with us so you'll have to put up with Mr James and me helping you. And we're not brilliant at folding things into drawers, either, so we may all have to wear crumpled clothes some of the time.' He glanced questioningly at Logan, who immediately nodded.

The boy relaxed visibly and beamed at them in turn. 'That doesn't matter at all, as long as I'm not in trouble. And coming with you means I'm nearer to being grown up. I've been longing for that so that I can enjoy some more interesting activities, like the things you do.'

'As long as you're not unhappy about it.'

He did a little jig on the spot. 'I'm the opposite, Father. I'm very, very, very, very happy.' He flung his arms wide and twirled round several times to illustrate this.

Ellis was rather touched and he had to admit to himself that Logan was right. He did need to get to know his son properly, and the lad did need a more interesting life.

Hmm. He'd try letting the boy sleep in his room. Logan was probably right about that as well: Gil shouldn't be sleeping alone in strange hotels.

9

Since it was a sunny day and they had nothing pressing to do, Walter Crossley and his wife set out mid-morning for their favourite walk round Jubilee Lake. They stopped at the upper end and sat down on the bench that had been put there so that people who needed to could rest comfortably for a while when they got halfway.

The Crossleys were old enough to appreciate this convenience sometimes but they stopped there more often simply because they loved the views over Ollerthwaite. They could look straight ahead across the water to the town itself, or look to the right and see their own farm in the distance. It had been Walter's home from birth and now a much loved home for his wife as well.

Although he still owned it and lived there, however, Walter left it to the younger Crossleys these days to run the farm and its allied businesses, like cheesemaking.

The house was big enough not only to house them all but to give Walter and his wife a wing with a small sitting room of their own. They'd married late in life and Ollerthwaite had quickly begun to feel like Flora's home town as well, because she fell in love with both Walter and the town where he lived almost as soon as she got there. After a long and busy life as a nurse, ending as a matron in charge of nurse education, she'd been more than ready to settle down.

On sunny days they often sat on the bench partway through their walk simply to chat quietly about some private subject because it was rare that anyone interrupted them here, as they might have done as they strolled about in town or chatted at home.

People seemed to know instinctively that they came here to relax quietly together – well, Lancashire weather and rain permitting – and left Walter and his wife in peace there with no more than a wave or cheery greeting as they strolled past.

Once they'd sat down, Flora took Walter's hand as usual and raised it to her lips. 'Things are going well in Ollerthwaite lately, don't you think, darling?'

'Yes. Having you here to help me has made a big difference to how quickly I've managed to finish several useful projects in the past few months, small arrangements but they'll help those poorer families to live more comfortably.'

'It's good to be able to do that, isn't it? And the district nurses have settled nicely into most areas of the town. But we now need to decide what to work on next. Sadly, one man and woman can only do so much. I wish we could find more people both able and willing to help improve living standards for the poorer folk.'

He smiled and raised her hand to his lips, giving it a quick kiss. 'You're not moving into peaceful retirement yet, are you? I'm guessing this chat is going to be about your pet project, the one you've been wanting to tackle for a while. Is it time, do you think?'

'Are you a mind reader?'

'If I am, yours is the only one I'd ever want to read, Flora darling. Now tell me, am I correct?'

'Yes. I'd very much like to do something about Eastby End, as you well know, and I know you would too. That part of town has been improved a little in the past few months by the few minor changes that we and some others have managed to get implemented, but that's not nearly enough.'

'No. I agree with you on that. Sadly, major changes are still needed, and some of them would be to refurbish and even rebuild completely some of the worst buildings. Those jobs will take much longer to sort out and finish properly than simply improving a few places.'

She nodded. 'And then afterwards, the homes and people living there will need time to settle into new patterns of decent behaviour. We don't want to improve things if they're going to be damaged and neglected afterwards.'

'That won't happen easily in the centre of Eastby End, will it? Poor behaviour seems to be ingrained there. So what's the first thing on your list that you want to tackle?'

'We have no choice about that do we, Walter love? Before we can continue encouraging the necessary improvements, we'll need to find another district nurse to replace Rachel. Sick people aren't able to be of much use.'

'You're right.'

'And I want to make sure the small clinic is put to better use. Lally has recovered now and is doing a good job as caretaker, but we need someone with nursing skills to live there and look after people who're ill.'

'The town council should make more effort to help us with that,' Walter grumbled. 'It's not right leaving so much to private individuals like ourselves.'

'Sadly, there are enough old fogies still serving on the council to slow these changes down dramatically. It'd be so easy for them to provide better funding to pay the district nurse and someone to help her at the clinic. Are they blind? Can't they see what a difference it's made having Rachel going out and about to help people in their own homes?'

'There's none so blind as those who deliberately avoid looking.'

'Her visits have been especially helpful to the older people who aren't able to get around easily any longer, or the women with small children and babies. She's going to be sorely missed.' She shook her head regretfully. 'We have to find a replacement for her.'

'And as quickly as possible. Some don't have relatives willing or able to help them get to the clinic, even.'

'Some mothers don't even have prams to push their babies round in, and it's especially difficult for them when they have two children in quick succession and need a pram that will fit both their offspring in it. We should look for some more second-hand prams and this time lend them to families so that feckless people can't pawn them!'

She still got indignant every time she thought of a couple of people who'd done that with the prams brought in, some of them, from outside their valley at considerable cost.

'You'd think the idiots on the council would have worked out that it's a lot cheaper to care for sick people in their own homes, than to run a hospital or residential poorhouse as they did in the old days.'

'I still wish we had a proper clinic in Eastby End.'

'One step at a time.'

They were both silent for a moment, contemplating the various problems, then Flora shook her head sadly. 'The trouble is, Walter love, now that Rachel's condition is starting to show, it's upsetting some of the stuffy, old-fashioned people that she's still going out to work at all. Do they think women want to sit quietly inside their houses for nine months and grow their babies in cupboards?'

'In cupboards!' He laughed out loud at that.

'Some of the things people have said to me about how women should deal with child bearing sound nearly as stupid as that. But nature's timetable is inexorable and it dictates that even Rachel won't be available for much longer. However lively she still feels at the moment, her body will gradually slow her down and having that baby will become the most important thing in her life. So we do need to find someone to take her place permanently as quickly as possible.'

'I suppose so.' He rolled his eyes, thinking of one man in particular who'd been annoying him not only with what he said but how publicly he trumpeted his opinions whenever he got the chance. 'Evan Tidby is still telling people that it's against nature for women to go out to work in jobs outside their homes after they're married and even more shocking if they're expecting.'

'That man causes more trouble than a cage of monkeys would and his latest complaints are against the lower classes because he's having difficulty finding and keeping servants. And is it any wonder, the mean wages he's offering and the poor living conditions in his attics?'

'Do you know, he cornered me only last week at the market and he had some other men with him, nodding agreement with everything he said. He was demanding that I stop Rachel going out to work in her condition. He shudders and brays like a particularly noisy ass at the thought of her gadding about flaunting her belly, as he called it.'

'How else does he think we can get a new crop of young-sters without women bearing babies?' Flora spread out her arms indignantly and gazed at the sky for a moment. 'I think she's looking wonderful, blooming with health and promise.'

'He doesn't think at all, that one, just swills ale and wants a woman only to stay at home, cook his meals and do his washing, then leave him in peace to get drunk, as his own wife does,' Walter said.

'It's no wonder he's only had two children and they're subdued little creatures too, undersized for their age. I don't think they eat very well because he spends most of his wages on booze.'

'I feel sorry for them and their poor mother.'

'I actually heard him say the other day that women should leave thinking to their husbands. Does he think that women's brains stop working once they marry?' she exclaimed indignantly.

'He and some of his cronies seem convinced that women don't have brains, though I don't know how they can say that after seeing what women like you and Rachel are capable of achieving. I can't understand their blindly old-fashioned attitude at all. It's nearly the twen-tieth century now, after all.'

He paused, watched her and chuckled. 'You've done it again.'

'What?' Flora looked at him in surprise.

'You always let out a huffing sound and toss your head back when something particularly annoys you, as the thought of Evan Tidby did just then.'

'Do I? Well, it does annoy me when these dinosaurs try to act as though we're still living in the dark ages, no, before the dark ages. I've recently heard some of them worrying about the motor omnibuses they're going to bring into the valley, saying how dangerous they'll make it for pedestrians even to walk along the footpath near them. They'll do even more damage than motor cars have done, apparently.'

'Cars have done surprisingly little damage, I think. At least they don't deposit piles of dung like horses do. I worried about motor cars at first, for obvious reasons, but I needn't have done. Accidents happen with all sorts of vehicles, after all. And even in the home.'

'I'd love to learn to drive a motor car.'

He stared at her in surprise. 'Would you really?'

She smiled. 'Is that foolish at my age?'

His voice grew chill and he said firmly, 'Well, I don't want to drive one and I'd rather you didn't either, and that's not because you're a woman but because it's too dangerous. At least bus drivers are properly trained experts with the necessary skills, who will be less likely to cause accidents.'

They both fell silent for a moment, because Walter's son and grandson had both been killed a few years previously in an accident involving a motor vehicle and every now and then that memory hurt him badly.

Then he took a deep breath and went back to his original subject. 'From what most people are telling me, they're looking forward very much to having reliable public transport. They can't all afford their own ponies and traps, after all.' He sighed and stared into the distance.

Flora gave him a few more moments to set his sad memories aside then said, 'Well, Walter love, people with more money are starting to expect to have their own motor cars. There are several in the valley now. And personally, I look forward to seeing what other new inventions will be produced to make people's lives easier.'

They sat in silence for a few moments, then she remembered what she'd overheard and went on scornfully, 'One omnibus in each direction every hour up and down the valley isn't going to make much difference to our world, yet some fools are getting all het up about it and asking the town council to forbid the introduction of more services than that.'

'It won't happen.'

'Well, why should they be banned? There was an article in the Sunday newspaper the other week describing how they've had omnibuses in London and Paris for decades, lots of them going in every direction, into and out of the central areas of the cities. And it doesn't seem to have wiped out the population there, does it?'

'On the contrary. It's not the omnibuses I worry about most, but amateur drivers. I still feel they should have to pass a test and prove that they really do understand how to drive safely.'

'We're in complete agreement about that,' she muttered.

'And you'd be pleased with me if you were able to be there invisibly sometimes at council meetings, Flora love, because I've scolded more than one chap about their old-fashioned ideas about women. I wonder what changes we'll see to our world in the coming years.'

'I think women are already changing a lot.' She was still obviously simmering with fury, however. 'Do you know, Walter, last week when I was waiting to be attended to in Mrs Selby's cake shop, one man came up to me to say that I should have a word with Rachel and tell her it's dangerous for the baby if she carries on working.'

'What did you say to that?'

'I told him to mind his own business, but he got angry and said loudly that women should stay out of sight of normal people voluntarily when they're expecting. As if it isn't normal to have a baby!'

'I'd like to have been a fly on the wall and seen you tell him off, Flora.'

'I certainly didn't mince my words. Nor did the other women in the shop.'

She smiled reminiscently. 'When Mary Cartwright gave him what for as well, some other women applauded. She has a sharp way when she's scolding someone. He muttered something about having better things to do than stand around gossiping and left suddenly without buying anything.'

'Good for all of those women.'

'That's what I said to them.'

'I love it when you're steaming with fury. It makes your eyes sparkle.' He leaned across to plonk a kiss on her cheek, then added, 'Rachel's looking particularly rosy and well, don't you think?'

'Yes. She's absolutely blooming and carries a baby well. Though I'm beginning to wonder if she's expecting more than one, she's putting on weight so quickly. I bet she'll have a beautiful child.'

'And you'll be the first in the queue to cuddle it,' he teased.

Flora smiled. 'Or them. I never can resist cuddling babies.'

They sat happily for a few more quiet minutes then he said, 'We do need to find someone to take over permanently as the district nurse in Eastby End, though. Rachel can't work for much longer, even in this modern world.'

'I know. I wrote to Pearl Grayson again last week, telling her we still hadn't found a replacement for Rachel, but so far she's only sent a quick postcard in reply, saying she's doing her best.'

She pulled a face. 'Unfortunately, not many of the people who train in Bristol are happy to move this far north and work in such a small town, let alone spend their lives in a place as bad in parts as Eastby End.'

He frowned. 'We need to continue sorting out some of the other problems there too, only you can't fix everything at once, can you? Parts of Eastby End are still unsafe after dark. I'd not like you to go out on your own in the central area at night, Flora my love.'

'I agree. And I'm not stupid enough to take that risk.'

'And what are we going to do about somewhere for the newcomer to live? It'll need to be reasonably close to Eastby for her to walk to and fro, and will need to house an assistant as well, to accompany her on night calls.'

'Well, that's one problem that has been solved in advance. I forgot to mention that I saw Rachel at the shops yesterday and she told me that whoever we appoint in her place can take over her former flat. Her landlady is happy about that.'

'Yes. That's good but we still have the difficulty of finding a new district nurse.'

'Will Hanny become the assistant to the new one? Have you spoken to her?'

'No. Joss and Rachel are going to pay for her to train as a nurse, so they'll even make the room in the basement available for another assistant to use and not ask for rent on that either.'

'How generous of them!' He smiled at her. 'We have some lovely people living in our town, don't we?'

'Yes. But Rachel said she doesn't want to stop work until she's handed over properly to her successor, so it's getting urgent that we find someone suitable. It's worrying that our first advertisements in the national newspapers didn't bring any replies at all.'

'Once we find someone, though, you'll be able to keep an eye on things, if only to make sure the new nurse is up to scratch in every way. You and I are lucky to enjoy good health, unlike some people of our age. I can't believe I've turned seventy when most of the time I still feel like a lad inside my head, though I will admit that my body tires more easily these days. And you certainly don't look your age, Flora darling.'

They were silent for a moment or two as they exchanged more of those loving glances that said just as much as words, then she gave him a nudge with her elbow and said provocatively, 'I'm not nearly as old as you.'

They both chuckled at that because she was only a few months younger than he was but teased him regularly about being 'an older man' during the part of the year when he'd moved on to a higher age number than hers.

He tugged her to her feet. 'Come on then, young lady. Escort your elderly husband home. We can't sit here all day and anyway, by the time we get back it'll be midday and I shall be more than ready for something to eat.'

'You definitely have a young man's appetite!'

He stopped to gaze at her and say in a low voice, 'In more ways than one.'

And she blushed as well as smiled.

10

Pearl's alarm clock, loaned for the occasion, sounded gently from under a folded towel next to Livia's bed the following morning at quarter to five. Even that faint sound woke Janie in the nearby bed and she jerked upright, staring round anxiously in the semi-darkness of only an outside gas street light shining dimly through the window.

The two young women got up and tiptoed round the bedroom, getting dressed and packing their night clothes in their suitcases by its faint light. They'd got washed and set their clothes out the night before, so were soon tiptoeing into the kitchen to grab a quick snack and their packets of sandwiches for the journey with the help of another street light.

It felt strange to Livia having to fumble their way round the kitchen without switching on the modern electric lighting Pearl had had installed. She was going to miss that, it was so wonderfully convenient. They did light a small candle and stand it in a holder on the floor in a corner of the kitchen well away from the window.

They'd tried it out before they went to bed and the candle wasn't bright enough to show from outside, so no one would know the occupants were already up and about.

Pearl had said goodbye to them the previous night and left food on the table ready to take with them. Sandwiches were wrapped up in oiled paper, then in a tea towel.

They had been supplied with dark outer garments from the second-hand box, the sort of clothes people wore to attend funerals. Their dowdy old-fashioned hats had heavy veils that pulled right down over their faces, something that was also still common wear for some mourners at funerals. It was hoped that this wouldn't attract any attention particularly and yet would conceal their identity, as well as helping to hide the livid bruises on Janie's face. It didn't hide them completely, though.

As they finished getting ready, she whispered, 'I'm frightened of going outside, miss. Do you think he's paid someone to keep watch on us?'

'He's not sure where we are and even if he was, would he go to the length of keeping watch all night? I doubt it. Anyway, how would he watch all the entrances to this building? We'll be going out the back way, don't forget.'

'I wouldn't put anything past him. He might have paid someone to help him. He goes mad if a woman bests him and takes his revenge in nasty ways later, whatever he can manage to do without getting caught. I don't want my face slashed. I heard that he did that to one woman.'

Livia had never seen anyone as afraid and said comfortingly, 'Well, our faces will be hidden not only by the veils but by the fact that it's not light yet. So if anyone is around and sees us at the station, we'll just look like a pair of women going to a funeral. And it's only just after five in the morning, so there aren't likely to be many people around, now are there?'

To her relief, Janie nodded and relaxed a little.

After a brisk walk through the back streets, during which they met only one other person, an old woman hobbling along with the aid of a walking stick, they found a few people standing around at the station. They too were huddled in warm clothes and scarves because it was still chilly at that hour.

Not only did no one seem at all interested in anyone else but Janie and Livia already had their tickets to London, thanks to Pearl. They found a darker part of the platform their train left from and waited there.

The other platform, which was only for local trains, looked to be busier, with several small groups of people standing around waiting for the next one, but there were only an elderly couple and a trio of men in business suits waiting for the London train on this platform, besides Livia and Janie.

When it arrived, the men all got into a first-class carriage. The elderly couple got into a carriage on their own, and Livia and Janie did the same, relieved to find that it was a corridor train with several empty compartments in the third-class section.

But even after Livia had put their cases up in the luggage net and they'd both sat down, Janie still kept her face covered by the veil and huddled into the middle of the bench seat with her back to the outside window of their compartment, although she didn't look at all comfortable there.

It wasn't till the train had pulled out of the station that she moved into a more natural position and stared at Livia, saying in a whisper, 'Do you think we really have got away?'

'Oh, yes. No doubt about it. And there's no need to whisper from now on. I kept an eye on the station and saw no one get on or linger anywhere nearby after the passengers we saw waiting had got on this train at the same time as us.'

She waited a minute, saw the uncertainty still on Janie's face and said very firmly indeed, 'I'm quite sure we're safe now and we're going to have a nice, peaceful journey.'

She crossed her fingers as she made the last comments, hoping she wasn't tempting providence.

Janie gulped and reached under the veil to dab at her eyes with a bit of clean rag Pearl had given her for a handkerchief, but she still made no attempt to uncover her face.

Livia had never seen anyone as afraid as this poor woman was and promised herself that if it was humanly possible she'd never let the man who'd attacked Janie so brutally get near her again, whatever it took.

In the meantime, the train chugged along and they weren't even visited by a ticket inspector, so Janie relaxed still further.

It would take under two hours to get to Paddington Station in London, and then they would have about an hour to wait between trains.

'We'll change our outer clothes in the ladies' room of the station we arrive at in London, then we'll take a cab across to Euston station,' Livia said. 'Pearl gave me the money for that.'

This information seemed to distract Janie from her own troubles. 'It seems strange to think that there are other stations in the same city. London must be a huge place.'

'It is. I forget how many stations there are in London itself, but there are underground railways taking people around there as well as railways going to other towns. I haven't been there before, either, but I've read about it and seen photographs in magazines.'

'I'd never been anywhere, hadn't even left my area of Bristol before except on Sunday school picnics to the nearby countryside. I'm so glad I've got you to show me the way. I'd be utterly lost on my own with all these hurrying people. And thank you so much for helping me, missus. I'm that grateful.'

'My name's Livia. You don't need to call me missus.'

'It doesn't feel right for me to use your first name.'

'Of course it is. I'm not the queen.'

'You're better than the queen to me. You saved my life.'

'I don't think he'd have killed you.'

'Not this time, maybe, but he was getting worse each time he attacked me and I knew he would definitely kill me if I stayed.'

Livia stared at the bruises on her companion's face. 'Why was he so cruel to you this time?'

'Because I tried to get away from him. He normally didn't want people to see the bruises he left, so he didn't hit my face, but this time he was so angry he didn't seem to care if they showed.'

'Such a horrible man. But I reckon you've succeeded in escaping now and I doubt you'll ever see him again, Janie.'

'I hope and pray not. I'd throw myself off a cliff rather than go back to live with him.'

She meant it too, Livia realised. That was very obvious.

When they got on the second train they were once again lucky enough to find a compartment to themselves and as it set off, Livia said, 'There. We're now out of London heading north.'

Only then did Janie relax and gradually fall asleep. But she'd still insisted on keeping the hat with the veil on and it was now twisted crookedly sideways on her head as she huddled in a corner, fast asleep. She must have slept badly the previous night to be sleeping so heavily now. Or perhaps she'd been sleeping badly for a long time and was only now starting to feel safe.

Livia had been hoping to throw the horrible hat away and had stuffed a beret in her bag to give to Janie in its place. Unthinkable that a decent woman would go out without some sort of head covering, even if it were only a headscarf. But she didn't even try to make her companion change hats yet. If keeping that horrible thing on her head made Janie feel safer, then she could wear it night and day for as long as she needed its comfort.

Surely he'd not find them now?

Livia was looking forward to arriving in the north and starting work again. She was also longing to live in a home, or at least a room of her own, rather than a dormitory. It had been hard to live in a group of single women again after being married for several years.

She'd stopped turning to cuddle Nigel in the mornings now and was growing used to being alone in the world.

I I.

Logan was starting to feel comfortable in the company of Ellis and young Gil now. They needed to get to the station in time to catch the first train heading north towards the area where they could change to the minor northern railway line that was the final stage.

To his surprise, Ellis had given him an alarm clock and explained ruefully that he could sleep right through its noise, and had done more than once in the past. He asked if Logan would mind taking charge of it and waking them all at five o'clock in the morning.

He didn't mind at all because he always woke early anyway. He set the alarm for ten minutes before five and woke immediately it sounded. He felt bright and alert as usual first thing in the morning, and often felt sorry for people who seemed to struggle for a while before coming fully awake. Though he paid for that later in the day because his early start usually meant he was ready for bed well before most other people, except for early risers like himself.

He got up at once, beaming in anticipation of the day to come.

Ah! He suddenly realised that his headache had now gone completely, and thank goodness for that. Last night he'd enjoyed some wonderfully restful sleep in the most comfortable bed he'd ever in his whole life snuggled down into. That had put him in fine form to face a busy day.

Best of all to wake up to was the thought that he was going home today. Home! To slow northern voices, friends and relatives living nearby to turn to if you needed help, or just to share a cup of tea and a pleasant chat with for no reason at all except the pleasure of it. Most of all he was longing for one of his mother's big, warm hugs. He'd missed those dreadfully.

As soon as he could manage it, he was going to go for a long walk, striding out across the moors and sucking in lots of crisp, fresh air. That always felt as if it was clearing out his lungs, and this time that'd mean the final traces of the smoke and dirty air of London would be gone.

Once he got back he'd have to confess to his family that he'd failed in what he'd set out to do, and he wouldn't be less than honest with them about that. He never lied to them or to anyone else if he could help it. That way he stayed comfortable inside his own mind.

He hadn't made much money at all, but what Ellis would be paying him for this trip would at least give him a start after his new employer and young son had left the north, as they no doubt would.

Logan would then have to find a more permanent place to live, though he could sleep on the hearthrug at one of his sisters' houses for a while, if he had to.

And at first he'd simply have to take whatever work was available to earn his daily bread, but there was nothing wrong with honest toil – except that it could be tedious or even dangerous in some jobs. He'd just have to put up with that and hope for the best.

Mind you, his trip hadn't been a waste of time in some ways. He'd learned a lot by visiting other parts of England, not just from having different experiences, but by learning all sorts of small new skills. He enjoyed learning anything at any time. You never knew what might come in useful one day and what would simply give you or your family pleasure or extra comfort. There was nothing wrong with pleasure and comfort.

He looked back at his life occasionally, sighing at the thing he regretted most deeply: he hadn't been able to take up the scholarship he'd won when he was ten to go to the small local grammar school. It would have paid all the fees and the cost of books, but not the cost of the uniform and of other scholarly items you had to provide. That would have been too much expense by far for his family and anyway, they needed his wages simply to feed everyone.

However, he'd continued to learn whatever he could because he enjoyed gathering knowledge for its own sake. He didn't think anyone else would care about the unseen benefits gained by his foray into the south of his own country, but his travelling had given him great personal satisfaction and taught him a lot about the rest of England.

He glanced at the alarm clock. Ah! He'd better get on with what needed doing before they left and stop day dreaming. You had to be both time and money rich to be able to lose yourself in thoughts and memories just because you felt like it.

He got dressed then went to wake young Gil first, which wasn't hard. The lad jerked upright in bed, remembered what was going to happen today and rolled out of it without needing any further urging, beaming at him.

When he suggested a quick wash and then getting dressed, Gil nodded but Logan grabbed his arm before he could rush off. 'Can you manage all that on your own?'

'Of course I can. I'm ten years old, not ten months. I'm ten years and four months, actually!'

'So you are. In that case, do it properly and don't forget to clean up the bathroom after yourself. People do that automatically as they grow older and don't need telling or reminding like younger children do. There will be no servants on this trip, just us three, so you'll have to get used to looking after yourself. Only the smallest children and babies get waited on when their families are travelling.'

'I know that,' Gil said indignantly. 'And I do know how to clear things up. It was just that my nursemaid said it was her job and she wouldn't let me do any of it. I don't need a nursemaid now, thank goodness.'

'I can see that when you stand up. You're quite tall for ten, aren't you? People would think you were at least eleven.'

That brought a beaming smile to the lad's face, as it would to any child of that age who'd been told he looked older. Logan didn't allow himself to smile at how well that ploy had worked. It nearly always did with youngsters.

'You'll be sleeping in your father's bedroom while we travel, so it'll be even more important that you look after yourself properly.'

'I can do that.'

He allowed himself a quick grin about young Gil's determination to seem grown up, though, as he was walking along the landing to wake Ellis who had the big front bedroom in their home.

When he'd done that he went downstairs. There was no sign of the elderly butler but Cook was in the kitchen, still wearing a dressing gown under her pinafore but determined to see them off properly. She must have got up even earlier than he had, because she'd already made them bacon sandwiches for a quick, hearty snack before they left.

Logan's mouth watered at the mere smell of the kitchen. And a pot of tea was brewing nicely on the already warm top of the kitchen range, just waiting for him to pour himself a cup. Sheer luxury, this, for him.

She nodded a greeting. 'Morning, Mr James. I've made packets of sandwiches for each of you and wrapped them in waxed paper to keep them fresh. They should be the last things you put into the tops of your knapsacks so that they won't get badly squashed.'

'That's wonderful. Thank you so much,' Logan said at once. 'I love your cooking.'

She beamed at that as he'd guessed she would. Who didn't enjoy being complimented?

Ellis had come into the kitchen in time to hear this and said at once, 'That was beyond the call of duty and it's much appreciated, Mrs Gretton. Have a restful time while we're away. You've earned it.'

'You take care on your travels, sir, and look after that lad.'

She seemed perfectly at ease with her employer and it was another sign that Ellis treated his servants well. Which didn't surprise Logan. The more he got to know the other man, the better he liked him, too. He was unlike most of the other affluent people that Logan had met, not at all stand-offish.

He turned at the sound of footsteps and managed not to smile at the sight of Gil hefting his smaller-sized knapsack into the kitchen and trying not to show that he found it rather heavy.

The lad smiled at the two men as he set it down. When told which were his sandwiches, he at once knelt to put them in his pack, working with earnest care so as not to squash them, tongue sticking out of one corner of his mouth he was concentrating so hard.

That lad had been deprived of so many little experiences and tasks like this outing. It was as if he'd lived in another country to the people Logan had grown up with. That didn't seem to be a good preparation for adult life for any child, rich or poor.

Logan wondered suddenly whether Ellis would expect waiting on during their travels. The man he was starting to think of as a friend would go down in his estimation if he expected too much fussing over. No, surely he wouldn't? He hadn't been at all uppity so far. No, Ellis would fit in well wherever he went. That was Logan's guess anyway.

You had to do what you could to help one another because life could be gruellingly hard at times. But unless they were unable to, ordinary people fended for themselves in the details and personal chores of their daily life and those they met would expect Ellis to do the same for himself. And Logan would ensure that he did it himself as well.

But he had to stop getting lost in thought because the taxi that had been booked arrived and Ellis helped him carry out the luggage, then they were off within a couple of minutes.

The two men exchanged glances and smiles at Gil's excited comments more than once on the way to the station, and Logan felt secretly happy, fairly certain now that he'd been wrong to doubt Ellis, who was in no way lazy or the sort of person to take being waited on for granted.

He was also delighted to see how happy Gil was, fairly fizzing with excitement.

The train journey didn't seem all that long from London to Manchester, only just over five hours, and young Gil spent a lot of the time staring out of the window, and occasionally asking questions about what they were seeing outside the train. Clearly he hadn't seen much of the world outside his home, and a couple of times Logan saw Ellis frown as if surprised by his son not knowing something.

At Manchester they had to change to another line as far as Preston, with yet another change still to come from there to the final stage on the small single line that led only into the valley.

Ollindale at last! Home. From Manchester onwards Logan relaxed and gazed as eagerly out of the window at the scenery as young Gil had been doing, ignoring most of what was going on inside the carriage.

Nearly home now.

And then they were on the final train, a shabby little one which chugged slowly along the final single line that only ran through a narrow valley set between low hills. There were small villages here and there, all of which the train stopped at to let people on and off, most of them women carrying big shopping baskets full of purchases.

'Ah! We're almost there now!' Logan exclaimed involuntarily and began pointing out places and in the distance the gleam of Jubilee Lake. 'I'll be able to take you two on some splendid walks across the moors on fine days. There's nothing like it. And it's grand to stroll round the lake, too.'

His two companions both seemed interested so he didn't attempt to rein in his enthusiasm and kept telling them more about his world.

'It's stark scenery and yet it has its own beauty,' Ellis commented at one stage. 'A beauty of line and form you might say, rather than of details that are beautiful in themselves.'

'And when you're out there on the moors, you're surrounded by soaring spaces that take your soul flying,' Logan murmured.

Ellis smiled at him. 'I've never seen anyone so enthusiastic about their home town.'

'Yes, I do love it. I didn't realise how much until I left. I hope never to be forced to go away from Ollindale again, even if I have to live in a hut at the end of someone's garden to stay there.'

Happy anticipation at the prospect of seeing his family also filled Logan's heart but he managed to keep that mostly to himself, at least he thought he did. He left keeping an eye on Gil to his father as much as possible and feasted his soul on the sights of his beloved home.

The other two murmured to one another from time to time, and then suddenly they were drawing to a halt in Ollerthwaite station.

He stood up the minute the train stopped. 'We're here now, Ellis. I'll pull down our suitcases.'

'You're sure there will be a cab to take us to the hotel you spoke about?'

'If there isn't one waiting outside, someone will send a lad to fetch one. It's close enough to walk to the hotel but we've got a lot of luggage and a rather tired lad to take there. Eh, I don't know about you but I'm beginning to feel tired myself as well. It's been a long day, hasn't it?'

'Yes, I'm not only tired but hungry again too. Those sandwiches have worn off and so have the bits and pieces of railway food. Will the hotel provide us with an evening meal?'

'Something simple and tasty, yes. Nothing at all fancy though.'

'Who cares about fancy stuff? Any sort of hearty food will do for a man as hungry as me.'

'And for a hungry boy!' Gil rubbed his stomach to emphasise this.

His father smiled. 'Yes. Clearly we have a ravenous boy on our hands. After we've eaten I'd like to stretch my legs. It should be light for long enough to do that at this time of year.' He smiled at Logan. 'And you'll no doubt want to go and see your family?'

'If that's all right with you, sir?'

'Of course it is.' Ellis ruffled his son's hair. 'I think I can keep this one in order, don't you?'

Gil leaned against his father, something he'd never been encouraged to do before they came on this journey. He shot a quick, shy glance sideways that showed Logan how much this meant to him.

Ellis put an arm round his son with equal shyness but also looking happy and leaving his arm there for a while.

Logan had known someone needed to speak about the lad needing his father and this journey had already proved it beyond doubt. His companion had been missing a lot by leaving others to raise his son and was now beginning to find that out – as was young Gil.

Maybe one day he'd have a son. Logan hoped so, hoped that so desperately it hurt at times. He'd always done his duty by his family. Now he wanted something purely for himself: and a different family of his own, not just a wife but children, sons or daughters, it didn't matter which. He would love them all.

He had so much love inside him bursting to be let loose on a family.

When he'd seen the others settled and a meal ordered, Logan couldn't bear to stay a minute longer. He didn't bother to eat with them and when Ellis flapped one hand at him to leave, he was out of the hotel as quickly as he could, striding away towards the outskirts of town.

He would try his favourite sister's home first and hope that his mother was still living with her. He picked up some fish and chips on the way and ate them in huge snapping bites as he walked along the street.

He hesitated briefly at the front door, then knocked and waited. He'd not have done this before his trip to London, would have just tapped the family's special double knock and walked in. But Betty wasn't expecting him tonight and he didn't want to give her and whoever else was here too great a shock.

It was his mother who opened the door. She gaped for a moment, then let out a happy shriek and fell into his arms, bursting into tears of joy, stroking his hair and face, saying his name over and over. It was a while before either of them talked any sense.

'Why didn't you let us know you were coming, Logan love?'

'It happened so suddenly there wasn't time. I've come with my new employer, you see. He wants to see something of the north and only decided on this trip yesterday, would you believe? Talk about impulsive. I have to get back to him tonight, I'm afraid – we're all at the hotel

– but I couldn't resist coming to see you and our Betty straight off and he understood that. He's a kind chap.'

He broke off as there was the sound of a baby crying from inside the house. 'Has she had the new one already?'

'Yes. It's another little lad. He came a bit early and had to be cosseted a bit, but he's all right now and starting to put on weight nicely.' She pulled him further inside calling, 'Betty love, our Logan's back!'

That caused a shriek from the far end of the house and he grinned as he went towards the kitchen. 'Now don't pretend you're glad to see me again, our Betty.'

She was sitting on a low chair feeding the infant, looking rosy and happy. He paused for a few seconds to enjoy the sight of her holding her child, then went across to hug her carefully. He kissed her cheek gently then studied the baby. 'What have you called him?'

'Oliver Logan. You're still going to be his godfather, aren't you?'

'Of course I am. Eh, to think I missed being nearby for the birth.'

'There was nothing much to miss. He came so quickly he took us all by surprise.'

She reached out to finger his sleeve. 'You're well dressed, Logan love. Did you make plenty of money down in the south, then?'

'No, I didn't. I failed miserably, but I've got a new employer, Ellis Quinn he's called, and he's a really nice chap. He's paying me to show him round and he bought me some new clothes because mine were so shabby. You'll like him. And he's got a son. Ten, young Gil is. Lively little lad. You'll like him too. We'll need to find him some playmates.'

'I shall look forward to meeting them but it's you who matters most to us. Um, where are you staying tonight? We're a bit short of space here, I'm afraid, what with the new baby and Mum still living here.'

'I've a bed at the hotel in the room next to my employer's. I'll still be working while I'm here, you see, but I'll be able to spend time with you and the others now and then.'

He told her a few things about the last day or two, then stood up and said regretfully, 'I need to get back now. I'm a bit tired after all the travelling. I'll see you sometime tomorrow, I hope.'

His mother walked to the front door with him. 'I'm glad you're back home in the valley, son. The money doesn't matter nearly as much as you do. I've missed you dreadfully.' She hesitated, then asked tentatively, 'And he really is a decent chap, your new employer? You're sure of that?'

'Yes. He and I are close to becoming friends, I think. He's good at making money but he's lacking in real friends. And as I said, I'm sure you'll find him a pleasant chap. And the son's a nice lad too.'

He strolled back at a brisk pace whistling happily, enjoyed another snack from those set out in the guests' sitting room. Gil was already in bed and the landlady promised to keep an eye on him while the two men took a quick stroll round the town centre.

For the second night running, Logan slept soundly and didn't stir till the hotel's maid woke him with a morning cup of tea.

Now, that was an excellent way to start the holiday, a fine night's sleep and being waited on by a maid bringing him tea in bed. He grinned and took another gulp of tea. He could get used to this sort of life.

12

The Crossleys might be in good health but unfortunately the owner of the house which contained the nurse's flat wasn't at all well, and Dora Prior collapsed in the street when she was out shopping a few days later.

Rachel didn't hear that her friend had been rushed into hospital until the following day. She went to visit her straight away, knowing that Dora didn't have any close relatives left.

When she arrived, the sister in charge of that ward intercepted her. 'I thought I'd better warn you that Mrs Prior isn't doing at all well and is desperate to speak to you. And never mind those rules.' She indicated a sign on the wall. 'You can spend as long as you wish with her.'

They stared at one another and as Rachel realised why she was being told this, tears welled in her eyes and her voice wobbled as she spoke. 'Oh, dear. I'm so very sorry to hear that.'

Like all nurses, Rachel and the sister had both had to deal regularly with people who weren't likely to recover. Some of the patients realised what was coming and accepted it, which made things easier for all concerned. But naturally it was much more upsetting, even for an experienced nurse, when the person dying was a close friend.

'Our task has been easier, if you can ever call it easy, because she's one of those who understands instinctively what she's facing,' the sister went on. 'I thought I should let you know, though, so that you could be careful what you say to her.'

'You were right to do that and I'm very grateful for your warning. Poor Dora!' Rachel had thought her friend was looking rather pale and lethargic last time she'd chatted to her while shopping in town. She'd noticed that she'd lost a lot of weight too, but hadn't realised how serious the problem was because Dora always faced life in a positive way and didn't burden other folk with her worries.

She followed the sister into a small room at the far end of the ward, a quieter, more peaceful place they used for patients who were more likely to die than recover.

'I've brought you the visitor you most wanted to see,' the sister announced in a firmly cheerful tone.

Dora's face brightened at the sight of Rachel and she stretched out her hand, saying in a thread of a voice, 'Oh, good! I wanted – so very much – to say a proper farewell to you.'

Rachel didn't try to pretend not to understand. 'I feel the same so I'm equally glad to be here.'

'I feel as though I'm getting worse by the hour, and I wanted to tell you myself –' she paused to catch her breath for a moment, then continued – 'that I'm leaving everything I own to you.'

Rachel was startled. 'Are you sure that's the right thing to do? Shouldn't your house and other possessions go to someone in your own family?'

'I'm very sure. I have no close relative to leave them to, either on my side or my husband's. There are only distant relatives, people I haven't seen for years. I didn't get on particularly well with them anyway so I don't feel they have any right to a legacy. All they'd do would be sell the house and spend the money on their own pleasures. So I want you to have it and to do something with it for me, something worthwhile.'

'Oh. I see. That's, um, very kind of you.' Rachel guessed what was coming. 'I'll be happy to do whatever you want with it, you know I will.'

'Yes. And I know you and Joss aren't short of money – so I'd like you to make sure that the house is still of use to help people. Maybe the district nurses could continue to live in it, if you don't mind. They don't get very well paid because our town council won't help with their wages. What do you think? You told me you were wanting to get two of them for Eastby End and there are two flats.'

'I think that's an excellent idea.'

'Oh, good. And if you come up with any better way of using the house or money that would be useful to people in the town, well, I trust your judgement to make any necessary changes. And there's some extra money just come in.'

'I'd be happy to use your legacy to help people. What a kind idea!'

Dora's face brightened, for all its pallor. 'I knew I could trust you and I'm so glad you approve. You've been kindly paying me rent since you moved out, so that the flat would be available if it was needed for a nurse new to the area, but you won't have to pay that now and can use your former rent money for some project of your own, though perhaps you'd make sure the council rates have been paid on my house first.'

'Yes, of course I will.'

The sick woman smiled and relaxed visibly, for all her weakness. 'Thank you, dear. I'll die feeling that I've helped Eastby to keep and look after its district nurses. And I'll also feel that because of that legacy my life hasn't been completely wasted.'

'Your life hasn't been wasted at all. You've been a good friend and I'll miss you very much indeed.'

'You've been almost like a daughter to me – the daughter I never had.'

The grip on Rachel's hand tightened for a moment. She didn't say anything but she knew it was a deep sadness to Dora that she'd never had any children.

'So letting the town's district nurses live there rent free will be my ongoing contribution to the town I love. That's good.' Her eyes fluttered shut.

Rachel patted the limp hand and waited until Dora had opened her eyes again to repeat, 'As I've said already, I think this is an excellent idea.'

That won another smile from the dying woman. 'Thank you, dear. I can go in peace now.'

She took a few more gasping breaths before continuing to speak. 'Strangely enough, I received a legacy myself a few weeks ago, quite a nice amount of money. I didn't expect it at all. It's too late for me to use that legacy but I felt sure I could ask you and your husband to manage that money and use it wisely to help people in whatever way you see fit.'

She paused to gather her strength again but it looked to be taking all her willpower to continue speaking. 'The new lawyer, Mr Schofield, has my will and I've told the sister here how I've left things too. She's going to let him know when I – when his services are needed.'

Rachel couldn't hide her sadness from Dora or stop tears welling in her eyes.

'Don't look like that, dear. I feel so utterly exhausted that I'm quite ready to go now that I've spoken to you and you've set my mind at rest.'

Rachel took Dora's hand and gave it a loving squeeze. 'I promise that I'll do exactly as you ask. I think you've done really well by our town with this will and I'm proud to be your friend.'

That brought another of those gentle smiles and Rachel kept hold of the hand for a few moments, then felt it gradually slacken and slip away, as if the sick woman didn't have the strength to keep hold of her any longer.

Rachel didn't stay long after that. Poor Dora was so weak that she kept closing her eyes and sighing, not quite falling asleep, then jerking fully awake again, but she wasn't able to stay awake for long.

As her visitor stood up to leave, however, Dora suddenly said, 'I nearly forgot to tell you that I've left you a letter. The lawyer has it. And he's arranged the funeral for me. You won't have that to do.' Then she closed her eyes and her next sigh sounded even weaker than before.

Rachel waited but her companion didn't rouse properly again, so she spoke to the sister then left the hospital. Outside she paused to blow her nose and wipe her eyes, then went along the street to find her husband, who'd said he'd buy a newspaper and read it while he waited for her, sitting on a bench in the small public garden near the hospital. When she'd finished her visit they were going to walk home together.

He stood up at once, setting down his paper and hurrying to put an arm round her. 'Darling, what's wrong? What can I do? You look so unhappy.'

'I am. Dora's much worse than I'd expected and I'll be surprised if she's still alive tomorrow.'

He pulled her into a hug and continued to hold her close. 'She's that bad? I'm so sorry to hear it. She's a good woman. Did the doctor tell you about her prognosis?'

'I didn't need to speak to him. Sometimes people get a look on their faces when they're nearing the end, and . . . well, poor Dora has definitely got it. The sister of the ward agrees with me.'

She stood in the shelter of his arms for a few more moments, feeling better just to have him with her. She had been so lucky to meet him and he said the same. 'Can we call in at the church on the way back and say a prayer for her?'

'Yes, of course.' Not that he felt that would do any good, but her beliefs were stronger than his and he knew it would comfort her. He picked up his newspaper and folded it neatly then held out his arm and she took it. They began walking out of the park and along the street, moving comfortably together as always.

Life was short and nurses perhaps saw more of the problems some people had to suffer when involved in caring for the sick, he thought. And kind, caring people like his wife would be particularly deeply affected by such situations, he was sure, especially when they involved a friend.

He was happy to support Rachel's efforts to help everyone she could, because he agreed with that approach to life. From time to time they managed to help sort out the problems of someone in trouble and that pleased them both.

He wasn't what he'd call rich but he was comfortable, had enough money to spare some of it at times.

He believed that everyone who was living comfortably should help needy people or their families from time to time, because sometimes people had times in their lives when things went badly wrong for them through no fault of their own.

But occasionally, as now, there was nothing you could do to help the person except allow nature to take its course and be ready to help further if needed.

Dora died two days later and as soon as he heard the news from the sister at the hospital, the lawyer informed the funeral company. Jonas Schofield then sent his clerk with a note to give Mrs Townley the details of the funeral proceedings and ask her to contact him at her convenience re Mrs Dora Prior's will once it was over.

Rachel had been informed of her friend's passing by the sister as well, so the message from Mr Schofield came as no surprise. Her husband's arm round her shoulders was yet again a welcome expression of support. How did people cope when a loved one died, she wondered, if they didn't have family or close friends to help them through it?

'We'll go to the funeral together, darling, and say a proper farewell to your friend. I'll book a cab to take us to and fro.'

'Thank you. And will you come with me to see the lawyer too, Joss? Not only do I feel sad about poor Dora but guilty that I'm going to be benefitting from her death. I'm sure it'll be helpful if we both hear what's involved, then we can discuss it together without me needing to go through it all again for you. After all, we deal with our other finances together now, don't we? Both yours and mine.'

'Of course we do. And you're really good at dealing with figures, definitely better than me, I reckon. I'm happy to come with you anywhere, anytime, but you shouldn't feel guilty about benefitting. From what you said about this inheritance after your visit to Dora in hospital, it'll be the town's district nurses who'll benefit most, with your help, and through them, the poorer people in the town. You'll simply be acting as your late friend wished.'

He gave her a sudden hug, something he did occasionally and which she absolutely loved. 'I'm always happy to help you in any way I can, as you well know, my darling, but it's especially satisfying to deal with such a worthwhile cause.'

He scowled and said, 'Your friend's generosity only emphasises that the local council does the bare minimum to help provide the town with district nurses. I've sometimes wondered if I should stand for the council. If I were elected, I'd give those reactionary old fogies on it a good shaking up, I can tell you.'

'Ooh, yes, why don't you do that? Apart from anything else, it'd do everyone good to have a younger voice speaking out about how our town is run and what's needed.'

'There are some good, forward-thinking older men on the council too,' he protested. 'Walter Crossley, for one.'

'Not enough of them to form a majority, though. They could do with a few women on it speaking out about their needs, too. Some of them haven't a clue about the modern world.'

'As usual, I agree with you about that.'

'Tell it to the government,' she said bitterly. 'I don't understand why women aren't allowed to help run this country? When they tried and actually got two women elected to a council in London about a decade ago, they were deemed ineligible and prevented from taking part. That made me so angry when I read the history of it in the newspapers, and I still get upset when I think about it.'

'That newspaper article made me angry too,' he said. 'It was absolutely unfair. After all, people had voted for those two women and over half our population are female, so they should be represented.'

'We've agreed about that before. I suppose it'll happen one day. The reactionary idiots can't hold the floodwaters of modern life back for ever, can they? And it can't come soon enough for me. I'll stand too once women are allowed. In the meantime, we need men like you on our council, men with a modern attitude towards the world, not ones like that horrible Evan Tidby.'

They stood close together for a few moments till she was more in control of her emotions, both anger and grief, and ready to continue with her day.

'When would it suit you to go and see Mr Schofield, Joss?'

'What do you think about first thing tomorrow morning? We'll both be fresh and alert then, and have recovered from the funeral. We'll need to have all our wits about us in case there are important matters to be decided straight away. I never take money for granted, always like to look after it carefully.'

'I agree absolutely.'

They sent a lad with a note in reply to Jonas Schofield, asking whether that would be a convenient time for them to call.

'It's a good thing there are usually lads wanting to earn extra pennies for running errands and taking messages across town, isn't it?' she said idly.

'It is, but I've wondered a few times why more girls don't do it. After all, nowadays they ride round on bicycles like the lads do. And they've started wearing shorter skirts to do that more easily.'

She looked down at her own skirt. 'One can walk about much more easily in shorter skirts as well ride bicycles. I certainly prefer the feel of it.'

'You'd look lovely whatever you wore.'

She rolled her eyes. 'You don't think you're a trifle biased, do you, Joss?'

He grinned and blew her a kiss. 'Maybe just a teeny bit. Do you mind?'

'It delights me every day. And to answer your question about girls: their families don't usually like them going to strangers' houses or businesses, and I can see why. Sadly, girls are more at risk of encountering problems from strange men than boys are.'

She was silent for a moment or two, because she'd been one of the girls who'd suffered from a cruel man attacking her on her way home one evening many years ago.

He gave her another hug, understanding how she felt, as he had before when something reminded her of that dreadful incident. The next time she spoke, he could tell she was trying to sound more cheerful so he followed her lead, letting her change the subject.

She gave him a wry smile. 'Apart from any other consideration, older girls are the ones who get lumbered with looking after their younger brothers and sisters, not the older boys, so they aren't usually free to run errands. I always wished I had a lot of younger brothers and sisters, though. I'd not have minded looking after them.'

'Since you've been so well while carrying this one, I'm daring to hope that you and I will have more children afterwards, then at least ours won't be as lonely as you obviously were at times.'

She gave him one of her glorious smiles. 'I hope so too. I'm not lonely now, though, Joss. You make me very happy.'

'We make one another happy,' he corrected. 'You're the joy of my life.'

13

The following week Flora received a letter from a friend who had gone to work as a doctor in America a few years previously. She read it quickly, eager to hear the latest news, and beamed when she found out what Anthea was asking her to help with. Perhaps fate was about to take an active hand in their affairs here in Ollindale, and by blind chance was favouring her own pet project.

Her friend had a colleague whom she hoped Flora might be able to help. This man was also a doctor, and a good one too, though getting a bit old now. Ernest Stanton had been working in America for over a decade and wanted to move back to England permanently. He admitted that he was slowing down physically and intended to prepare for a peaceful retirement in his own country, for whose scenery and people he had developed an intense longing.

However, he wanted to do this in a way that would benefit a young relative of his, who had recently qualified as a doctor in America. Alex had studied there because it had been easier to gain a place in medical training in a prestigious establishment and to be near Ernest, who was the closest relative who led a settled life.

Ernest's son and daughter-in-law were still more interested in travelling than settling anywhere permanently.

They were now in Australia and were a pair of 'permanent gadabouts', not good parents at all. In their time, they had worked here and there across half the world, and had thoroughly enjoyed the differences, so it was no use moving to live near them because they'd only move on again after a year or two.

Alex had worked in America for an additional year after qualifying, valuing the mentorship offered by a highly respected doctor at the same university. But now also wished to make a permanent home in England to stay near Ernest.

Anthea had written to beg Flora's help for her two friends in their move. If Flora would kindly ask around and check the newspapers, trying to find a medical practice for sale in some pleasant country area in the north, Ernest would buy this and the two of them would run it together. That way, by the time he decided to retire, he'd be able to reduce his hours of work and gradually hand over the practice to Alex.

Flora read the letter again, slowly and carefully, then passed it to her husband and waited impatiently while Walter read it twice as well. He nodded from time to time and when he'd finished he looked across at her and grinned.

'Perfect for our purpose, isn't it? Well, it will be if your friend's doctor friend will change his plans slightly to come here and let us help him to set up a new practice rather than buying an established one.'

'I should think he will. He's a north country chap himself originally, though from Northumberland not the north-west, I gather. We could offer to help him financially when it comes to setting things up, because he doesn't come from a wealthy family. Anthea has talked about him before and said he had always worked to help people get better and not bothered much about whether he was making a lot of money from his work. Though he's attracted monied patients as well because of his fine medical skills, she said.'

Walter waved one hand dismissively. 'I can take some of the charity money that was given into my care a while back and use it to help those two doctors. Having them here will be an excellent way of improving the medical side of poorer people's lives in Eastby End and the area around it, don't you think?'

'Indeed I do. I'll write back to Anthea straight away.'

'No. Send a telegram, Flora. This is too important. Invite these people to come and offer to help them set up the new medical practice. And ask them to come as soon as possible. I know you wanted to find a woman doctor but the chance to get two coming here at the same time is too good to miss. We'll find a woman later.'

'You're right.'

'I definitely am. They can stay with us when they first arrive to make things easier. If they accept our offer, we can surely find an older house we can purchase with some of that money to give them a permanent home and perhaps large enough to use for running their practice from as well.'

'You're sure of that?' Flora asked.

'Of course I am. What else is this special fund I'm managing for but helping people?'

'We've never met this man so we'll be taking a bit of a risk. Still, if my friend considers him worth helping, and she's talked about him before, saying he's a good doctor and a kind person, I promise you. And she's nobody's fool.' Flora beamed at him then decided this wasn't enough, so darted quickly across the room to fling her arms round him and twirl him round.

When they moved apart again he said thoughtfully, 'We could drive into Ollerthwaite and send the telegram from the main post office straight away. I'm sure these people will accept our offer – what doctor looking for a practice wouldn't? – and they might as well get started on their preparations to leave America as quickly as they can. We'll be able to do all sort of things to help them set up the new practice once they get here.'

She frowned. 'We'd better work out the shortest way of saying it or the telegram will cost a fortune.'

'Not too short, Flora my love. We want our message to be persuasive.'

'But they must be told that there's a poor area in that part of town, which is why we're getting involved. We don't want them taking one look at the place and running for their lives.'

'Yes. I suppose so. I wish we could just pick up a telephone and speak to people overseas as we can to some people in England these days. Now, that's what I call progress.' He sighed.

'People will be able to make telephone calls directly to America one day, I'm sure, though perhaps not in our time. Oh, I wish I could live for long enough to see some of the changes coming to the medical world as new cures are invented and more women tread the path to becoming doctors. They're bound to bring changes in the way female patients are treated as well.'

His smile had faded a little as she spoke. 'Unfortunately, when I think about the future, I can't help worrying about the war that's brewing in South Africa, unless I mistake things. There have been some worrying articles about it in the national newspapers lately. I can happily do without seeing the results of war, and that's an area where young men are the main sufferers, not older ones or young women.'

He sighed and it was a minute before he continued speaking. 'Oh well. Let's go and send that telegram. That's something positive we can do for the world. Come along, wife!'

'Very well, husband!'

They chuckled at this joking way of addressing one another, as they always did. This sometimes made some people stare at them in puzzlement. Sharing a similar sense of humour made for a very good marriage, as they'd said many a time to one another. Some people showed no sense of humour in their dealings with the world, which was why the two of them got on so well.

They set off for the stables and Walter said regretfully as he and his grandson harnessed the pony, 'If we weren't so old, we could cycle into town.'

'Well, you are, and no one's ever found a cure for old age.'

'You're right, and I doubt they ever will.' He shrugged and drove Flora into Ollerthwaite to the central post office.

After some further discussion, they sent a telegram that had the young chap behind the counter goggling in astonishment at how many words it contained and how much it was costing them.

'That's one useful job done,' Flora said in satisfaction as they walked back to their pony and trap.

'We'll have to wait to see if they accept, and then wait again to find out how quickly they can sort out their lives in America and book places on a steamship to come to England.'

They drove home along the road that bordered the lake, stopping for a few moments to enjoy the view of the sparkling water, then continuing up the hill to their farm.

Both of them smiled often as they chatted, happy as always to be spending time together without interruptions from well-meaning people. You weren't supposed to feel romantic towards your partner at their age, but they did. Their love for one another had ignited quickly once they met and grown very deep indeed.

When the telegram was delivered to its recipients in America, Ernest opened it anxiously, worried that a telegram might be bringing bad news. He read it quickly then let out a yell of joy and called for Alex to come and join him at once.

The door was flung open. 'What's wrong?'

'Oh sorry! Nothing's wrong.'

'Something very good indeed must have happened, Gramps, to bring a smile that wide to your face.'

He held out the longest telegram either of them had ever seen. 'Read that.'

Alex read it, gaped, then read it again. 'Oh, that's wonderful! I like your friend Flora already.'

'She's a wonderful woman. I'm told she's done a lot of good for people in trouble all through her life.'

'What's her husband like?'

'I don't know in one sense because I've never met him. But if she's married him, a woman who my friend says swore she was never, ever going to get married, and with her attitude towards helping people in need, then he must be a very special sort of person too.'

They had another quick hug then he pulled away. 'We need to get a bustle on, as she's asked. We'll start by having a chat with Paul and finding out how quickly we can leave, then we'll find out about steamers and book our passage. Or I might even contact my rich friend and see if he's got any travelling planned. If ever a man loved gadding about on his yacht it's him that was. Sadly, it could still be weeks before we get there.'

Thanks to his cousin Paul's kindness in letting them leave the practice almost immediately, which was far more quickly than they'd ever have expected, their discussions led to another, much briefer telegram winging its way across the Atlantic the following week. It said they'd be coming to England on the next available steamer and would send details of their arrival date and time as soon as they'd sorted it all out.

'The thing that pleases me most is that by going to this place in the north, I shall be able to start work as a fully fledged doctor straight away,' Alex said quietly, as the two of them sat together sharing a late supper snack one evening shortly afterwards. 'In the meantime, we can start preparations to break up our home here. If we like this place in England, maybe we can set up a permanent home there, the two of us together. I'd like to put down roots now that I've finished my training.'

'You've finished your formal training, yes, but you should never finish learning anything and everything as a doctor. We can do so much good in the world.'

'I agree.'

He gave Alex a proud, loving smile. 'I've been told what a good doctor you are by those medical folk who've worked with you here. Don't forget to get references from them all, just in case we have to move again.'

'I hope we won't have to do that.'

He raised his mug of cocoa in a salute. 'I do too.'

A short time later, he chuckled.

'What's so amusing?'

'I think you were born to become a doctor, Alex. Your mother used to say that you were always bandaging your teddy bear, even as a small child. And the cat! And an old dog we'd had for years.'

'Oh yes, I'd forgotten that.'

'That cat put up with a lot. And you were lucky the dog was so old it couldn't be bothered to fight you off.'

'He was a lovely old fellow. I've never stopped missing him.'

'We were all sad when he died. But for a dog he had a good long life. Now, let's get back to sorting out our coming changes. We'll need to make several lists and I think we should send off some of our things even before we leave so that we can use them in our work.'

'I'll get a pad and pencil, and we can make a start.'

They smiled at one another. They were both known as and teased about being inveterate list makers among their groups of friends and neighbours. But they both found it a very efficient way to deal with the world.

14

The day following Dora's funeral Rachel and Joss walked along the main street to the address the new lawyer had given them at the far end of it to see what he wanted. She saw it first, stopping with a smile. 'Ah, here we are. That's a nice shiny new name panel on the wall, saying whose chambers are located there, isn't it? I wonder if it's the first business this Mr Schofield has owned.'

'Perhaps. But I don't think the panel is nearly as nice as the person walking past it into the building at the moment,' he teased as he held the door open. He flourished an over-elaborate bow at her as she stopped briefly on her way in to blow him a kiss.

'Fool,' she murmured, smiling.

'Besotted fool,' he admitted happily.

The clerk hurried along to inform his employer that they'd arrived, then came back and showed them straight through to Mr Schofield's office at the rear of the building.

It was a spacious room which looked out on to a small, neat rear garden. Mr Schofield was a man of only about thirty from the looks of him, young for a lawyer in this town. He had a slight Scottish accent and a very pleasant smile.

When he came forward to greet them, he shook Rachel's hand as well as Joss's, which made her like him immediately. So many men virtually ignored women and concentrated all their attention on the men, something which immediately lost them her future custom.

'Why don't we make ourselves comfortable?' He gestured to some armchairs covered in maroon velvet set round a low table in the bay window.

All the furniture looked brand new, Rachel thought, and it was a tasteful collection.

'Thank you for coming so promptly after the funeral, Mr and Mrs Townley. Um, I gathered from Mrs Prior that she had already told you she was going to leave everything to you, Mrs Townley?'

'Yes. But she told me only a couple of days before she died and I'd far rather have had her alive for a while longer.'

He nodded. 'I found her very pleasant to deal with.'

He waited, letting her take her time to reply as she fought back tears, then said, 'There has been an alteration made to the will even in the short time since she spoke to you. Mrs Prior did tell you she'd received a legacy recently, didn't she?'

'Yes. But she didn't give me any details of it.'

'She'd inherited some money from a distant cousin and also some valuable but extremely ugly jewellery. She didn't like or want the latter, and felt quite sure you would feel the same about it, so she asked me to sell it for her. The sale was finalised later the same day that you saw her, so we added a quick codicil to the will, which she signed that afternoon.'

'She didn't let me know about it.'

'No. She passed away before she could give herself the pleasure of surprising you with the news of the extra money.'

'She loved to give people happy surprises. How did this happen?'

'Someone bought the jewellery rather more quickly than anyone had expected, a French gentleman I believe, from what the jeweller said.'

'I see.'

'The transaction has now gone through the relevant banks and its value has been added to the bank account into which your legacy has been paid. You will need to visit the bank and complete some paperwork before you can access the money.'

'I'm glad she got the pleasure of looking forward to doing that, at least.'

'Yes. She was pleased about it.'

It was out before Rachel could stop herself. 'What a pity it didn't happen a few years sooner. Poor Dora was desperately short of money during the time I was renting a flat in her house and she could have lived so much more comfortably.'

'She had the rent money you continued to pay her so that you could keep the flat vacant in case it was needed suddenly. You'll need it now to house the district nurse who replaces you and you won't have to go hunting for accommodation or turn someone else out of it to let her stay there.' He was carefully avoiding looking at her stomach.

Rachel flushed slightly but smiled too as she often did at the thought of the reason for that. She hadn't expected to start a baby so quickly after her marriage, but was delighted about it, as was Joss.

'Do you have any idea how much the jewellery sold for?' she asked. Maybe they could put some of it away to start a trust for their children.

When Mr Schofield told them approximately how much the extra legacy would amount to, she was so astounded that she couldn't speak for a moment or two. This was far more than she'd expected.

'Oh, my goodness! That much?' She turned to Joss and could see that he was equally amazed. 'What are we going to do with all that money?'

There was silence, then she answered her own question. 'We can put some of it towards helping fund the district nurse, I suppose.'

The lawyer smiled. 'I haven't had time to tell you yet but I just heard that a few of the town's leading citizens have apparently contributed more money this time than they did when you were appointed, Mrs Townley.'

'The council should be providing all the money for that. Councils in other towns do.'

'I agree, but apparently your work has made such a visible difference here, especially in Eastby End, that some of the councillors are beginning to appreciate the value of having a district nurse to tend to ordinary people in their own homes.'

'We have enough work for two district nurses in and near Eastby, but unfortunately we have difficulty finding even one who is willing to move to such an isolated place as our valley.'

Joss gave her hand a quick squeeze to show his unspoken support. 'There's no urgency to do anything with that money for the time being, is there, Mr Schofield? We can use a generous amount like that to finance something really worthwhile but it'll need careful planning.'

'There's no hurry at all, Mr Townley. It'll gather interest every quarter, after all. Um, there was another reason

Mrs Prior delayed discussing with Rachel what specifi- cally she wanted her to do with this money when it came.'

'Oh?'

'There was something a little unfortunate that you need to know about,' Mr Schofield sighed. 'She insisted that we create the codicil straight away and she signed it at once, because she wanted to make sure that no one else could claim the inheritance and try to take it away from you.'

'Why would she worry about someone doing that?'

'It puzzled me too, so I asked her for more details, explaining that I didn't want to risk being taken by surprise if there were another person claiming a right to the legacy.'

He paused then went on, 'And I think you need to know about that as well. She didn't like to blacken someone's name but in the end decided that she'd better tell me about the second wife of the cousin from whom she'd inherited it. The woman had died before him but she already had a son by her first husband when they married, and he's about your age now.'

They waited and the lawyer heaved another sigh. 'This son is apparently something of a scoundrel who tried at one stage to trick money out of his own family and he had his eye on Mrs Prior's money too, even though he isn't actually related to her.'

'Really?'

'From what I've been told, he broke his mother's heart when he was much younger by being arrested and accused of theft, though the police were unable to prove it so they had to let him go.'

'He's not a good person, then?'

'He's definitely the black sheep of that family and has been disowned totally by most of them these days.

Mrs Prior told me he tried to get into her good books at one stage, but though she agreed to meet him, she disliked him on sight. And she remembered what she'd heard her cousin say about him, so refused to have anything further to do with him. After all, there was no blood connection whatsoever between the two of them, was there? So why should she feel any obligation to help him?'

He gave her a wry grimace. 'She told me all this in confidence when I had the privilege of becoming her lawyer after her former lawyer had died. I'm quite sure, however, that she would want you to know the facts about him. Forewarned is forearmed.'

Rachel nodded. 'Kind as she was, Dora could always tell when someone was a liar. So if she didn't like him, then he must be a really bad 'un. She had such a kind heart, always used to see the best in people, yes and she brought out the best in some of them too.'

'Well, he's been boasting that he's in line to inherit a house and money in Ollerthwaite, and I've been informed that he told someone it was Mrs Prior's house. So you need to be prepared for trouble, just in case.'

There was dead silence as this sank in, then Joss said, 'You'd better tell us what he's called, then.'

'Jeb Lytton.'

'I don't know of a family in Ollerthwaite with the name of Lytton.' He turned to Rachel. 'Have you met anyone by that name on your rounds as a nurse?'

'No, but I'll remember it from now on. I trust Dora's instincts about people absolutely.'

'I, um, have already made a few enquiries because I like to be prepared and I've discovered certain other facts,' Mr Schofield went on. 'Most of the Lyttons live in one of the other villages along our small railway line, Merrinfield. It's two villages along from this end of the line, I gather. These members of the Lytton family won't have anything to do with this chap either, it seems.'

'His own family won't?' Joss didn't try to hide his shock. 'Do you know why?'

'Apparently now that he's bigger and older, he's turned into a bully who gets into fights regularly. Some members of his family invited him to a gathering a year or two ago in an attempt at reconciliation and in the hopes of finding him an honest job. But he apparently stole a few small items from them while he was there. They didn't report this to the police but most of them have said they'd never speak to him again after that, let alone invite him into their homes.'

'Then how has he ended up in the Ollerthwaite area?'

'Unfortunately, he's married a woman from a rather unsavoury family he works with, if you can call what they do work. They live here in Eastby End. She's a Janet Preece by birth, but her name's Lytton now, of course.'

'Well, I've definitely heard of the Preeces,' Joss said. 'Who hasn't? They're another bad lot. So we'll keep our eyes open for both him and his wife.'

'We're grateful to you for sharing this information,' Rachel said.

'You should definitely take care if he tries to deal with you. Refer him to me, perhaps. He's a big chap and is known to be extremely violent and to carry a knife. I will make sure he doesn't get his hands on any of the money by legal pretences, I promise you.'

He frowned and added, 'Though I can't see how he'd find any credible reason for making such a claim.

Anyway, I'm sure you'll use the money wisely, as my late client would wish.'

'Yes, of course.'

'On a happier note, Mrs Townley, it may please you to know that Mrs Prior told me how much she'd enjoyed having you as a tenant in her flat and staying in touch after your marriage. She told all her friends and neighbours about her lovely visits to you for tea. She didn't seem to be an unhappy person, or a greedy one, and she did me the honour of becoming one of my earliest clients when I opened my own business. I shall miss her.'

'Yes, she was a lovely person. Our invitations weren't offered out of duty or pity but because we enjoyed having her to tea.'

They all stopped speaking for a moment and then the lawyer frowned, seeming to be still thinking things through. 'There are just a couple of other details to sort out then we're done. I presume, since you've still been renting the flat, even though not occupying it, that you have one of the new front-door keys from when she had all the locks changed?'

'Yes.'

He held out a small parcel that clinked. 'These were her spare keys to various internal and external locks, to which I've added her personal set of keys, so now you'll have all the keys that I know about. If any others turn up, they'll have been unlawfully acquired and don't let anyone tell you differently. Report anything like that to the police immediately and refer the latter to me for confirmation. We want to keep things safe.'

'You sound as if you expect someone to try to break into the house,' Rachel exclaimed.

'I don't think it's very likely, but I always prefer to be prepared if there is any possibility of a problem arising at some
future stage. I'm certain my client felt a bit worried about
that too or she'd not have had all the external locks changed.'

'Very well. We'll take care.' Joss took the parcel from
him and put it on the small, low table round which they
were sitting.

'Her own flat seemed to be in a reasonable condition,'
the lawyer said. 'I had a quick check round.'

'As she grew older, I went into it to dust around and
help her do the floors every now and then,' Rachel said.
'Though I haven't been in since she died.'

'I don't think the poor lady had been keeping up with
the housework very well during those last few weeks and
the room in the cellar needs some attention too.'

'I'll see to it,' Rachel said at once.

'No, we'll hire someone to clean it for us,' Joss corrected firmly. 'You promised me to lead a less strenuous
life from now on, given your condition, and I'm going to
insist on it.'

He always made her feel so cherished, she thought,
smiling at him. She saw the sentimental look on the lawyer's face as he watched them but she didn't mind at all.
There was no shame to being loved by your husband.

Mr Schofield continued his explanations of what he
was handing over to them. 'I'm afraid Mrs Prior's health
declined so suddenly and catastrophically that she didn't
have time to sort out her possessions as people usually try
to do before they die. That fretted her during her last day
or two of life, the sister at the hospital told me, but Mrs
Prior told her she didn't trust strangers to go through her
things and would have to leave them for you to deal with.'

He let that sink in then went on gently, 'It was very clear that she trusted you absolutely, however, so I've therefore left her possessions exactly as they were when she was last in the house.'

Rachel looked at him anxiously. 'I've never done that sort of thing before, Mr Schofield. Is there anything I need to know about the tasks involved? Anything I should bring to you if I find it?'

'No, nothing at all like that, Mrs Townley. Since Mrs Prior had no close family, you now own the house and everything in it outright, so it's entirely up to you what you do with the contents and how you do it. But she did manage to leave you a letter.'

He held out a second envelope with Rachel's name printed on it in neat letters, not her old friend's handwriting. 'I'm afraid her handwriting was very shaky by the time she wrote this, which upset her, but she wanted to say a proper farewell. It tired her, so she asked me to put your name on the envelope for her, which of course I was happy to do.'

'I shall treasure this letter.' Rachel stared at it, then slipped it into the pocket of her coat, murmuring, 'I'll read it later.' She had no doubt it'd bring tears to her eyes and she didn't want to cry in front of him or walk home through the streets showing she'd been weeping.

The lawyer leaned back, nodding. 'Anything else you wish to ask?'

'No. You've explained it all very clearly.'

'Then that's everything I needed to go through with you sorted out, my dear lady, but if I can be of any further help, please don't hesitate to contact me. I'm entirely at your service. Your friend was a delightful person and helped me to get a start as a lawyer here in Ollerthwaite, recommending my services to other people. I shall always remember her kindly.'

It was good to hear him speak so positively about Dora and he'd done so with unmistakable sincerity. Even that brought a lump to Rachel's throat.

When they left the lawyer's office, Joss said, 'Let's go to the house straight away and find out what we'll be facing. I don't want you lying awake tonight worrying about what we'll find there.'

'Good idea. And I'd like us to read the letter in the cab on the way there before we do anything else, so that we arrive knowing whether she wanted us to do anything else specifically. Or perhaps we should walk and read the letter there. Yes, that seems appropriate, don't you think?'

'I'm sure the letter was meant only for your eyes, my darling.'

'And I'm equally sure Dora wouldn't mind at all if you saw it as well. She understood what a wonderfully close marriage we have already.'

She paused then said, 'I have to admit, though, that I'm not looking forward to going through the contents of her part of the house. I shall feel like an intruder when I'm dealing with someone else's intimate possessions. However, if Dora wanted me to do it rather than anyone else, then I shall give it my best go.'

'I doubt we'll find any unpleasant surprises from a woman as nice and kind as she was. And there's no hurry, so we can stop work for a time if we feel we'd like a break from the various tasks involved. The upstairs flat won't have much to clear away, now you're no longer living there. Clearing out her things is bound to make you feel sad. It may take longer than a day to do it anyway.'

'You're always so sensible, Joss dear.'

'Am I? I could say the same about you. But if we're still going to use the place to accommodate any new district nurses, we'd better get on with the job of clearing up her flat on the ground floor fairly soon. At least we shan't need to get rid of the furniture, just her personal possessions and the contents of the drawers and cupboards. And there's the cellar. Don't forget the room down there is going to be used again as well for the new nurse's assistant.'

'Oh, yes. Shall we walk over to the house? I feel like some fresh air.' She slipped her hand in his, surprised when he didn't start moving. 'Is something wrong?'

'I think perhaps you'd better save your energy in case we find there's a lot to do straight away.'

Rachel stared at him in surprise. 'Have you changed your mind about the house? Do you now think there will be something unpleasant there?'

'I doubt it but in your condition you should tread carefully when facing the unknown.' He put one arm round her shoulders and gave her a quick hug. 'It's my privilege and pleasure to cosset and protect you at a time like this.'

She lifted her hand to lay it against his cheek. 'And you're doing it very nicely too. Thank you very much, kind sir.'

'So we'll take a cab there. And when we arrive, please don't go rushing into the house till I make sure everything is safe. If the place has been standing empty, even for only a few days, someone may have broken in or objects may have been left where people can trip over them.'

He laughed at her grimace when she heard this and admitted, 'I doubt there would be anything in a small house like that to attract a burglar, Rachel love, but do please humour me and let's be ultra-careful in our approach to the world during these last months of waiting time.' He patted the soft swell of her belly, which was now starting to show and they smiled at one another. They'd done a lot of smiling about the coming child lately.

'All right then, Mr Fusspot. We'll take a cab there. And I'll tiptoe slowly round the house. Actually, that means I can have a quick glance at her note on the way there.'

A cab was easy to find in the centre of Ollerthwaite at that time of day, and as soon as she'd settled inside it, Rachel took out the letter.

Dora's farewell was only a few lines long, but her kind words about how much she'd valued their friendship brought tears to her friend's eyes, tears which overflowed until Joss gave her his larger man's handkerchief to mop them up with.

Once she'd calmed down, he tucked the crumpled piece of damp cloth back in his jacket pocket and sat holding her hand again.

'What a delightful person she was,' he said.

'Yes. She didn't have an easy life and she was fairly short of money but I sometimes think loving friends and relatives rank high among the true riches of this world. And she certainly had those.'

'Plenty of them,' he said softly. 'And well deserved.'

15

Dora's house wasn't a large one and it stood in a row of similarly neat detached dwellings, each surrounded by a small garden. Today her house looked slightly shabbier than its neighbours, as if it hadn't been properly cared for recently. The windows were rather dull and that showed, even with the curtains fully drawn across all of them.

'I wonder who drew all the curtains? I don't think any of the neighbours had been going in,' she said quietly as Joss helped her down. She took out her own front-door key, leaving him to pay the cab driver, and went to unlock the door.

'The house looks as if it's missing her, doesn't it, and— Oh!' To her surprise the front door wasn't locked or even closed properly. It swung back a little as she touched it, which caused her to call out in shock.

Joss turned round quickly, taking an involuntary step away from the cab in her direction. 'What's the matter?'

'The front door isn't locked or even closed properly. That's strange because Dora was always very careful about locking up. If she couldn't do it herself, I'm sure she'd have got one of the nurses to contact her lawyer about it and he'd have arranged for someone to lock every single door and window.'

He moved across the rest of the short distance between them and stared at the door suspiciously. Then he looked at the windows but they were all fully covered by curtains. There was no one to be seen in the houses on either side but both they and their gardens looked much better cared for.

He clasped his wife's arm and tugged her away from the door. 'Don't even try to go inside, Rachel. This is usually a very peaceful street but we're not taking any chances. Someone has opened this door at a time when no one should have been able to get inside. I'm not risking anything where you're concerned.'

He turned to the cab driver. 'Would you mind waiting in case we need anything else? We'll pay you for the extra time.'

He took out another coin and went to drop it into the cabbie's hand. The man gave him a quick nod and slipped it into his inner pocket. 'Happy to stay here for a while, sir.'

Joss went across to Rachel and tugged her gently away from the house. 'Stay near the cab while I have a quick look round inside, darling.'

He held the door still and bent to examine the lock, muttering, 'You'd surely see faint scratch marks if someone had broken in this way?' Only he couldn't see anything like that.

'You'd think some neighbour would have seen a stranger fiddling with the lock, only there doesn't seem to be anyone else around in the street nearby. If there is someone inside, I reckon they must have got in elsewhere and opened this door from the inside.'

'Even if the neighbours were keeping an eye on the place, sir, they'd not see anything if the intruder came here in the middle of the night and worked quietly,' the cabbie called. 'Locks like those are easy to pick open if you have time to jiggle them round a bit and listen for the sound to change. It's quiet enough in this street even at this time of day to hear the faint clicking noises they'd make. The place would be even quieter at night.'

Joss bent to examine the inside of the lock but there were no scratch marks there either. Perhaps the cabbie was right, but if so that meant the person who'd got in was used to breaking into houses, which probably made whoever it was more dangerous to confront.

The cabbie watched him for a few moments then said in a low voice, 'If this is your house now, sir, you should get those locks changed for more secure ones straight away. I'd change every single one of them, if it were mine, and put bolts on the inside of the windows too. Yes and bigger bolts on the insides of the doors as well.'

He glanced sideways at Rachel and added, 'If you're going to be moving in here, you can't be too careful to make it safe, especially with your missus in a delicate way, if you don't mind me saying so.'

Joss looked at Rachel. 'He's right. You're the most precious thing in my world.' He saw the cabbie give them a sentimental smile at that but he didn't care who saw how much he loved his wife.

After a while, the cabbie cleared his throat to get their attention but Joss was studying the lock again so Rachel turned back to the man. 'Thank you for your advice. We're not going to live here ourselves but we'll definitely do as you suggest and change the locks to keep any tenants safe.'

After checking again around the outside lock and finding no signs of tampering Joss said thoughtfully, 'This definitely hasn't been forced. Perhaps a burglar got in the back way and opened this door from the inside?'

'Wouldn't he still have left scratch marks?'

'I'm not sure. If someone is very skilled and they can take their time, I'd guess that they can pick the lock without having to force it in any way.'

She shivered. 'I don't want to risk that, either. We have to be utterly certain that any nurses we put in here will be absolutely safe.'

'No, I don't like the thought of it, either. But let's face it, if someone is determined to break into a house, any house not just this one, and that intruder doesn't mind causing damage, it's not easy to stop them, whatever fancy locks have been installed. Intruders can always break a window to get in when the house isn't occupied and at a time no one will hear them.'

Joss sucked in a deep, slow breath and gave the door a quick shove to open it fully, then took a step forward. 'Well, here goes.'

'Be careful!' she called.

He took a couple of steps forward, glanced quickly at the inner side of the lock, shaking his head when he saw nothing untoward. He then peered through the internal doorway on the right, calling back to the others, 'I can see no sign of anything having been disturbed in the front room of Dora's flat. I reckon whoever it was must have got in through the back of the house, had a quick look round the front, where there's mainly furniture and ornaments, not good pickings for an ordinary burglar, I should think, and then gone away via the rear.'

He turned, saw her take a step forward and called, 'Stay where you are, Rachel.'

She would normally have protested and insisted on going inside with him, but after he gave a quick glance down at her lower body, she muttered, 'Oh, very well.'

For some reason she felt uneasy as she waited, however, and she didn't care if he thought she was fussing unnecessarily, so she called, 'Stay in the hall, though. If you go out of sight, I will follow you in.'

Joss frowned at that but she frowned back at him, so he walked to the front door again and looked across at the cab driver. 'Would you come in with me? I'll pay extra.'

The man shook his head. 'Sorry, sir, but I'm a bit old to be acting as a bodyguard an' I need to keep a-hold of my horse in case there's any loud noises because that sort of thing might unsettle him. Nor I've never been much of a fighter, so I'd not be a lot of use to you even I did try to help. Hmm. Maybe I can find someone else for you, though.'

He gestured along the street then turned back to Joss. 'From up here I can see a likely looking lad standing at the other end watching us in case we need an errand running. They often do that round here, stand around hoping for a chance of a little job. Do nearly anything for sixpence, the local lads will.'

Joss looked at him thoughtfully. 'Do you know that one who's standing at the end looking this way?'

'Yes, I do. He's a strong young chap, nearly a man now, and I've used him myself to run errands and carry messages. Very reliable he is, too. Ted Miller, he's called. Shall I give him a wave to join us?'

Joss looked along the street to where he was pointing, checking what he'd said. Yes, his first impression had been right. That lad did look strong and had a nice fresh open face. That was all he could tell from this distance, but if the cabbie knew him, he'd be all right, surely. He wouldn't want to hire a bullying type of young chap.

'If you agreed to pay him a shilling, he'll help you do anything you need for an hour or so,' the cabbie said persuasively.

Joss looked at his wife and she called, 'Yes, do ask him to join you!' She gave him a stare that said how determined she was that he should not go into the house on his own.

He knew by now when to give in and do as she wished about something so rolled his eyes at her and murmured, 'Very well, Madam Fusspot,' then said more loudly, 'I'll take your word for it, then, cabbie. Please signal to him to join us. And thank you for pointing him out.'

Rachel took hold of Joss's sleeve to keep him with her till the lad arrived because she still felt anxious, though she'd kept watch on the house as best she could from here and hadn't heard or seen anyone moving about inside it.

These days she was enveloped in Joss's loving care from the minute she got up in the morning to the minute she fell asleep at night. He was such a lovely man and she hoped she'd have a son just like him. In her turn she'd look after him in every way she could.

She didn't know why she was so nervous today about him going inside that house on his own, she just was. And even if he laughed at her afterwards, she wasn't going to let her Joss take any risks, not even a tiny one, if she could help it. He was far too precious.

Doors didn't unlock themselves, so someone must have broken into dear Dora's house? Who could it be and why?

This wasn't a rich neighbourhood. And Dora's possessions were not only very ordinary but well used, with no valuable ornaments or fancy silver pieces. After her husband died, her poor friend had had to sell the few more valuable pieces she'd once possessed to make the upper floor into a flat that would bring in an ongoing income. And that was well known round here so a local man committing burglaries would surely have found it out too.

The lad came dashing along the street in response to the cabbie's signal and proved to be nearly as tall as Joss, to Rachel's relief.

He announced, 'I'm Ted, sir. How can I help you?'

When Joss explained the situation and offered him a shilling for an hour's work, Ted happily accepted the task of accompanying him inside and staying around for as long as needed, beaming at the idea of money so easily earned.

And as Ted was almost a man grown, Rachel felt happier about the situation now. She was amazed, though, that it was causing them all this trouble to get into Dora's house, a place where she'd once lived happily in the upstairs flat and popped in and out of all day long!

Ted must have noticed her worried expression because he said earnestly to her, 'I can see you're anxious, missus, but I won't let anyone hurt your husband. An' I know how to take care of myself. You have to when you move about in Eastby End.'

Joss grinned at her. 'There you are, my dear. I'm perfectly safe now with this fearsome bodyguard, so you can go and sit in the cab.' He winked at the lad, who gave him a nod and smile in return, then they both turned back towards the house. Joss went more slowly this time, moving quietly and followed closely by his new helper.

Rachel didn't move far away from the house, how-ever, and had no intention of getting back into the cab till her husband came back safely. You couldn't rush to the aid of anyone if you were shut up inside a vehicle.

The driver watched her for a few moments, then got down and tied his horse loosely to a lamp post. He came to stand protectively beside her, a small whip in his hand, saw her glance at it and said, 'You can't be too careful, can you? And the mere sight of me carrying this has helped put some villains off attacking me.'

'I agree that you can't be too careful. Do you often need a whip?'

'I always have one next to me on the driving seat but I've rarely had to use mine, missus. I always have it very visible and easy to grab when I'm in Eastby End, espe-cially that central part. Once a few rogues there have found out the hard way not to attack me or my passen-gers, the others tend to stay clear.'

'I'm glad to hear that.' Only if there were anyone inside the house who shouldn't be, they'd not be able to see the cabbie, only her Joss.

She turned to stare through the front doorway, the door to which was now wide open, so she was able to look right along the hall to where the cellar steps began to go down at the rear.

Joss was out of sight now and she didn't like that, but at least he had that tall lad following him.

'Strange, that door being open,' the cabbie muttered. 'You were right to tell your husband not to go in on his own, missus. It pays to keep your eyes open and be on your guard when you see something you can't explain like that.'

This remark didn't make her feel any less anxious. 'Yes, and I'm sure someone would have checked that this house was properly locked up while Mrs Prior was in hospital.'

'Stands to reason. So some stranger must have opened that door and I'm glad your husband has got Ted with him.' He shook his head, still frowning, but didn't say anything else, merely waited, alternating between glancing up and down the street, and then into the house. 'I wonder who that chap is?' he muttered. 'He's been here as long as we have but he's not with anyone or doing anything.'

Rachel saw the man and she didn't like the looks of him. 'I wonder why he's hanging around?'

The cabbie suddenly snapped his fingers. 'Don't have anything to do with that chap,' he murmured. 'He has a bad reputation round here.'

'What's he called?'

'Wally Perkins. Though he changes his name to suit, so you never know what to call him.'

'I'll remember his face, though, and what he looks like generally.'

She turned back to stare at the front door, wishing Joss would come out again. She hardly dared breathe deeply, she was listening so carefully for sounds from inside the house.

And it didn't reassure her that when she looked back down the street, Perkins was no longer there.

The cabbie was still frowning and twitching his whip. He kept watching the house and looking along the street.

'Where are you, Joss?' she muttered. She was getting increasingly anxious about her husband.

The house didn't matter, but he did.

★ ★ ★

When Joss walked into the hall of Dora's house, he paused to sniff the air then whisper to his companion, 'Can you smell anything, Ted?'

The lad sniffed, nodded and whispered back, 'Yes. Someone's been smoking cigarettes inside this house, an' not long ago, either.'

'There shouldn't even have been anyone inside and that front door should have been locked, would definitely have been locked till someone tampered with it.'

'Whose house is it now, sir?' the lad whispered. 'I heard that the old lady had died.'

'It belongs to my wife and me,' he whispered back. 'Mrs Prior kindly left it to us and we didn't give anyone else permission to come into it. But you and I had better keep quiet as we go further in to search for the intruder. There shouldn't be anyone in the cellar, but there's a room down there too, which we need to check. It's where my wife's assistant, Hanny, used to live, but she's moved into our house now, so that she can go out with my wife on night calls. She doesn't have a key to this place now, no one should but us, so how did anyone else get inside?'

He looked round the hall and saw a walking stick and umbrella poking out of Dora's old coat stand. They looked dusty and unused, but solid enough. 'We might need to defend ourselves,' he whispered and pulled out the walking stick. After hefting it in his hand, he nodded approval and took a firmer hold, then put one finger to his lips to remind the lad to stay quiet, before gesturing to him to take the umbrella.

Eyes fairly sparkling with the excitement of all this, Ted picked it up, managing to do that without causing anything to rattle. He had large hands and was quite tall already, was definitely going to be a big man in every way once he'd finished growing, Joss thought.

Ted picked up the umbrella by the point, moving the carved wooden handle to and fro quietly, as if practising hitting someone with it. Then he held his makeshift weapon ready to use, waiting for further instructions.

Joss moved on and beckoned Ted to follow him further into the house, both of them walking carefully so that their feet would make little if any noise.

The hall was slightly wider than average, containing two flights of stairs, one near the front door leading upwards. Joss had been up them a few times when courting Rachel, calling round to take tea with her and Dora.

He'd known that the other flight took people down into the cellar and that Rachel's assistant Hanny had had a room down below but he'd never been down there and this had been intended to be his first visit.

At the moment there were no sounds coming from further inside the building, either upstairs or down, but he still wanted to check the place. 'Stay here,' Joss whispered to Ted and moved back through the doorway to the right of the front door, remembering happy visits to this flat during his days of courting Rachel.

It made him feel sad to think of that kind old lady being dead now. And it made him feel angry that someone would break into her former home when she'd only just been laid to rest.

He made a quick check of the flat just to be sure there was no one hiding there, taking care not to make any noise. It didn't look as if anything of hers had been disturbed.

Why had the front door been open, though? Who had unlocked it and were they still in the house?

Unfortunately, that seemed likely. If so, the person was probably down in the cellar now.

But what did he want there? The stuff he'd find down there would be mainly worthless bits and pieces that Joss and Rachel had been intending to go through and throw most of them away.

16

When Ted let out a faint hissing sound from the top of the stairs, clearly trying to attract his attention, Joss moved quickly back into the hall towards him to find out what was wrong. At least he was sure now that there was no one hiding in the flat, so they wouldn't be attacked from behind.

The lad was still standing near the top of the cellar stairs. He now pointed to his nose, grimacing as you do when you smell something bad, then mimed puffing a cigarette and looked down the stairs.

The cabbie had been right about young Ted. He was a smart lad who hadn't needed telling to keep extra quiet now that they'd found where the intruder still was.

Even before Joss got to the top of the cellar stairs he too could smell tobacco smoke and strongly too. Ugh, cheap tobacco at that. All tobacco smelled horrible but to him the cheap stuff smelled worse, ghastly it was. He'd not want that stink in his house.

Nodding, he gestured to the lad to step aside and moved past him to stand on the top step. Whoever had broken into the house hadn't gone away then because there were occasional shuffling sounds of feet moving around below as well.

He drew in a long breath, grimacing again at the nasty reek. He wrinkled his nose in disgust, already disliking this person, whoever he was. Not only had he broken into the house of a woman who'd just died, but had added insult to injury by smoking there.

All the smokers Joss knew went outside other people's houses to do their puffing when visiting, as a courtesy to the people living there. Most housewives tried hard to keep their homes smelling fresh. And yet this intruder was daring to smoke inside a house which most people would consider a place of mourning, and therefore doubly deserving of respect in the small ways neighbours and friends could show it.

Actually, another thing about the smoking puzzled him. He couldn't remember ever hearing of a burglar stopping his search for loot to have a smoke. They usually wanted to get in and out of a place as quickly as they could to avoid being caught, and tried to leave no traces of themselves behind.

In fact, this situation didn't make sense in more ways than one.

He couldn't help giving a wry smile. As if a burglar would care about such niceties as being polite! Or about whether what he was doing made sense to anyone else. He supposed this chap must know that the owner of the house had died recently and perhaps he'd felt himself safe staying here for a night or two.

There had been no sound of voices from below, so he was hoping there would only be one person to deal with. He wasn't an aggressive person, but by now he was feeling very angry indeed about this intrusion.

He paused to turn round and put one fingertip against his lips, tapping them a few times to emphasise the need to keep quiet, then he started down the rest of the stairs trying not to make any noise at all.

The lad followed him so silently that he paused again to make sure Ted was still there. Yes, he was, and grinning broadly, obviously enjoying this adventure. Joss held up one hand and made a jabbing gesture to tell him to stop there and come no further, and got another nod, then shaded his eyes to show the lad he wanted him to keep watch for anyone else appearing from any direction. That immediately got another nod.

It looked as if Ted would be well and truly earning his money today. With his help, Joss hoped to catch this intruder and hand him over to the police, though the fellow would probably try to run away as soon as he found he was facing two people. Well, Joss would prefer to catch him even if that did mean a struggle. He definitely didn't want the fellow coming back again when the house was empty, or even worse, when a nurse was living there.

Hmm. Had the intruder broken in to use the place as temporary accommodation or was he here on the off-chance of finding a few items to pinch? In a small house like this there wasn't likely to be anything valuable, but if the intruder wasn't an experienced enough burglar to figure out the situation and he wasn't intending to sleep here for a night or two, what other reason could anyone possibly have for breaking into this ordinary house?

Joss couldn't think of one at the moment. Maybe he'd find out the hard way, by discovering what was missing.

He continued down the stairs but stopped a couple of steps before he got to the bottom, because he saw a scrawny, scruffily dressed man was standing with his back to them at the outer side of the lower area, his whole attention seeming concentrated on fiddling with the lock of the cellar door that led out into the lower half of the sloping back garden.

The nearby window was broken, with enough glass stripped from the frame to allow someone who wasn't too big to get inside through it. Now, he seemed to be trying to open the back door, not by breaking one of its panes but by carefully picking the lock.

Joss took a sudden decision and asked loudly, 'Looking for something?'

The man jerked in shock then spun round and glared at him before yelling, 'Who the hell are you? What are you doing in my boss's house?'

'This isn't your boss's house; it's mine.'

'Oh, yes it is! His aunt has just died and left it to him, so those lawyers should have given it to him. It's you who don't have any right to be here.'

Joss glared right back. 'The former owner didn't have any nephews, so she can't have been your boss's aunt, let alone have left it to him.'

'Her husband was my boss's uncle by marriage, so what else do you call that relationship but being his aunt?'

'It makes no difference even if you're telling the truth, because the former owner didn't leave the house to him.'

'She promised his mother faithfully that she would, yes, an' she wrote that down in a letter, witnessed by his mother's neighbour. So it is his!'

'Mrs Prior did no such thing.'

'He has a letter from her that proves she did, so I'm here to watch this place while he gets his own lawyer to speak up for him, then that new lawyer what doesn't know the folk in this town yet will be forced to do what's right an' hand this place over to the rightful heir.'

'As I just told you, that isn't true. Mrs Prior left a will, written only a couple of days before her death by her lawyer and witnessed by him and his clerk, leaving the house to Mrs Townley. Even if there had been another will before that, or a letter, they'd no longer be valid.'

'His ma gave him the letter and said the old lady was an honest soul as wouldn't try to cheat anybody. So the right thing for you to do is follow what she said in that letter an' get out of his house.'

When they made no attempt to leave, he picked up a mop that had been leaning against the nearby wall and brandished it at them. Joss jerked back instinctively and moved up a couple of stairs, even though he wasn't within reach of a blow landing on him.

'Think I'm frightened of a softie like you an' a scrawny lad like him?' the man taunted. 'Well, I ain't frightened of no one, even if they are bigger than me, an' you'll find out why if you don't get out of here quick smart. That's what the new owner pays me for, keeping watch over places for him. You should be afraid of me, you should. I deal with folk like you every week, an' get rid of them for him too, if necessary.'

Joss was astonished by this tirade and the man's absolute refusal to hear the truth. He was of medium height and scrawny, his narrow face ugly and his expression filled with what looked like hatred. How could you hate someone you'd only just met – or did he simply hate anyone who got in his way?

'Go and find a policeman,' Joss muttered to Ted. 'Tell him we need help with an intruder.'

The lad whispered, 'I don't like to leave you alone here, mister.'

'I'm not staying here for long, believe me. I'll be following you outside in a minute and I'll wait for the policeman nearby. Anyway, this chap is smaller than I am, so I doubt he'd be able to do me much physical harm. I'm not a fighter by choice but I can defend myself against someone like him.'

He gave a quick flap of his hand behind his back and heard Ted run lightly away up the stairs, then he turned to scowl at the intruder. 'I'll be coming back shortly with my lawyer and a policeman. This is definitely not your master's house.'

The man sniggered, stood the mop against the wall again and bent down to pick something up. 'We'll see whose house it is. You'll not be in a fit state to try to take it when I've done with you. Try this for starters if you don't believe me!'

Before the fellow had even finished speaking, he flung a chunk of rock at Joss, taking him by surprise and hitting him on the side of his forehead. The rock was thrown so hard and accurately that it knocked Joss backwards against the wall.

He was surprised by how sharp the pain was, seeming to spread down the side of his head and neck to his shoulder. It knocked him sick and when he tried to move he found that he was dizzy, so had to stand still again.

Something warm and wet began to trickle down his cheek. He brushed his fingertips against it and stared in surprise at a large smear of bright red blood. Thinking it wise to get further out of reach, he began to edge back up the stairs.

The man let out a peal of mocking laughter, but didn't throw any more rocks, thank goodness, because Joss couldn't have jerked away quickly without risking a fall.

He brushed more blood from near his right eye while keeping a careful watch on the man, who had stayed at the bottom of the cellar stairs. When he saw Joss brush away more blood, he gave another scornful laugh and bent to pick up a second chunk of rock.

'Get out of this house an' stay out or you'll get more of these! I've already proved that I'm a good shot.' He brandished the rock but didn't throw this one.

Joss moved back up the final few stairs to the hall as quickly as he could, which wasn't very quickly because he was still feeling dizzy and didn't want to fall down the stairs.

He wasn't stupid enough to stay and try to fight back when he was feeling like this and had blood trickling down his face.

He found no sign of Ted outside the house, but Rachel and the cab driver were waiting for him a short distance along the road and the cab driver had a sturdy-looking whip in one hand. He was arguing with Rachel and holding her arm with his other hand, clearly trying to keep her from going into the house to find Joss.

When Joss appeared at the front door, she again jerked her arm away and this time the cabbie let go of her.

She ran along the street to him, holding his arm and studying his face. 'What's happened? You're bleeding, and quite badly too.'

'The intruder took me by surprise and threw a chunk of rock at me. He's a scrawny chap and I wasn't worried about a fist fight, but don't let him get near you.'

More blood trickled down his face and he fumbled in his coat pocket, pulling out a crumpled handkerchief with his bloodied fingertips and quickly wiping away the worst of the blood from the right side of his forehead. 'Has Ted gone for the police?'

'Yes. He said there was a man inside and you'd sent him to fetch them. He went running off along the street as soon as he'd told us. He didn't say you'd been injured, though.'

'He didn't know. It happened afterwards.'

'How did the intruder get in?'

'He broke a window in the cellar. He's down there now and the strange thing is he's claiming that the house has been left to his employer by Dora, not to you. He said she was the man's aunt.'

'She didn't have any nephews that I ever heard of. Or children of her own. She'd have told me. How did you get injured, darling?'

'I was hit by a rock.'

She glanced along the street. The other burly man was back there, smiling broadly now and shaking his fist at them.

'Do you know who he is?' Joss asked.

'No. He's been watching but has kept his distance.'

'I wonder if he's the one claiming to be the owner. Let's get a bit further away. I'm in no state to defend you.'

Joss began to move away from the house but could only seem to shuffle along slowly and had to clutch his wife's arm because everything seemed to be wavering about.

When they paused near the cab, she said gently, 'I need to look at that injury on your forehead, Joss love. You still look woozy.'

He couldn't help smiling, in spite of the pain. 'What sort of word is that?'

'It's a new one the younger folk are using and I seem to have caught the habit of using it, too. I think it's American.' She'd used it to distract him from his injuries and it seemed to be doing the job because he had a slight smile on his face now as he moved along.

'It certainly sounds like I feel. Woozy, eh? I'll remember it.' He paused and leaned more heavily against her for a moment or two. 'Sorry. Thought I was going to fall.'

'I think you've got concussion, love, so we should get you somewhere you can lie down for a while, perhaps even see a doctor.'

'I do feel a bit unsteady still. And this blood keeps getting in my eye.' He'd had to keep using his handkerchief to staunch the trickle of red liquid and he patted it against the painful part of his forehead yet again.

'We'd better get you into the cab, Joss. I don't want you standing out in the open and especially not lingering close to the house when there may be a violent lunatic inside it still. Or perhaps that horrible man down there is the most dangerous one.'

He looked back along the street. 'You'd think he'd have come to see if he could help us, if he were just a passer-by.'

'At least he's only staring, not coming to attack you. Some people don't like to get involved in helping others and are just plain nosy,' she said soothingly.

'I reckon he must be the chap claiming to be the new owner. Oops!'

Joss swayed again and she held him up, standing still as she waited for him to start moving again once he felt up to it. 'I don't care who he is. I want to get you away from here before you fall down.'

He moved a little further and stopped again, so she asked, 'Have you recovered enough to get up into the cab now, Joss love? You'll be safer there and you're far more important to me than any house could ever be.'

'I didn't realise we'd reached the cab.'

She had to help him get up into it by giving him a shove from behind, and he half collapsed on to the seat inside the vehicle, which was now standing close to a trough of water so that the horse could lip up a few mouthfuls while waiting.

But the driver was still standing beside it, holding the whip at the ready and keeping a watchful eye on what was going on so at least no one could come after Joss.

'Hurry up, missus,' he called in a low voice. 'Can you get him settled there or do you need more help?'

'We can manage, thanks.' She climbed in after Joss.

17

Once seated inside the cab, Joss leaned back with a groan against the faded upholstery. She could tell that his head was still hurting from the way he winced when he tried to wipe the blood away.

'Are you still feeling badly dizzy?' she asked.

'Not as much now I'm able to sit still. But my forehead hurts.'

The driver closed the door for them, then clambered up on to his seat at the front and swapped his weapon for a bigger whip, calling out to his passengers, 'Stay where you are and we'll wait here for the police. I've got a bigger whip now in case he tries to attack us.'

'Well done!' she called out.

'I've had to learn to keep myself safe. Anyway, that new constable usually patrols the town centre at this time of day, so I don't think it'll be long before young Ted finds him.'

'Will one policeman be enough?'

'He's a strong fellow and I'm sure Ted will help him if he needs it. They'll come here as quickly as they can, I'm sure, missus.'

'Good,' Rachel said. 'I bet the intruder runs away when a policeman turns up and where's that man gone from the end of the street? Has he gone inside the house as well? We'll ask the policeman to check the house and find out how that intruder's left things before we even try to go inside. Did you recognise the man you saw there, Joss?'

'No. The intruder was a stranger to me, but I didn't like the looks of him at all. He had a really nasty face.' Joss frowned, trying to remember more details. 'He had a bit missing from the bottom of one ear. I think he must have got the injury in a fight when he was younger perhaps, because it didn't look like a recent scar.'

The cabbie must have been listening to them through the little flap on the back of the driving seat, which was there to speak to passengers, because he chimed in suddenly, 'That chap standing along the street who just left looked familiar to me but I can't quite place him. Did you know him at all, sir?'

'No. I can't remember ever seeing him before. Did you recognise him, Rachel?'

'No, but why a stranger would keep giving us dirty looks, I can't work out. It was as if he had some reason for disliking us or resenting us being here.'

She turned her husband's head gently towards her. 'Never mind him, let me see your forehead. I've been wondering whether this cut is going to need stitches but I think the bleeding is slowing down, so maybe not.'

'I hope it won't need them. I don't like doctors fiddling around with me. Surely you can take care of anything that needs doing to it?'

'Stop pretending you're fine. You're not. That lunatic must have thrown that rock very hard and you're definitely concussed. Was it a big one?'

'I didn't see it clearly. Everything happened so quickly.'

'Well, it must have had sharp edges to make a jagged cut like this. I think you should lean right back in the corner and let me keep an eye on you.'

'Don't try to do anything to the cut now, Rachel. It's more important to keep an eye on the house in case he comes out the front way and tries to attack us.' He raised his voice and said, 'Can you be ready to drive off if he does, cabbie? I'm in no state to help fight him off.'

'I certainly can, sir. And I've got my whip at the ready, so he won't be able to get close to us without getting hurt. Believe me, I know how to use it to defend myself.'

'Good man.' Joss turned back to Rachel. 'If you've got a clean handkerchief, love, can you lend it to me? I'll hold it against the cut while we're waiting. Mine's rather dirty, I'm afraid.'

'What am I thinking of? I should have sorted that out myself by now.' She got out a neatly folded handkerchief from a pocket in the side of her skirt, shaking it partly open before handing it to him. 'Best to press the folded part firmly against the injury. Don't try to speak unless it's essential, just rest and let yourself recover.'

'All right.' To tell the truth, he was still feeling occasional waves of dizziness, though not as bad as before, and was finding relief in simply sitting quietly.

After a couple of moments he glanced sideways and caught her watching him with a frown, as if she knew he still wasn't feeling at all well. 'Never mind me, Rachel love. You keep an eye on the front door of the house and the ends of the street. I don't want that fellow creeping up on us and chucking rocks at you or the cabbie.'

To his great relief, however, the chap didn't follow him
out and there was no sign now of the fellow who'd been
watching them from the end of the street.

The intruder must have been lying, though. Mrs Prior
would never have told Rachel she'd left her the house if
she'd already left it to someone else. And her husband had
been dead for years, so even if the stranger was related
to Mr Prior's family he couldn't be considered a close
enough relative to inherit anything. No, he was fairly sure
that had all been a pack of lies. It might have frightened
away a timid heir but it wouldn't frighten him and his
wife away.

Indeed, the more Joss thought about it, the more certain he was that Dora would never have had any dealings at all with a fellow who looked so rough, whatever
he claimed. She'd been a gentle, utterly decent person
and like many widows had mainly associated with other
women, shopkeepers or people from church.

He'd guess that the would-be thieves had heard about
the death of the owner and the man who'd been watching
had sent his tame thug to break in and lay claim to the
house. Anyway, Joss didn't think anyone would ever have
believed him when he said he'd been left the house.

He was one of those people you instinctively mis-
trusted. And besides, if he'd been to visit it before, the
neighbours would have recognised him because some
people had lived here all their lives and their families
before them.

Joss had thought he knew his own limitations, but even
so he'd overestimated what he could do. The intruder had
taken him by surprise and injured him. Done it easily,
too, to his embarrassment.

The older he got, the more he loathed even the idea of being caught up in fights started by idiots who saw no better way of dealing with the world when they had problems. He'd defend himself, if he had to, and would never give in to threats, but he'd never start a fight or voluntarily join in one.

He was still feeling bouts of dizziness, however, though a bit less severe now that he was able to rest, so he'd have to leave it to the police to deal with this situation. He wished they'd hurry up and get here because he felt helpless to protect his wife and his unborn child.

'This is going to give us another problem,' Rachel said suddenly. 'How can we lodge a new nurse in this house if it's going to put her in danger?'

'Well, I'm sure that man's claim that he was working for the new owner wasn't true because you're the new owner, not that fellow who was watching us. Surely he didn't think he'd get away with such a claim?'

'They must have thought they had a chance. Mr Schofield did warn us.'

He shook his head then wished he hadn't as his head throbbed again.

Rachel said what he was thinking. 'What will he do next, do you think? Just go away or attack the real owners and their tenants, and try to drive them away?'

'Who knows? But we've been hoping to hire two nurses, and there are two flats in that house. I feel quite sure the two villains will have come from Eastby End. Maybe this attack will spur on the town council and the local police to tackle that place much more forcefully, yes and quickly too. We all know that most of the people committing serious crimes in the valley came from there. It's the only part of the area that's so bad nowadays.'

'And yet the authorities are making only a half-hearted attempt to deal with the problems. What else are councillors elected for and household rates paid but to provide the necessary services and to keep the residents safe via good policing? They aren't doing a good job of it.'

He scowled at the thought. 'I'm going to write a letter to the council complaining about the situation and demanding that they do something about it. And maybe, just maybe, I really should consider standing for election to the council.'

'You'd make a good councillor. I'd vote for someone like you – if I had a vote, that is.'

'Or I might just make a fool of myself and not get many votes.'

'I think it'd be worth a try and—'

She broke off suddenly as the cabbie yelled, 'There's someone coming!'

Joss and Rachel stared out of the cab windows and saw a man in a dark uniform pedalling furiously towards them on a bicycle.

'It's that new young policeman!' she exclaimed. 'Oh, thank goodness!'

The man was smartly turned out, his uniform looking brand new and he looked sturdily built. 'Constable Waide at your service, sir. I believe there has been someone causing trouble and has attacked you. Did he give you that injury?'

Ted ran up to join them just then, puffing but still looking excited and ready to join in the fray.

Joss and Rachel explained exactly what had happened, then the constable left his bicycle with them and went into the house with Ted, who still had that eager look on his face.

'He's certainly earned his money today,' Joss muttered.

The two of them came out again after a while.

'There's no one in the building now, sir, so you're safe to go inside, but you'll need to get that broken window mended.'

'But will our new nurse be safe there?' Rachel worried. 'We were hoping to house the first one in a flat in that house very soon.'

'I'll report all this to Sergeant McGill and I'm sure he'll he happy to advise you. I've not been posted to the valley for long, so I'm not yet aware of everything that's going on as well as he is, I'm afraid.'

'Thank you for coming so promptly anyway.'

'I was happy to be of service.' He hesitated then said, 'You might like to consider hiring the young chap who came to find me as a nightwatchman. He seems to have a good understanding of the situation. He said he's hoping to join the police force when he's old enough and was asking me how to do that.'

'I think we shall have to hire him,' Joss said. He beckoned to Ted and paid him for his time then asked if he would like a job keeping watch. 'We'll pay you five shillings a night.'

Rachel smiled at his eager expression. 'And we'll arrange for you to have a breakfast waiting at the corner shop just down the road as well.'

If his expression had been eager before, it was full of enthusiasm now.

Rachel fumbled for one of the spare keys to the house and gave it to him. 'Keep the outer doors locked at all times.'

'Yes, Mrs Townley. You can rely on me.'

'I'm sure we can.'

She turned to the cabbie. 'Can you take us home now, please? My husband needs to rest and recover from the attack.'

'I'm happy to do that, and I'll spread the word to look out for those two villains. I come into contact with a lot of people during the day.'

'Good idea.'

When they got home, she dealt with Joss's cut then insisted on him lying down for a while. But she didn't send for the doctor because her husband was already looking a bit better and had got his normal colour back.

18

The few days after their walk round the lake were rainy on the whole, and Flora did a lot of thinking about the future of her adopted town. The main thrust of her attention at the moment, now that they'd sorted out two new doctors, was how she and Walter could help speed up the much-needed improvements to the tumbledown houses in Eastby End. It was no use looking after people's health alone; they also had to improve their housing and general surroundings or they'd keep on getting ill.

Eastby was the area in which the least attention was paid by local councillors to law and order, and even the police weren't often seen there. Sadly, there were simply not enough policemen to keep order everywhere. That aspect needed attention too, but though Walter was a councillor, as he'd told her, the men proposing improvements did not have the backing of the majority of councillors, so they found it hard to get anything more than minimal changes voted in, and only then because these might win a few votes from property owners.

There was less maintenance carried out in Eastby End than was usual because the landlords in that slum were more interested in making as much money as possible from their tenants than spending it on them. So the poorest people continued to live in appalling conditions and that could not be allowed to continue.

There had to be something done, and thinking about it seemed to have woken up a whole series of ideas in her mind for possible actions, but not yet for how to persuade certain men to look after their tenants better. She let Walter tend to various other matters and sat by the window staring down from their farm across the valley she'd grown to love.

The problem she had felt should be tackled first had been solved, which had delighted her – or would if the two doctors now hired were as good as they sounded from their letter and the recommendation from their colleague in America. They would, she hoped, soon be on their way here, the sooner the better as far as she and the valley were concerned.

She'd have preferred one of them to be female, but it was so hard to find doctors willing to come here that she'd not quibbled when Walter helped her to 'snabble' them as he phrased it, using one of the old semi-obsolete words he loved to find and toss into conversations. And the two doctors who'd become suddenly available would be setting off soon, surely?

They could help these doctors to settle near the Eastby End part of the town and open a surgery there so that it would be easier for poor people to reach it if they needed help. Some of the charity funds Walter managed could be used to set up a properly stocked clinic, but that would be best done by the doctors themselves so that they had what they considered necessary to run it.

The doctors plus the new district nurse and assistant would mark a huge step forward medically for the poorest area of the valley and would, Flora felt, even make a difference to Eastby End.

She sighed. It would have been better, though, if one doctor had been female, who'd probably have had more understanding of the problems women and their families faced. Women usually had more problems than men did, at least that was what Flora had found in her many years of experience as a nurse and later on, an organiser of medical services.

But there you were: it hadn't happened. Dr Coxton had paved the way for people to accept women as doctors but she was getting old and tired and couldn't manage to do any more on her own. However, she'd told Flora that patients who wouldn't be easily able to afford a doctor didn't usually care whether they were seeing a woman or a man, as long as the services they needed were free.

There was quite a lot of money at Walter's disposal to use for any charity he saw fit to help. So trusted was her beloved husband by most people in this valley that he'd been left more funds to use since the original large bequest. But you couldn't do much until you had the necessary doctors and nurses to do the job properly.

Unfortunately she felt that the goal of full acceptance of women in the doctor's role would probably take a long time to achieve, even in a fairly civilised country like England. And at the moment, there were simply not as many female doctors around as male, so in some areas they were still unknown.

She went to make herself a pot of tea, still thinking hard. One of the barriers to bringing in any changes to help the poor, unfortunately, was a group of the more affluent men in the town, whom she considered ludicrously old-fashioned in their approach to life in general. Dinosaurs, she called them in her own mind and sometimes when speaking to her husband.

These men had fought actively against any improvements that might have helped the poorest people on the grounds that such things cost too much, and it was their job to deal frugally with council funds. Some of them were totally without scruples about what they would be prepared to do to get their own way and above all make money, and had blocked council funding for other projects, not just the medical ones.

But one day she would find a way to get past them and fortunately the council had no say about a woman's qualifications being accepted as equal to a man's, only about use of council finances. So she and Walter could continue to look for a suitable and willing female doctor and fund her from those charity funds. Together with a few like-minded people, they could also cover her expenses and accommodation as needed.

She and Walter would slip changes into their valley gradually, and sneakily if that was needed. She had no scruples about doing that for the good of their community.

And just let those men complain about anything she was doing, as they'd tried to do when she first came here. She wasn't afraid of telling such people to their faces and in public that they should be ashamed of not doing more for their fellow human beings. She'd held her tongue for long enough out of respect for Walter's position in the valley, but was about to start letting it loose.

When she'd warned him she couldn't hold back much longer, he'd simply grinned and told her to go for it, and not to hesitate to ask him for help or money if she needed them.

'I can't do as much as I'd like to help you, love, because I'm too busy already.'

'I know.'

'But I can slip you some extra funding if you find you need it.'

'I shall hold you to that,' she warned him.

'I wouldn't offer if I didn't agree that more is needed.'

It wasn't right, though, that you had to resort to plotting and planning to help people. If only women were allowed to become town councillors that would have made it easier, but they were as hamstrung about that as they were about every official position of power! The government had a lot to answer for and needed to bring the voting laws up to date.

She had a few bees buzzing in her bonnet about the world she lived in, as her husband phrased it: she wanted to make sure that married women were allowed to continue going out to work, not just the unmarried ones. And to her delight, women were gradually learning that they didn't need to stay at home permanently after marriage or to bear one child after another. There had been some progress for them about that, at least.

It also absolutely infuriated her, however, that some people were still trying to keep the information about how to control unwanted births from the less well-educated folk, and yet they were often the ones who needed it most. Well, she intended to work out ways to spread that information, too. Oh, yes.

However, she would have to be rather careful how she set about this and avoid falling foul of the law, as one of her personal real-life heroines, Annie Besant, had done a couple of decades ago.

Flora wasn't optimistic enough to expect the necessary changes to happen more than sporadically in her lifetime, but she did think – and Walter agreed – that she could help make some small difference before she shuffled off this mortal coil.

She'd discuss how best to take any steps with him first, of course. Her husband was a shrewd fellow, dealing pleasantly with everyone, whether male or female, old or young, and good at getting his way without causing too much trouble. He often amazed her by succeeding when other people had failed to get something done.

She smiled, remembering how she'd fallen in love with him within a few days of meeting him, in spite of them both being past the age when people expected to find someone to love.

And her love for him had only grown stronger with each day she spent living with him after they married.

But she hadn't stopped working to change what she considered injustices, and she never would. Nor would he ever ask her.

Every small step helped, she believed. So she would continue taking them.

19

When their train at last pulled into Ollerthwaite station, both Livia and Janie heaved a sigh of relief at exactly the same time, which made them smile at one another at the same time too.

They were a lot more comfortable with one another already, Livia thought, and she was finding Janie not only a pleasant companion but an intelligent one, too, interested in anything and everything. Now that she wasn't afraid of upsetting the person she was with, she asked questions openly when she didn't understand something. And she was quick to grasp the ensuing explanations.

She had told her how happy she was that she'd be able to take an interest in the wider world now that she'd escaped from Billy Doyle, as she called it. Fancy being forced to stay with someone you hated and having to endure him beating you!

However, when a burly man walked along the corridor outside their compartment, Janie huddled suddenly down.

'What's the matter?' Livia asked.

She shuddered. 'That man reminded me of Billy. For a moment I thought he'd found me.'

'But you've got away from him now. It couldn't have been him.'

'I know that here.' She tapped her forehead. 'But I'm still terrified of him here,' she tapped her chest. 'I find it hard to believe he won't come after me and find me one day. He'll be so furious at being bested in any way by a woman. And other people will know about me getting away, you see, which will make it worse to him.'

'He'll get tired of searching for you, I'm sure.'

Janie shook her head. 'No, I don't think he'll ever let the matter drop completely till he's got his revenge on me, so I don't think I'll ever feel totally safe.'

Livia could only stare at her in shock. Surely no one could be that stubbornly vindictive? But then she caught sight of Janie's bruises and her heart sank. He hadn't been afraid to do that to her quite openly, had he? She needed to at least bear it in mind as a possibility that he might come after them, but she also wanted to build Janie's confidence in her chances of making a better future for herself.

'He'll have to find us first, and we're going to be a long way away from Bristol by nightfall,' she said. 'Is he clever enough to track us down, do you think?'

'He won't do that till he's sure where I am, but he'll keep his eyes and ears open and chance might one day give him some idea of where we are.'

'But that's not likely, surely. And he won't bother about chasing you for ever. Think of how much that would cost him, apart from anything else.'

If he ever gets to hear about me, he will come after me, whatever it costs, if only to demonstrate to the other people he preys on that no one can get the better of him. He can be absolutely unreasonable and stubborn when he wants his revenge and he prides himself on that, boasts about it.'

That left Livia worrying too, though more about Janie worrying for ever than about that brute succeeding in finding her.

However, even her concerns about safety didn't stop Janie alternately chatting and taking little naps during the journey. By the end of it she had started looking better as well as more relaxed, as if her fears had subsided a little at least, and that was allowing her body to start recovering.

As soon as the train stopped a porter moved quickly along the platform opening the carriage doors so that the passengers could start getting out. Livia had already stood up to lift down their luggage from the overhead racks by the time theirs was opened.

She looked across at Janie rather doubtfully as she set down the shabby suitcase, wondering if her companion would have the strength to carry it. The poor thing still looked pale, even if a trifle brighter in mood. However, several bruises showed so clearly on her face they made people who noticed them stare. There was nothing that could be done about that and only time would fully erase the livid purple marks, which were currently at their worst.

Janie seemed to realise what she was worrying about. 'Don't worry. I'm all right to carry my suitcase. Just a minute.' She settled her hat more firmly on her head, pulling the veil down to cover her face, and peering into the small mirror in the middle of one side of the carriage, just above the seats.

She shook her head at what she saw, sighing unhappily. And well she might because once you got close to her, the bruises looked horrific. But at least people who passed them in the street would not now have their attention drawn as quickly by the sight of the marks.

Janie put into words what Livia had been thinking. 'The further we've got away from him, the better I've felt. Truly. I'm so very grateful to you and Miss Grayson.'

'We were both glad to be able to do something to help you – and to stop him being so cruel.'

Janie nodded, then caught sight of her own reflection again in the carriage window and turned quickly away from it, murmuring, 'I'm ashamed of my current appearance and I hate the way people stare, but his marks will fade, and if I'm very lucky indeed, I'll never see him again.'

She didn't sound optimistic, though.

After staring blindly into the distance for a moment she said quietly, 'I try to believe that I could be that lucky but even now I don't like to say his name aloud.'

'I was surprised at how many people living near you seemed to be not just afraid but absolutely terrified of that man.'

'And with reason. I should have told you this before you got involved. I wasn't thinking clearly, as I'm sure must have been obvious.' She took a deep breath and went on, 'There's no doubt in my mind that he's killed several people, mostly women.'

Livia gaped at her in shock. 'Killed several people! Surely not!'

'Believe me, it's true. I thought I was going to be his next victim. He gets . . . well, angry if women defy him and I knew he was feeling furious at some of the things I'd said or done. Every now and then I couldn't hold back on speaking out to him, or arguing, you see. And I was better with words than he was. If I used long ones that he didn't understand that made him even more furious, so I used them on purpose sometimes. He was going to thump me anyway so why not upset him as much as I could?'

She picked up her suitcase and hefted it in her hand. 'Oh well, let's not talk about him any more. See. I'm fine carrying this. It isn't all that heavy because even with the clothes Miss Dawson has given me I don't own much nowadays.'

'Did you ever?' Livia asked gently.

'Yes. Well, I didn't own a great many clothes or other possessions compared to someone like you, but I did have more than this when my parents were still alive. And even after, when I was on my own in lodgings, I had at least double this number of clothes and possessions.'

She paused, looking even more unhappy. 'When he forced me to live with him, he pawned or sold some of them without asking me and that included an ornament that had been my mother's, the only thing of hers I had left. I came home one day and they were gone. And he laughed when I got upset, then thumped me till I shut up.'

'The more I hear about him, the worse he sounds.'

'Yes. He's the most wicked man I've ever met, or even heard of in real life. I'm surprised one of the men he's upset over the years hasn't killed him.'

Livia waited, knowing Janie needed to get it all out if she was to recover properly. Sure enough, she began speaking again.

'I begged him not to take any more of my things, but he laughed and said I didn't need that many clothes and he liked me better without any on at all. Ugh. The memory of all that makes me feel sick. He said the other clothes were just a waste of space and he'd enjoy spending the money they brought.'

Anna Jacobs

She paused and said quietly, 'That was when I grew absolutely determined that one day I'd get away from him – one way or another.'

'Why did he need so much money?'

'To spend on boozing with his friends. He had enough money to do that and treat them even when I was going hungry.'

Tears came into her eyes. 'And he was planning to sell the rest of my things, a few bits and pieces I'd inherited from my mother. I heard him talking to someone about them, so I hid some of them in the church vaults. That's why he hurt me so badly this time. I may never get them back again, but he won't find them, either. He hates going into churches. And whatever he did to me, I wouldn't tell him where they were. I'd have died rather than done that. Literally. They're still there, I suppose, and I'd far rather they rotted away than he got them.'

Livia realised suddenly that they were standing talking instead of getting off the train. 'Oh, goodness! This is no time to talk, even about such important matters. Let's start moving. I'll get out first and you can slide the suitcases along the carriage floor towards me.'

Once that had been done, Livia picked up her own case and started walking slowly along the platform, trying not to go too fast for Janie to keep up. She kept an eye on her companion but couldn't help continuing to ask more questions as they walked slowly along. She would need to know everything she could to help keep them both safe.

'How has that horrible man got away with so much wrongdoing for so long, Janie?'

'People who tried to stop him simply vanished, people from the poorer areas, that is. After a while other people guessed what he was doing until there wasn't anyone in our part of town willing to risk speaking out against him. He was very cunning about what he did, he seemed to have been very careful who he stole from or attacked too. And he stayed clear of upsetting anyone with more power or money than him.'

When Livia stopped walking to stare at her in horror, she stopped as well and said quietly, 'But no one has ever managed to find proof of that, not even the bodies of the missing people. They don't know where he puts them. After a while, folk from our part of town didn't even try to go against him, didn't dare. Some folk who saw the way he was eyeing their daughters as they grew towards becoming women left the district suddenly, hiding where they were going even from close relatives.'

It was a moment before Livia could even form a word, she was so shocked, then she stammered, 'That's . . . it's absolutely appalling. I'd not have believed it if I'd read about it in the newspapers.'

'You can see why I was – and still am – so afraid of him.' Janie waited while Livia showed their tickets to the smiling man at the exit, though there was no actual barrier there to stop people walking out without having tickets.

'They said they'd send someone to meet us so we should wait here.' Livia went to stand near a sign at the end of the platform, which said that heavy luggage would be unloaded and placed here.

They stood quietly, watching the people who passed by or waited like them for the rest of their luggage to be unloaded. Livia kept an eye on Janie when she didn't try to continue chatting, and saw that she was looking exhausted again, poor thing. You could see how pale she was even through the veil. That seemed to make the purple of the bruises even more vivid and shocking.

A couple of minutes later, an older woman came towards them, smiling and nodding as if she recognised them.

When Janie stiffened and glanced sideways at her anxiously, Livia patted her arm. 'It's all right. I bet this will be the person who's supposed to be meeting us.'

The woman stopped in front of them and said quietly, 'You two must be Livia and Janie, because no other pair of young women has got off the train. I'm Flora Crossley and I'm really happy to welcome you to Ollerthwaite.' She glanced at Janie's face for a second time, looking upset for a moment or two at the sight of the bruises, but didn't comment on them.

'Pleased to meet you, Mrs Crossley. I'm Livia Blake.'

She held out her hand so Janie did the same and said, 'I'm Janie Clayton.'

Livia watched and thought yet again what a quick learner her companion was.

After that they had to move quickly to one side to get out of the way of two men walking out of the station.

'I hope you'll both be happy here,' Mrs Crossley went on. 'My husband is outside with the cart waiting to take you and your luggage to the place where you'll be living. We've arranged for accommodation in a house owned by a friend of ours. Rachel has left it to us to take you there and show you round. She's expecting at the moment, so gets tired more easily.'

'Thank you for helping us,' Livia said at once.

Mrs Crossley nodded and continued her explanations. 'There's a flat for you, Livia, and a room in the same house for you, Janie. I presume you've got trunks in the luggage van? The porter will be bringing the heavy luggage along in a minute or two. There isn't usually a lot of that. Do you need any help with your hand luggage or can you manage?'

Livia smiled. 'We don't need any help, thank you. There's only the one suitcase and a shopping bag each, and there's only one trunk in the luggage van, which is mine. Janie doesn't have anything else because she was, um, robbed recently.'

'I'm planning to buy more clothes as soon as I can afford them,' she said quickly, ashamed of how little she had. 'I shall need to in order to wash my dirty clothes.'

Flora didn't show any surprise at this. 'Actually, I can help you with that, well I can if you don't mind second-hand clothes, that is. My husband owns a couple of shops and he collects clothes with plenty of wear in them still, keeping some of the garments which have been discarded by better-off folk for decent folk in need of more clothes through no fault of their own. Some of them are rather old-fashioned, but they can easily be altered. He keeps them and some smaller pieces of furniture in the back room of one of his shops. I can take you there to choose a few more clothes, if you like, Janie. There's no charge.'

She didn't ask about the bruises but from the sudden flash of anger on her face when she'd first glanced at them, she'd obviously guessed how they must have been caused.

Janie had been watching her carefully as she spoke, gradually relaxing. 'I'd be very grateful to have a few more clothes, I must admit, Mrs Crossley. I'm so short of them. Do you, um, have any underclothes as well as top clothes?'

'Oh, yes. We have all sorts of clothes.'

'I'll be extremely grateful for a few of those as well, then, and I don't mind second-hand items at all, as long as they're clean. In fact, I'd welcome anything that's decent and wearable.'

'They wouldn't be allowed into our shop if they were dirty, and they've been mended as necessary, too, by a couple of ladies who volunteer to help there. We'll take you to choose some things – perhaps tomorrow, if you're not too tired?'

'Tomorrow or whenever is most convenient for you. That would be a wonderful help.'

'You look exhausted at the moment, if you don't mind me saying so.'

'I don't mind anything said with such obvious good-will,' she told the older woman frankly. 'And yes, I am tired, very tired indeed. I've been ill but I'm on the mend now and the future is looking much brighter, thanks to Livia helping me to escape from that dreadful man.'

'I could see that someone had hurt you when you arrived. That sort of thing can't be hidden, but we stop men who try to behave that badly round here. Some of them move here thinking they can continue to hurt people openly, but they can't, not in our valley. Your attacker must be a vicious brute to have done that to you.'

'He is. I will tell you that he's called Billy Doyle, but I'd rather only tell his name to one or two people unless he ever comes here after me, that is. If he does, I don't know what I'll do. Run away again, probably.'

She added in a low voice, as if she couldn't help thinking aloud, 'Or I'll simply throw myself off the nearest cliff. It'd be an easier way to die than letting him get hold of me again, that's for sure.'

'There will be no need to go to that extreme here, my dear.' A warm hand rested lightly on hers for a moment. 'Indeed, you won't ever need to think like that again, because people here look after one another. You'll be considered one of us from now onwards, I promise you.'

Janie gulped audibly, clearly fighting tears at this unexpected and very unambiguous statement of support.

'Thank you,' she managed in a husky whisper. 'I'm so grateful.'

'We'll tell my husband and our very efficient police sergeant about this man if you don't mind. Then, if that brute ever does come to our valley, they'll make sure some of our younger and stronger men are waiting to deal with him. They'll keep him away from you, I promise.'

Janie looked at her so doubtfully when she heard this final remark that Flora said, 'They've had to do that before with other bullies and have always managed to keep the person being pursued safe. Always.'

She waited and when Janie still looked doubtful, she repeated, 'We really do look after our own in Ollindale.'

'Our own?' she whispered, looking both surprised and wistful at the same time. 'Even though I've only just arrived?'

'Yes. So welcome to the valley, my dear. Consider yourself at home from now onwards. I hope you'll be very happy here, both in how you live and with whatever job you find.'

Tears welled in Janie's eyes and she could only whisper, 'Thank you,' once again.

Flora reached out to clasp her hand again and it felt to Janie as if the two of them were sealing a promise. Then Mrs Crossley let go as there was a rattling sound from further along the platform, and the porter began wheeling the trolley loaded with heavier items from the luggage van slowly towards their spot near the exit.

The moment of rapport might have been over, but the warmth of this welcome seemed to linger inside Janie as if someone had wrapped a warm shawl round her shoulders. The feeling that she really, truly wasn't alone both lifted her spirits and made her want to weep.

Flora beckoned and a man who'd been waiting to one side came across to join them.

'Will you and your friend bring this lady's trunk out to our cart, please, Harry? There's only the one.'

'Happy to do that, Mrs Crossley. Can the young lady point out which one it is, please.'

Flora turned back to the two newcomers. 'Can you show these men which is your trunk when they've been unloaded here, Livia, then you can come across and join us? I'll go ahead and get your friend settled on the cart.'

And Janie, normally timid with strangers, felt happy to go off with this kind lady and be introduced to Mr Crossley, who was driving the cart. His wife had such a kind face you could never be afraid of her, and Mr Crossley also had a kind expression. His love for his wife showed clearly and further added to Janie's feeling that she had no need to be afraid of this man.

She felt lucky to have been brought here and to be safe with such good people, so very lucky. Would it last? Oh, she did hope it would. It was like her best dream come suddenly true.

20

The two newcomers were quickly settled on a small bench in the cart. It was attached to the rear of the driver's seat and there were a couple of bags full of shopping sitting next to it, as well as their luggage now.

They looked round with interest as they were driven first through the centre of the town, then out towards the slightly wider streets of what were clearly better residential areas. The Crossleys pointed out a few places of interest on the way, including a building which had been a shop but was now used as a clinic. Mostly, however, they were left in peace to take in their new surroundings as the pony ambled along.

The streets they turned into next were narrower and that happened quite quickly, it seemed, with most of the houses in this part smaller. But these were definitely not slums. The houses were well cared for with clean windows and neat little gardens measuring about two yards by one at the front.

When Mr Crossley reined in the pony in a short street on a slope, Flora didn't get down straight away but gestured towards the house next to their cart. 'Stay where you are for a moment, ladies, because you'll get a better first view from up here. This is the house in which you'll be living.'

'It looks nice,' Livia said. 'The outside is well maintained. I always look at that as a guide.'

Janie also thought that it looked good but couldn't help asking, 'What's the rent, please? I don't think I can afford to live in a house as nice as this, even if we share the costs, because even when I find a job I'm not likely to earn enough.'

She took a deep breath and dared to put her ambition into words. 'At best I'll be able to afford a clean room lodging in a decent home in a respectable area, and believe me, I won't complain about that.'

'The house is split into flats,' Mrs Crossley told her. 'And there is a room in the basement as well which might suit you.'

'Even so, I only have a few pennies left and I feel I need a day or two longer to recover properly before I can start work.' She looked pleadingly at Livia. 'I'm hoping I can maybe sleep on the floor somewhere because I haven't enough money even to pay for the cheapest lodgings and I'm . . . well, a bit run down healthwise.'

'More than a bit,' Livia said gently.

'Yes. I suppose so. Or maybe – will the owners let me owe them my share of the rent for the basement till I get settled, Mrs Crossley? I would pay it all back, every single penny, I promise you. And even then, I can't afford to pay a lot of rent.'

She was looking so distressed, Flora patted her shoulder. 'You won't need to pay any rent at all, my dear. This house belonged to a very kind lady who died recently. She left it for the use of any district nurses and their assistants or helpers working in this part of the town. They don't have to pay any rent at all, just look after the place carefully.'

After a pause to let that sink in, she added, 'You can stay here for a while rent free.'

Relief shivered through Janie and with it a tiny thread of hope. Was this possible? Was it really possible? 'You'd . . . let me stay here? Even though I'm not a nurse?'

Something else had caught Livia's attention about that remark and she interrupted, looking at Mrs Crossley in puzzlement. 'You speak as if the nurses always have personal assistants. That isn't usual in my experience. In fact, I've been nursing for years and never had one.'

'The nurses need them for protection in the part of our town where you'll be doing a lot of your work. I'm afraid that area is rather rough. It's safer to go about in pairs, but the nurses have also found that they can deal with more patients and problems if they have an experienced helper, so it has its good side as well.'

Walter joined in. 'You two definitely shouldn't go out on your own in Eastby End after dark, though. Never, ever do that, however urgent someone's message seems that they need help. In fact, sadly, it'd be better to go out accompanied by an assistant at all times if you're called to the central part of Eastby, even during the day. We have one or two families living there who contain men who hang about the centre at night sometimes and even cause trouble in the daytime. We don't trust them at all, not with our nurses' safety at stake. It's hard to catch them out, though, because they seem to sense someone like me or a policeman coming.'

The two newcomers were both staring at him in open dismay now.

'We're gradually improving the area, so it's getting better but it all takes time. We'll find you an assistant as quickly as we can, I promise, Livia, and we'll find you a job somewhere safe, Janie.'

There was a moment's silence as he waited for an answer.

'Actually, I may be able to find my own assistant.' Livia turned to stare at Janie and gave a little nod as if she approved of what she saw. 'Would you like the job of being my assistant?'

Janie gaped at her. 'Do you mean it? Really?'

'Of course I do. I'd not have asked you if I didn't feel happy at the prospect of working with you. I'm not asking out of blind pity, believe me. I'd never do that. The patients' welfare is too important. I've just spent several hours alone with you as we travelled, however, so I've got to know you more quickly than I usually would. Well? What do you think?'

'I'd love a job like that. It'd be so interesting and worthwhile. But how do you know I'd be good enough? You must realise that I've had no experience of such work and I only attended the village school and wasn't able to go on to any secondary education. I must seem very ignorant to someone as clever as you.'

'I've been talking to you while we travelled and I've seen how your intelligence shines out, given the chance, and how interested you are in the world around you now you're free to ask questions, and that's even now when you're under the weather healthwise. Besides, I don't think you're any more ignorant than the next person about most everyday things. And how you talk about other people shows that you care about them. That's extremely important in this job.'

The younger woman flushed with pleasure at the compliments. 'Oh. It's very kind of you to say such kind things, Livia, but surely there are others who would know much more than I do about the job and would make a better assistant for you.'

'Don't you want the job?'

She didn't hesitate. 'Of course I do. But I don't want to let you down, not when you've been so kind to me, when you've saved my life, literally.'

The Crossleys gave her shocked glances when she said that but didn't interrupt the conversation.

'I don't think you will let me down, Janie. I can teach you the specific skills you'll need and I enjoy teaching, by the way, but you have to be born with the right attitude towards people who need help to make a good nurse, and I should think that applies to an assistant as well. That attitude can't be taught, it has to be innate. Sad to say, training doesn't necessarily make a good nurse, only an adequate one.'

'Oh.' Janie gulped and seemed close to tears. 'If you'll give me a try at it, I'll do my best always, I promise, and I won't make a fuss if you think I'm not good enough and you need to find someone else better able to do the work.'

'I'm sure you'll be fine in that sort of job, and the best thing about me needing to teach you will be that you'll do things my way from the start. I warn you, I'm very fussy indeed about how sick people and injuries should be dealt with, and about cleanliness. But I shall have to give you a trial first to be utterly certain you're suitable, because lives will sometimes depend on your work.'

After a moment's pause she added slowly and thoughtfully, 'And I should think you'll want to give this sort of work a trial, too, before you start doing it permanently. It doesn't suit everyone, you know, and there's no shame to that. We see some very sad things and we can't always help people to get better, however hard we try.'

She paused and when Janie continued to stare at her as if still finding what she was saying hard to believe, she prompted, 'Is that all right with you, then?'

'Oh, yes. Yes, please. Very much all right. Thank you so much for giving me this chance.' She had to mop away more tears of joy.

They didn't see Flora nod at her husband in approval of what they'd just seen and heard, because the two younger women were too busy smiling at one another.

Livia didn't even look at the Crossleys for confirmation that this trial employment of Janie had met with their approval. It seemed so obvious to her that this was the best way to approach the situation, for both her and Janie. They'd already shown that they got on well, and that was important too, but it was how Janie worked with the patients that would count most, and it was the key thing about to go on trial.

Feeling certain the matter was now settled, because she thought both young women were decent sorts who would work hard and work well together, Flora took over again. 'Employing Janie and having her live nearby will make your settling in easier. Good idea.'

She continued to explain the situation, pointing to the house as she described its interior. 'There are two separate flats, one on each floor. They share a small bathroom, which is at the rear of the ground floor, but otherwise they each have their own cooking amenities and a kitchen sink, and of course stout entrance doors to each flat to give them privacy from anyone else coming into the building.'

She hesitated then brought their safety problem into the open. 'I'm afraid there has recently been an intruder here, so we've hired a young chap to act as nightwatchman for a while. That means you'll have to live in one of the flats at first, Janie, whichever one Livia doesn't want to live in permanently. We won't charge you for that, but as soon as the police have dealt with whoever it is causing this trouble, we shall have to ask you to live in the one-room dwelling in the basement. I'm sure you'll be happy in that, and it's rent-free as well.'

Janie nodded. 'I'll do whatever you say very happily, I promise. And just to reassure you, I like to keep where I live nice and clean, even if it's a dark place.'

'Good. The single room isn't in a dark basement, though. There is quite a large outer window there that's above ground level because of the slope of this street. There's a sink with running cold water in the cellar next to it, too, and a working gas ring, both of which the occupant of the room is free to use. There's also a privy across the yard in addition to the indoor lavatory in the bathroom on the ground floor. The occupant of the room is allowed to use the bathroom there if she will take on the job of cleaning all the public areas thoroughly every week. There's a geyser as well to provide hot water for baths or for cleaning the place.'

Janie stared at her in amazement and delight. 'A bath! A real bath with running water!'

'Yes. But as I said, we'll ask you to live in one of the flats until the intruder is sorted out, then move into the basement. The police are investigating the situation. All right?'

'I shall look forward to living anywhere in this house and enjoying what is a luxury to me of having a space all to myself, large or small. Thank you so much for your help.' Her voice wobbled on the last few words.

'You're welcome, dear.' Mrs Crossley got down from the cart with the ease of long practice and waited near the front door for them to clamber down more slowly and carefully from the back of the cart to join her. 'We're hoping to hire another district nurse once the other flat is available again.'

Janie wondered if she was worried she'd got the wrong impression about accommodation, so said, 'I do understand that this flat is temporary, Mrs Crossley. Even to have my own room is more than I've ever known before, so I won't be upset by having to go down to the basement, believe me. And if I don't have to struggle to find the rent money, that will make my life so much easier.' Easier than she'd ever had it up to now, she admitted to herself, but didn't tell them that.

'As I've already said, the room is free to someone doing your job, as is the use of the bathroom to you if you'll clean it thoroughly every week.'

A sob of joy escaped Janie and she had to wipe her eyes again. 'I'm a good cleaner, given the chance. Having a bathroom will be wonderful. And so will having my own room once the other problems are sorted out, believe me.'

Flora waited to speak again, trying to give her time for the good news to sink in. So many of the poorest people had to spend their lives in cramped, crowded accommodation and never got this sort of opportunity. She did understand that.

Some towns at least provided public bathhouses, where people paid a small sum to use one of the bathrooms, but the local council in Ollerthwaite had dismissed the suggestion of them doing that here out of hand. If only women were legally allowed to become town councillors they'd get a few more practical things happening, she thought for about the thousandth time. She felt sure they'd vote for things that would make a real difference to women's lives and the care of families.

She'd read about two women who had been elected to councils in London in – what year had that been? Oh, yes, 1889. But there had been legal objections to their becoming councillors and they had been deemed ineligible. Shameful, that had been, utterly shameful. She felt angry every time she remembered reading about it, but hadn't been able to forget about it. It showed what women were facing from some people.

Women ratepayers had been allowed to vote for council elections for a few decades, but only if they were single or widowed. Why could married women not vote as well? That was utterly stupid! Some men seemed to do everything they could, including making ridiculous rules like that, to keep women out of positions of influence and under their firm control. Thank goodness her Walter wasn't like that!

She realised the others were speaking and that she'd been lost in thought and not paying attention. Well, she had a lot to think about at the moment. She watched Janie stare from Livia to the Crossleys, beaming now, and the sight of that happiness made Flora feel good too.

'Oh, it'll be so wonderful to have a whole flat to myself. What a treat! Sheer luxury, that!' Janie exclaimed.

Flora had also watched Livia stare at her friend in surprise, then look away, clearly trying not to show her sadness at how heartfelt and joyful this exclamation had sounded. Luxury, indeed! One person's luxury could be another's idea of living in poverty. It just wasn't fair that some people had so much more than others!

After giving Janie another minute or two to pull herself together, Flora said, 'Good. That's settled, then. I'll tell Josh and Rachel that you'll be using both flats for the time being. Some household items are supplied but if you're short of any other things, they said you can use the bits and pieces you'll find stored in the cellar as well. There are blankets, some oddments of crockery and a couple of saucepans down there for starters. I don't think there's much left in the flats except for the furniture.'

She waited to let that sink in then continued, 'The flats are unoccupied because their former owner was living in the ground floor one when she died recently, you see, and Rachel was occupying the first-floor flat but has now got married. So her possessions have already been taken away, but there's still enough furniture there to be comfortable. She's letting my husband and me use the accommodation for the district nurses we're employing, so we'll be arranging things here.'

Janie gave her a blissful smile. 'Thank you so much. That'll be just wonderful.'

Flora turned back to Livia. 'You can have either of the flats, my dear, and Janie will take the other temporarily. It's your choice: upstairs or down. They're very similar inside and they come with most furnishings and household equipment. I'm sure Janie won't mind which flat she occupies. You can use items from the basement as well, of course, or store things there if you have too much clutter in the flat. But if you do the latter, please label your possessions so that no one will take them inadvertently.'

'I'd prefer to have the upstairs flat,' Livia said without hesitation.

'Don't you want to see them first?' Flora asked, looking rather surprised at her rapid response.

'No need. I think the upper flat is likely to be quieter, you see.' And it would also, she hoped, be safer, though she didn't say that. Single women were always more at risk than other people if they lived alone. You had to be very careful indeed where and how you lived.

Flora stared at her for a few seconds, then nodded. 'Yes, I suppose it will be quieter. Come and look at them both first anyway, then we'll take you down to see your room in the basement after that, Janie, just so you know what it'll be like there later on.'

'What was this kind woman called, the one who left her house for nurses to use?' Livia asked.

'Dora Prior.'

'I'll remember her gratefully in my prayers.'

'So will I,' Janie said very fervently.

'That's a kind thought.' Flora hesitated but they had to be told. 'Just so that you understand the details, the intruder claimed that the house belonged to his master after Mrs Prior died. This man had sent word that he was a distant relative of Dora's and he possessed her will leaving it to him.'

She saw both her companions look anxious again and said quickly, 'That was a lie, and the will we have was written and overseen by lawyers, and is indisput-ably genuine, so don't let anyone fool you. The will is legal and really does leave the house to be used for accommodating nurses and other people involved in medical occupations. What's more, the will was written only a few days before Dora died, so not only can't this man's claim possibly be genuine but even if it had been once, it would have been superseded now.'

They both nodded slowly as they took this in and relaxed visibly.

'I'm only telling you about it so that you pay no atten-tion whatsoever to anyone else claiming to own the house. It belongs to Rachel but Walter and I will be managing it.'

They were both still looking a bit worried, however, and she felt sorry at how fragile their trust in the world was.

'We'll make sure you're safe here, but you should be careful to keep the outer doors locked at all times. And since we didn't want to take any chances, we've already had better locks and extra bolts fitted, not only to the insides of all the external doors but to the entrance doors to the flats and to the basement room. That has given you a new set of keys that no stranger can possibly have copies of.'

Walter moved to his wife's side. 'What's more, we're still hiring Ted for a few days to keep watch on the house and make sure the intruder doesn't try to break in again. He kept watch last night but everything stayed perfectly quiet, you'll be glad to know. And we'll keep him on for as long as is necessary to keep you safe. He comes from a large family and lives in very cramped conditions, so he won't mind how long he keeps watch for us because he's earning more than he ever has before, and we're letting him catch up on his sleep during the daytime in the basement.'

They nodded and Livia said, 'We ought to be all right here, then.'

But Janie in particular still looked worried, though she was trying to hide that.

'Ted will come round this evening and introduce himself by telling you that I've sent my regards. He'll be catching up on his sleep at home at the moment. We've arranged to leave him a mattress and blankets to sleep on in the basement for as long as he's needed. He'll be moving up and down the stairs occasionally and because he's patrolling the stairwell of the house, he'll be able to hear anyone who tries to get in at the front or the back.'

Livia nodded. 'It'll be good to know he's going to be there.'

'We prefer to keep our nurses safe, whatever it takes. Is there anything else you'd like to ask about?'

'What do the police say about this?'

'They've promised to keep an eye on the situation and they're now making regular patrols of the central streets in Eastby during the night as well as in the areas nearby. That has recently been started and we feel it's made a bit of difference already. We've also given the police your names and this address, and have asked them to keep a particular eye on this house.'

Livia relaxed visibly. 'Oh good. We greatly appreciate the care you're taking, Mr and Mrs Crossley, don't we, Janie?'

Janie nodded and tried to look more confident than she felt. 'Very much indeed.'

'You're welcome. And if there's anything you'd like changed or improved in the flats or basement room, just ask me.' Walter looked at Janie and added quietly, 'If we weren't sure we could keep you as safe as you'd be anywhere else, we'd not have brought you to live here yet, believe me.'

'Thank you.' But she noticed how he phrased it and she had to accept that. No one was ever totally safe in this world, were they?

Mrs Crossley smiled at them. 'If you should see the neighbours coming and going outside, do introduce yourselves. We've told them your names and to expect you. They're already keeping their eyes open for any strangers loitering nearby, for their own sakes, but that'll help you too. You have well-respected families living on both sides.' She told them the names of the neighbours and which of them exactly lived where.

Livia nodded. 'We can't thank you enough for being so careful about our safety, Mr and Mrs Crossley.'

As Janie still continued to look faintly anxious, Walter shot a quick glance at his wife, but she shook her head and neither of them pursued the matter any further. Only time would make that poor young woman feel less afraid after what she'd been through during the past few months. They'd been informed about that before they met the two young women at the station and discussed it. Janie was, Flora had said, lucky not to have come away with a baby in her belly from that brute. That was the sad truth.

As they'd also said to one another rather sadly, nowhere in the world could be made totally safe for everyone, and especially for pretty young women.

Walter helped Livia carry her trunk inside and upstairs, then left them to take their own cases and bags from the hall where they'd been dumped and into their new homes. She didn't have much luggage anyway.

Flora lifted a shabby bag from the cart, took it into the house, setting it down in the hall. Walter followed suit and came back in with an almost identical one. The top of a crusty loaf poked out of each well-loaded shopping bag.

When the two young women rejoined them, Flora gestured to the bags. 'These are to welcome you to our town. They contain some basic food supplies to get you started, one bag for each of you, and you can keep the shopping bags for your own use afterwards.'

'That's very thoughtful of you. Thank you so much,' Livia said.

Janie stared at the bags then at Flora, looking overwhelmed by this largesse. Indeed, she'd looked so astonished that Livia had wondered if she'd not had many presents in her life, perhaps none at all, given her family's poverty. She could have been pretty but at the moment she was far too thin with that faintly hungry look you saw sometimes in people who didn't eat regularly.

Long-term hunger often showed on people's faces, Livia thought. You could tell some ill-fed children when they passed you in the street, well, she could after her years of nursing and others had said the same thing. And anxiety hung over some people like almost-visible clouds, as it did with Janie, which didn't do their health any good.

'Be careful how you handle the bags,' Flora warned. 'Each one contains a couple of eggs from our own hens and a bottle of milk. I wrapped the eggs in rags to cushion them and the rags will no doubt come in useful afterwards for cleaning. There should be enough food there to tide you over for a day or two till you can do some shopping of your own and stock up on your basic supplies.'

'How kind of you! And how practical!' Livia said. 'Thank you so much.'

'I like to help people. There's a little corner shop at the end of the next street which would welcome your custom – we helped the owner when she was struggling after being widowed. She's very obliging if you need anything regularly that she doesn't stock at the moment.'

Livia took the hint. 'We'll definitely do some of our shopping there regularly.'

'Good. That'll help her.'

'You've been so kind to us, Mr and Mrs Crossley. I can't thank you enough for your help. How can I ever pay you back?' Janie's voice sounded choked with emotion.

Flora shrugged and smiled. 'My husband and I are lucky to have enough possessions or access to discarded items to be able to spare some for others in need, so we're glad to help people. One day perhaps you'll have enough to be able to spare something to help others as well, which is the only way we would want to be paid back.'

She liked the thought of that. 'I'll do that. I promise.'

'So will I,' Livia added quietly.

'Good. Now, come down and have a look at your basement room, Janie, even if you won't be using it yet. If there's anything missing that you'll really need, don't hesitate to tell me now. After all, you'll be living there permanently once the situation is safer, so you ought to know what it's like.'

But the room was well set up, lacking no essential basic item and indeed, extremely comfortable by Janie's standards. It took up nearly half the space in the basement and was already very clean. She could only manage to stutter her thanks again as she stared round in delight at all that space for her to use on her own. She admitted to herself, however, that she was even more thrilled to be given a whole flat to live in for a while. She'd enjoy the novelty and luxury of all that space to herself greatly.

When the Crossleys left, the two young women waved them goodbye from the front door then Janie said to Livia, 'I'm so looking forward to having that whole flat to myself, just for a taste of luxury living. And wasn't it kind of them to give us so much food? I can manage for days on that if I don't eat too lavishly.'

'There's a difference between eating lavishly and eating enough to stay well and healthy. You're far too thin and I don't think you've been eating properly for a good while.'

She saw Janie flush and look embarrassed, so gave her a quick hug. 'You won't need to skimp on food or miss meals to eke it out from now on. I'll give you an advance on your wages, so you'll be able to afford to buy food regularly as needed. Mrs Crossley slipped me some money to get us started here.'

Janie gulped back tears at this further kindness and managed to say 'Thank you!' in a choky-sounding voice. She'd never met such wonderful people or been treated so well, not in her whole life.

Livia went on, 'We can visit that nearby shop together tomorrow, if you like, to buy some basics like flour. And there will probably be a market in the town at some point as well. I usually find I can pick up some good bargains at markets, especially if I go there just before closing time.'

Janie nodded agreement. She knew that already. She'd not only bought things cheaply at markets, but also regularly picked up spoiled fruit and vegetables from them after the stalls had been cleared. There was always edible stuff lying on the ground in corners and it was easy to cut away the bad bits.

A sudden yawn took Livia by surprise. 'I have to admit that I'm exhausted now. I think I'll have a rest and perhaps even a short nap even before I unpack anything and perhaps you should do the same. You look as tired as I feel.'

'I'm exhausted.'

Livia stared round the entrance hall. 'I think you'll be very cosy down in that basement room eventually, but I don't like the thought of that intruder.'

'I don't, either. I'm really glad we'll be having a watchman at night until they've sorted all that out. Surely an intruder isn't as likely to come back again if he's been chased away once?' Janie looked at her anxiously as she asked this.

'I doubt it's likely but you can never quite be sure, so I'm relieved we'll have the watchman. And remember, if anyone tries to break in during the day, there will still be two of us to deal with any trouble. I can scream very loudly if I need help and you should too. Want me to demonstrate?'

That won her a smile from Janie. 'No, thanks. I'll take your word for it. I can scream loudly, I promise you, but I hope we won't need to do that.'

Livia hesitated then said, 'I'm not taking any chances so I think I'll find something to defend myself with and leave it near the outer door of my flat. A cosh of some sort. And I'll carry it with me if I have to go out to visit a patient after dark, especially one in Eastby End.'

'That's a good idea. I'll do the same. A small rolling pin might be a good idea, especially one with thin handles at the ends. They're easy enough to carry and use. Or there may be some even more suitable items in the basement.'

'We'll look for something for you later. I don't think we're in danger at the moment. There's been too much coming and going here. People don't usually try to burgle houses full of people.' Livia was suddenly overtaken by another huge, long yawn. 'I need a nap quite desperately.'

Janie immediately yawned too, then smiled. 'People always say yawns are catching, don't they?'

'They seem to be. I wonder why. Well, never mind that. There are more important things in life to find out about. I'm really looking forward to having a proper rest on something that stays still under me. That last train seemed to bump and rattle even more than the others and the journey felt by then as if it was going on and on for ever.'

'I'd like a rest, too. Such a lot has happened in the past week I need to take it all in and grow used to my freedom.' She would especially appreciate the freedom to lie down in a bed on her own. 'I'll rearrange the furniture in the basement later when I move down there. The main thing will be that I don't want to sleep in a bed that can be seen from outside the flat.'

'I know what you mean.'

'Mr Crossley said if I wanted to change things around in that room, I could. It's wonderful that there are so many items stored for us to use if we need them, isn't it?

I shall feel as if I'm in heaven in the flat, but I'll be perfectly happy down in the basement when I have to move to my more permanent home, believe me.'

Livia smiled at the blissful expression on her companion's bruised face, reminded yet again that Janie would be pretty once the purple marks had faded, and when she'd put on a little weight. What a hard life the other woman must have had, though. It showed in the tense way she held herself and her expression when she was quiet and looked as if she was remembering something unpleasant.

'I'll rearrange things slowly when I move in. I shall need to make sure of what I want first, and also what's available among the piles of stuff down there,' Janie said thoughtfully. 'Except for the bed. The one in the flat is already out of sight from the window and there are net curtains as well as the normal curtains there. I like that.'

'I don't think they'd be able to see right into your room downstairs from outside the basement window, though.'

Janie's voice grew suddenly fierce. 'I'm not giving anyone the chance to see even one of my hands or feet when I'm sleeping.'

Her anger about some memory was almost a visible thing.

'It's up to you how you arrange things but if you need help moving the bed when you go down there to live, don't hesitate to ask?'

'Thanks but I don't think I shall. It's only a single bed and I'm stronger than I look.' She sounded calmer again now.

'I'll see you later, then.' Livia left her to it and went slowly up the stairs to her flat. She would welcome some time on her own, would really relish it.

Who'd have thought that helping another woman to escape danger from a violent man would bring her to the very north of the country? Still, she had to go somewhere and had no family to settle near. And the Crossleys seemed lovely people. They'd already been very kind to the two newcomers, and that felt like a good start in her new life.

And this was a very comfortable bed. She snuggled down.

When she was alone, Janie turned round slowly on the spot, taking in how the borrowed flat felt when she was alone in it. Safe, that's how it felt, which was much more important than comfortable. She turned round again, even more slowly this time. This place was clean already. Hmm. She was going to jam a chair under the bedroom door handle before she tried to rest in there, though. Just to be utterly certain.

On that thought she moved her case and shopping bags to one side of the bedroom and kitchen, then put one of the two upright chairs under the bedroom door handle and one under the front door handle too, pleased that the chair backs were high enough to jam tightly into place. There! That hadn't taken long. She'd unpack the food Mrs Crossley had given her later.

She lay down on the bed, sprawled across it, arms and legs stretched out, then sighed happily and snuggled down under the quilt.

Moving to Ollerthwaite would mean she'd not only be safer but have a job she would enjoy and enough clothes to keep herself clean. Imagine that! Could fate really have been so kind to her? How long would this last?

She opened her eyes again and stared round the room, enjoying the luxury of it. Even the basement room she would be moving to was larger than most of the rooms she'd shared with other people during the past few years. Who'd have thought there would be so much space inside and under what looked like a neat little house from outside? That was because of the slope and the big usable cellar. Wonderful.

She'd seen all sorts of objects piled up haphazardly in the open part of it. She'd go through them and tidy the place up once she moved into her more permanent home down there. She didn't like living in messy places. Not if she had any choice, that was.

She wriggled around on the bed. This flock mattress felt new and didn't have any lumps in it at all. So very comfortable.

She heard a noise and stiffened, then realised it was only children playing and shouting further down the street, and relaxed. Would she ever again feel completely safe? She wondered suddenly. Not as long as he was alive, that was sure.

But she wasn't on her own now and this flat or the room downstairs would give her a better life by a long way than any she'd experienced since she'd grown up. There were bad things about being a child, but far worse ones about being a woman without a family's support.

She let her eyes close. Just to rest them for a few moments. She'd be safe.

And she didn't open them again till Livia woke her by knocking on the door of the flat nearly an hour later, judging by the alarm clock Mrs Crossley had given her.

When Janie opened the door, Livia leaned closer and whispered, 'I was asleep too but was woken up by the neighbour knocking on the front door. I'm surprised that didn't wake you.'

'I didn't hear a thing.'

Now she'd been told, Janie could see a figure standing outside the front door of the house.

Livia spoke more loudly, 'Rhona next door kindly came to introduce herself and she wanted to meet you as well so that she'd know who had the right to come in and out of our house. She says they watch out for one another in this street, which is lovely to know, isn't it?'

That made Janie nod happily but another yawn took over her face muscles.

'Come on, sleepyhead,' Livia urged cheerfully, adding in a low voice, 'Rhona seems to be a very pleasant woman and we want her on our side, don't we?'

Janie wished the neighbour could have come a little later and let her stay asleep but forced herself to begin moving towards the visitor. Livia was right. You didn't turn down offers of friendship and mutual support.

'Sorry to keep you waiting,' she said as cheerfully as she could manage. 'It always takes me a minute or two to wake up properly.'

'I'm Rhona Perkins.'

'Janie Clayton.'

After they'd chatted for a while to Rhona she left them with a cheerful wave and Livia closed the front door with a tired sigh. 'What I'd really like to do now is get something to eat and go to bed early.'

'Me too.'

'Good. Let's do that. We'll explore our bags of food and maybe have something simple like a crust from the loaf with jam on it, and it's good quality jam too. And after that I'm going to bed and not answering the door again. If I don't lie down and get a good sleep soon, I'll fall down or go to sleep standing up, I'm so tired. Shall we eat together?'

'Yes. Why don't you come into my room?'

'I'll just nip up for my food. It'd be best to keep what we eat from our bags of food separate.'

Ted arrived just as they were finishing their snack and proved to be a big chap with a rather ugly face, which looked threatening till he smiled at them, then suddenly friendly and honest.

'You two ladies can sleep easy. I'll keep a careful watch,' he assured them. 'I really want to keep this job.'

'You'll keep that back door locked when you're in other parts of the house?' Janie said.

'For all our sakes, lass. I don't want to be attacked and taken by surprise, either.'

For some reason she trusted him. She went to bed properly this time, though she didn't forget to put the chair under the door handle. She lay there trying to get used to the normal sounds of this house and street, then she heard Ted come upstairs, well she thought it was him. So of course she had to get up and open the door of the flat a crack to peep into the front hall and check.

Yes, it was him. She watched him peer at the street through the narrow window next to the front door and when he turned round, she opened her door wide enough to give him a tiny wave. 'Just getting used to what the various sounds mean, Ted.'

'Good thing to do. I'd do it too.' He turned and went back down to the cellar.

He had quite a heavy way of walking. She'd recognise it and therefore him next time without even seeing him. After that she had no difficulty getting to sleep. Not only wasn't she hungry but there was someone she trusted guarding the house. Both those things felt absolutely wonderful.

It was the first night for ages that she hadn't had night-mares and she only woke a couple of times, once to listen and hear only silence inside the house and outside it, the other time to Ted's now familiar footsteps as he checked what sounded like a drunken passer-by from the front-hall window.

Each time she woke it was easier than she'd expected to fall asleep again, easier than it had been for a very long time.

21

On their first full day in Ollerthwaite, Logan, Ellis and Gil enjoyed a leisurely breakfast. It seemed wonderful to Logan to sit and eat bacon and eggs with his new employer, and then slather the leftover toast not just in butter but in some delicious honey as well. He'd lost count of the number of times he'd had to make do with a chunk of dry bread to satisfy his appetite.

It felt strange at first to be waited on by a maid but then he realised she was a lass he'd known when they were both small, all grown up now and pretty with it. She had a nice smile and chatted happily to them, unlike some of the starchy maids he'd encountered in his searches for work in London.

So he enjoyed Maddy's company and could see that Ellis was finding the casual atmosphere at their table very pleasant too.

Once their appetites were satisfied, they lingered over a final cup of tea and discussed how to organise their day. Young Gil had mainly kept quiet but Logan had noticed how intently he listened to everything. A smart lad, that one, he reckoned, but it was a bit sad to see how desperate he was for his father's attention and approval, how afraid of saying or doing something wrong.

Ellis said quietly, 'I'd like to get an overview of the town and its surroundings first. How do you suggest we do that, Logan?'

'Do you want to do it on foot or to hire a cart? I don't think there would be many fancy pony traps for hire in Ollerthwaite, though, so it'd be just a plain old cart. What do you think, Maddy?'

The maid nodded. 'There aren't enough fancy folk needing transport to make traps for hiring a worthwhile way of earning a living.'

Ellis frowned. 'Hmm. I don't want to do it on foot this first time because we won't see enough of it. Let's hire a cart, then. I'm not fussy about my dignity, I promise you, Logan. That way we'll be able to cover more ground and I can get a much better overview of what the town and its surroundings are like. Do you know someone with a cart who would drive us round?'

Logan hesitated, frowning as he considered this, then said, 'One of my cousins married a carter, who used to take passengers now and then, though I can't say whether Tait will be free today or not. And I have to warn you that it'll not be luxurious seating.'

'I don't mind that. Could you go and ask him if he'd be able to spend the day with us, please? I'll pay whatever he thinks fair to have his help for the whole day.'

'Yes, I can do that. But he lives a bit out of town so it'll take me a while to get to and fro. Eh, I could have sent a message to him yesterday when I went to see my mother if I'd known because she lives quite close to their home.'

'Never mind.'

Maddy had been clearing the table as they chatted and openly listening to their conversation as she piled their used crockery on a big wooden tray. She now stopped to say, 'Excuse me interfering, Logan, but I've got my bicycle here. It's old but works just fine and if you borrow that you could cycle out to see Tait. You'd be there and back within a quarter of an hour at most, I should think. I won't be needing it for a couple of hours, not till I finish my morning's work.'

He smiled at her. 'Thanks, Maddy love. That'd be a big help.' Then he looked at Ellis. 'Is that all right with you?'

'I think it's an excellent idea and it's very kind of this young lady to offer to lend you her bicycle.' He reached into his pocket, pulled out a coin and slipped it into her hand. 'Thank you.'

She didn't refuse it but chuckled and said, 'Young lady! I'm not often called that, sir. I'm just Maddy usually, especially to my cousin Logan, whose sister is my best friend.'

'I don't think our local folk are as formal here as you're used to, sir,' Logan said, winking at her.

'I'm beginning to realise that and I like it. But I thought you and I were on first name terms now as well.'

'I didn't want to sound too casual in public, not when you're my employer.'

Ellis rolled his eyes. 'Nonsense. If we're on first name terms, we're on them all the time.'

As Maddy again chuckled openly at this interchange, Logan grinned at her and then at his employer. 'Ellis it is, then. I'll nip off to see if I can catch Tait. You and Gil might like to walk round the town centre in the meantime. You won't want to sit around inside the hotel doing nothing. And I reckon if you even try that, your son will drive you mad with his twitching and sighing. I'd give him about five minutes to start doing that. He needs keeping occupied, that one does.'

Gil grinned at him from across the table then turned to his father. 'Logan's right. I don't like sitting still. Can we go out for a walk while he's away, please? We could see the centre of the town.'

He was getting more comfortable with his father, thank goodness, Logan thought and looked out of the window to check that the weather had turned out as fine as had seemed likely when he got up.

'It's a nice day so why waste the sunshine, Ellis? I warn you, we seem to get more rainy days than sunny ones here in Lancashire. If you'd like to walk round the town centre, go up the hill when you leave the hotel, and then keep taking the first turn on the left in each street you walk along from then onwards. That'll take you past a few shops and along by a small park, then bring you back here to the hotel in roughly the right amount of time for me to get back. Tait will be here soon afterwards with his cart if he's free, I should think.'

Gil's face brightened as his father nodded.

'Good idea. We'll do that.'

Logan turned back to the maid. 'Where's your bicycle, Maddy?'

'I'll show you.' When they were out in the yard, she said, 'Your Mr Quinn seems like a nice chap.'

'He is. Very nice.'

'The lad's a bit quiet for a young fellow that age.'

Logan couldn't help chuckling. 'That's because he's on his best behaviour at the moment. This is the first time he's gone away with his father and he doesn't want it to be the last. He'll be a lot more lively once they get used to one another, I'm sure.'

'Fancy having to get used to your own father,' she muttered, shaking her head in surprise and sadness. 'Rich people don't see a lot of their children, do they?'

'No. I'd not like that.'

'Me neither. Not that I have any yet. Me and my young man have only just started walking out together. He's got a good job, though, and he makes me laugh, so he seems promising.' She went back to her work and left him to set off on the borrowed bicycle.

Now he came to think of it, Logan decided as he pedalled along, it would be a good thing if he left Gil to spend time alone with his father as often as possible. Both of them were still rather tentative about how they dealt with one another, though things were improving.

The bicycle felt a bit strange at first because it was a lady's type in design. He'd ridden them before and in some ways they seemed easier to handle than the men's bicycles because they didn't have that central bar across between the seat and the handlebars. Some men preferred that, mostly the younger and more agile ones, but some of the older men didn't.

Who knew why they made them like that anyway? You just put up with such puzzling things because you could only buy what was being sold in the shops, which wasn't necessarily exactly what you'd have preferred.

Perhaps the women's bicycles had a more open style of frame to cope with the long skirts, and . . . ? Ah, who knew? He should stop trying to understand all the details of how the world around him got to be like it was. No one could do that completely, he was sure.

It was interesting to try, though.

Left alone with his father, Gil waited for him to speak, not even looking at Maddy as he pushed his empty plate slightly to one side to help her clear the table.

Ellis studied him, rather amused that Gil had eaten just as much as he had. He couldn't resist reaching out to ruffle his son's soft brown hair. 'You've been very quiet this morning, my lad. You are allowed to speak to me without asking permission, you know.'

The words came out in a rush. 'I'm trying to behave really well so that you'll let me stay with you all day.'

'Did you think I'd put you in the nearest cupboard if I got fed up of you?'

Gil stared in surprise at this response, then realised his father was teasing him and sniggered. 'I'm not always sure what to think about you yet because we haven't spent a lot of time together.'

'No. Far too little.' He regretted that deeply now but he'd not had a lot of choice when working for his uncle. 'I'm going to enjoy getting to know you better and I hope you'll feel the same about me.'

He pushed his chair back and Gil immediately did the same. 'Right then. Let's go and put on our outdoor things and go for a stroll round the town centre.'

The landlady came into the hall as they were coming down the stairs. 'Did you want a meal providing tonight, Mr Quinn?'

'Yes, please. Sorry. I should have remembered to ask you about that. And thank you for a fine breakfast. I enjoyed every mouthful.'

'I'm glad to hear it. I'll put a tin of biscuits in the guest sitting room in case any of you get hungry between meals.' She smiled. 'Even if you don't, your son probably will. That room will be open for you to use all day long if you want to sit and rest since you're staying here for a few days, and today's newspapers will be available there from this afternoon onwards. We get them a bit later here in the country. You have only to ring the bell if you want a pot of tea and someone will come and attend to your needs.'

'That's very kind of you.'

'No trouble, Mr Quinn. We do our best to keep our guests happy.'

'And you do it very well, too. I'm extremely happy with the service here.'

She beamed at that and her face went a bit pink.

Ellis and his son left the hotel and set off on a gentle stroll round town, which gave them time to look more closely at what they were passing. As they came to a bookshop he noticed that his son slowed down even more to stare longingly at the window displays. 'Would you like me to buy you a book or two?'

'Really?'

'Yes, really.'

'And can I choose one of them myself, please?'

That remark puzzled him. 'Who else would choose your books?'

Gil didn't say anything, just stared down at his feet and avoided his father's gaze.

'Go on. Tell me. You sound as if someone else has been choosing all your books for you. I can understand that for school books but not when you're reading for pleasure.'

'My tutors have all chosen the books I was allowed to read. They wouldn't let me have any books they didn't approve of.'

'Did they really do that? Well, I'm even more pleased they're not with us any longer, then. I'd far rather you chose your own pleasure books from now on, Gil. Reading can be fun but only if you really want to read that particular book. How about you choose two books now and I'll buy them for you? Then you can let me know when you've read the first one and we'll buy you another book or two. I don't know how fast you read.'

'I'm quite a fast reader.'

'Well, then, we'll have to make sure you always have at least one book in reserve apart from the book you're reading, in case there isn't a bookshop handy. And when we settle somewhere we'll both join the local library. For the moment, I intend to choose a book or two for myself as well. I love reading when I get the chance.'

'We'll be late back to meet the others.'

'Logan won't mind when we tell him what we've been doing. He enjoys reading too, from what he says.'

In the shop he watched his son's face light up with joy and stay alight as he began to study the titles in the children's section. He came to show his father *Black Beauty* and *Treasure Island*. 'Can I have these, please?'

Ellis was a bit puzzled. 'I'd have thought you'd have read those two by now. I've heard they're popular titles for youngsters.'

Gil stared at him apprehensively as if unsure where this was leading and the happiness faded slightly. He was now clutching the books as if expecting to have them taken away.

'My tutor said books like these were rubbish and he wouldn't let me read them. He insisted I read books he chose instead. Only his books were very boring, mostly about children going to church or Sunday school. I only read them because I had nothing else to do after my lessons ended.'

'Good heavens! They sound ghastly. Go ahead and enjoy these two. You can tell me all about them afterwards and I'll tell you about the books I'm reading.'

Gil brightened up again. 'Thank you, Father. I'd love that.'

'You're welcome. Come to think of it, you might as well choose a third book while you're at it to be sure of having something in reserve. And you're to tell me from now on if you're running out of books. When we go home again you can have a look through my bookshelves and see if there's anything you fancy reading there.'

'You'll let me read grown-up books!' He beamed at his father. 'Oh, goody!'

'Anyone can read anything, as far as I'm concerned. Well, as long as they understand it.'

'Thank you!' Gil suddenly flung himself at him and hugged him tightly, something he'd never done before.

It was one of the best moments Ellis had experienced for a long time, so he hugged his son back just as tightly and kept hold of him for a while, patting his back gently. And the boy cuddled closer, making no attempt to draw away.

After they'd pulled apart, smiling at one another almost shyly, they went on to choose several books each, not just two or three in the end, and Ellis paid for them with great delight.

★ ★ ★

When they got back to the hotel they found a cart out-side it and a man standing nearby chatting to Logan, who looked up as they got close, raised one hand in greeting and smiled at them.

Ellis waved the parcel of books at his friend. 'Sorry we're a bit late getting back. We got tempted into the bookshop.'

'Good for you. And the time doesn't matter. It's up to you what we do and when we do it since you're paying us by the day.' He gestured to his companion. 'This is Tait, who's free to take us out to look round the valley today. He brought me and the bicycle back on his cart. Tait, this is my friend Ellis Quinn.'

Logan named the price that would be charged and Ellis said at once, 'That sounds very reasonable.'

The man immediately held out one hand and Ellis shook it awkwardly because of the books.

'And this is Ellis's son Gil.'

Tait clapped the lad on the shoulders. 'Pleased to meet you, young 'un. Logan was worried that you don't know any children round here to play with, so if you'd like to come outside and kick a ball around one evening, I can bring my sons and some of the rascals they mess around with after school to the hotel to meet you. There's a nice patch of ground near here that they like to play on if they can get me to bring them here.'

'Really?' Gil looked at his father, clearly finding this hard to believe. 'I'd probably get a bit dirty, you know,' he warned him.

Ellis grinned and said, 'I should hope so, too.' Then he turned to Logan and his friend. 'Thank you. I think that's an excellent idea, Tait.'

He shrugged. 'Well, I'm sure a lad of your son's age won't want to spend all his time with the grown-ups. Are you any good at football, young 'un?'

Gil looked embarrassed. 'I don't know. I've watched other boys playing it in the park and it looked fun, but my tutor didn't like me to get dirty, so I wasn't allowed to join in. And anyway, there aren't a lot of places to kick balls around on near our house in London. I'd love to have a go, though, if no one minds me not being very good at it.'

'Well, the kids in my family will be happy to teach you, Gil, I'm sure.'

He hesitated then the words burst out of him, 'They'll think I'm stupid, though, needing to be taught the best ways to kick a ball around at my age.'

'No, they won't. I'll explain about you growing up in the city and having nowhere to play, plus an old misery of a tutor. They'll enjoy teaching you.'

'My tutor was definitely an old misery.' Gil's face stayed lit up and he repeated, 'A real old misery!' more loudly and with obvious relish.

Logan gave Tait a quick nod of thanks for his understanding then turned back to Ellis. 'Now, if you and your son would like to go to your rooms and fetch anything you want to take with you, I'll do the same and then Tait can give you the grand tour.'

He turned to their driver. 'We won't be long.'

Tait shrugged and smiled. 'If I'm being paid by the day, it doesn't matter to me whether I earn the money by driving around or waiting for you.'

Five minutes later they were all sitting in the cart, with Ellis and Gil sharing the front seat with Tait, and Logan occupying a pull-down seat behind the driver's bench on his own. He'd insisted on doing this so that both the newcomers could get the best view of the town, instead of relegating the lad to the rear seat as most folk would have done.

This was proving to be a very pleasant day, Logan thought as he relaxed. It was good to see young Gil enjoying himself with his father. And as for himself, he'd never earned his living so pleasantly.

At first the newcomers were silent, then they drove into what was clearly a poorer part of the town and Ellis said quietly, 'There was a lot of greenery in the town centre and the houses near it mostly had nice, neat gardens. We passed a small park where children were playing, but this area looks, well, run down. No gardens, no park either, though one would surely be even more appreciated here.'

'You said you wanted to see the whole town,' Logan told him. 'This is one of the poorest parts.'

'Yes. That's quite obvious. Not only the buildings but the people look run down and shabby here, most of them, anyway.'

'Yes. Another two streets further on and we'll get to the worst part of all: Eastby End. One or two decent people are trying to improve conditions there, and have managed a few repairs to buildings, but as you'll see there's still a long way to go and it all costs money.'

As he'd said, shortly afterwards the streets got worse, narrower and with litter blowing around or piled in corners. Some houses had broken windows covered in whatever material must have been handy – plywood, rough strips of wood or even cardboard in one recently broken window, where shards of glass were still scattered on the ground nearby.

'Respectable young women don't go out on their own round here at night,' Logan said in a tight, grim voice. 'I always made sure my sisters weren't on their own even in the daytime if they had to come through Eastby, which they didn't do if they could help it.'

Gil was staring round wide-eyed, not commenting, but Ellis couldn't hold back a disgusted grunt. 'I'm not surprised you kept an eye on your sisters. And some of the buildings look as if a bad storm would blow them down. Don't any of the owners do maintenance?'

'Only what's absolutely necessary to stop their properties actually falling down. It always makes me feel both sad and angry to see people so poorly housed and clad, only I've no spare money so there's nothing I can do about it, except try to make sure none of my own family are reduced to living round here. But this is the most direct way to get to the moors and anyway, I thought you might as well see the worst as well as the best of Ollerthwaite.'

'I agree. May I ask what places you consider the best?'

'Those closest to the moors, some of them not far away from here, surprisingly enough, because Eastby used to be a separate village. The majority of folk, even those comfortably off, seem to prefer to live near the town centre these days rather than near the countryside.'

'Can you show me an example of what you consider one of the best places near the moors?'

'Yes, of course.' He turned to their driver. 'Tait, how about we go into the grounds of the old Fairfield House when we leave Eastby and start up Moor Road?'

'Happy to go wherever you want. It's a nice old place, that house is, or it could be with a bit of care.'

Logan explained to Ellis why he'd suggested this one. 'You get excellent views from the grounds of a big old house at this side of one of the better areas. It has a larger garden than most of the homes nearby but because it's not near the centre of town, people who've made money haven't wanted to live there, at least we think that's the reason no one's bought it. It's been for sale for a few years.'

'Will the owners not mind us going to have a look at their garden and views?'

'There's no one living in the house at present to see us trespassing. It's standing empty. Such a shame.'

'I'm fond of the view from its front garden myself,' Tait went on. 'But it makes me sad to see how overgrown everything is getting. Last time I was there, it was just after someone had broken into the house. I sent word to the police but luckily whoever it was hadn't done any damage inside. I checked that carefully and they hadn't even gone upstairs. I could tell that because it was so dusty they'd have left footprints. But they'd broken a windowpane to get in, probably out of curiosity to see what it was like inside, and that wasn't right.'

'Did the police catch the ones who'd done it?'

'The police sergeant found out which lads it was and gave the trio a good old talking-to and a strong warning not to do such a thing again. But he let them off with that since they'd not done any damage, apart from the one small pane in the window to get at the catch.'

'Didn't he make their families pay for mending that?'

'Those families would have had trouble scraping enough money together to buy food and the broken pane doesn't really show.'

'Does them being caught keep others away now?'

'There aren't many lads who want to go that far out of town to mess around, and anyway there are too many trees in that particular garden to play a game of football properly, or even one of catch. I go there to eat my midday meal sometimes when I've made a delivery to that part of town because I really enjoy the peace and the views. I don't try to go inside the house, just sit on my cart under a tree or on the grass near it and eat my sandwiches.'

'I reckon you'll enjoy the place too, Ellis,' Logan said. 'We can pop into the drive and have a look at the outside of the house from there, then go further in and turn to look at the views, if you like. I enjoy stopping there as well.'

'Sounds interesting.'

They all fell silent again, except for occasional scraps of information offered by Logan or Tait about places they were passing. They had soon gone through the worst slum area, so it obviously didn't stretch very far, thank goodness.

'How sad to see a place so run down,' Ellis commented.

Gil didn't try to join in this discussion and continued to study their surroundings, but he listened with obvious interest to the three men's remarks.

The road now passed a few larger houses in better condition with bigger gardens too, then there were what looked like a couple of small market gardens near one bend. At this time of year there was produce for sale on tables set up close to their gates. The prices were listed on small blackboards, and old jam jars were at the front of the tables to put the payment money in.

'People must be very honest round here,' Ellis said.

'Most are.'

The road sloped gently upwards now and after a short time Tait allowed his pony to slow right down as they reached the entrance to a house on the left. Only one end of the building showed from the road, the rest being hidden behind some magnificent old trees.

He tugged gently on the reins and as his pony came to a halt he said, 'That's Fairfield House behind the trees, Mr Quinn. It looks pretty from here, doesn't it? Well, it is quite pretty still, though the garden gets more run down every time I come up here. It's sad to see that. It used to be a really lovely garden, with lots of flowers blooming at this time of year.'

'I've been away for a while. Do the Fairfields still own it?' Logan asked. 'They've been trying to sell it for a long time, if I remember correctly.'

Tait shrugged. 'I think a Fairfield does still own it and would like to sell, an old lady, that is. I've been told she's the last to bear that name, which is sad. We'd have heard about it if she'd sold the old place or even had anyone interested, I'm sure. You know how quickly gossip spreads round the valley.'

A light touch on the reins made the pony start moving again and this time he guided it into the drive.

As more of the house came into sight, he stopped again and said quietly, 'Who'd want to buy such a run-down old house now, though, even if it is being offered dirt cheap? It's too far out of town for most ladies these days, that's for sure. People who can afford houses this big like to be convenient for the town centre, and the ladies like shopping, calling in on their friends or taking tea in a café.'

The drive was greatly in need of maintenance, with big potholes here and there in its uneven gravel. Occasionally partly grown plants were thriving but not many. His pony continued at a slow pace, zigzagging to avoid the worst patches of ground, as if it already knew the terrain.

'It'll be too full of potholes and young plants to drive along at all by this time next year,' Tait said. 'Pity. As I said, I enjoy coming here on sunny days, when I'm not too busy. I can stop over there under the trees and eat my midday sandwiches while looking down across the town and hills. Even the queen doesn't have many views as magnificent as that in her palaces, I bet.'

After another short silence, he turned to look at Ellis. 'Would you like to stop here for a few minutes and look at the views, Mr Quinn? Your young fellow might enjoy stretching his legs as well.'

'Yes, I would. Good idea. Stay where you are till we stop, Gil.'

'I'm sure you know the best spot from which to show Mr Quinn and his son the view, Tait,' said Logan, 'so we'll leave it up to you to find a good stopping place. It's a while since I've been up here.'

'I can do that for you.'

22

Tait guided his pony round the slight bend in the drive so that the whole front of the house became clearly visible and Ellis said quietly, 'Can we stop here and look at the building first? I know it's shabby but it's very pretty even so. Georgian in style, isn't it?'

Tait shrugged. 'You're paying, so I'll stop wherever and whenever you like. I don't know what fancy words posh folk use to describe the style of the house, though I agree that this old place could be pretty if it were properly looked after.'

'Is that window pane still broken?' Ellis asked.

'Yes, it is.' Tait turned and his smile grew broader. 'If you're wanting to look inside, we could do that quite easily.'

'Without doing any further damage?'

'Yes, definitely. I'd never suggest doing something that damaged the place.'

'Do you think the old lady would mind us going inside?'

'Not at all if she knew I was keeping an eye on you. I always got on well with her. You might even want to buy the place.' He laughed at his own joke.

'I shall enjoy looking at it, that's for sure,' Ellis said. 'I've always admired houses built in this particular style. Are you really sure we could get in easily? You're not just saying that?'

Tait gave another of his gentle laughs. 'Well, there's that pane broken already and all you have to do is slip your hand through the hole to get at the latch of the window. They didn't bother to mend it, because they couldn't decide who would bear the cost. The lads' families couldn't afford to have it done properly, in the same old-fashioned style, and no one had told the old lady about the break-in or she'd have worried herself sick.'

'Why weren't they afraid of more damage being done by other intruders if we can get in so easily?'

'Not many people come this far out of town and the damage doesn't show from the front. It's at the back end of that side of the house and it's even sheltered from the worst of the weather. Besides, only locals would know about it and word has gone out from the magistrate to the young 'uns to stay away or else. They know better than to go against him, believe me.'

'Some stranger might break in, though.'

'We don't get many people visiting our town and why would they come up here? It's too far out and they don't know the old house exists, let alone that it's worth being looked at. And we don't tell 'em about it, not often anyway. I don't mind telling you, though. I'm sure you're not the sort of folk who'd damage it.'

'I'm glad you did tell me and if you and Logan don't mind, and I can do it without more damage, I would love to look round the inside. Houses built in the eighteenth century can have very pretty fireplaces and fancy plasterwork to the ceiling and cornices. Some are called Palladian in style. I don't know whether this place is a hybrid or true to that style, but it's my favourite style of architecture so it's worth a look.'

He fell silent again then said thoughtfully, 'I don't like the massive country houses of the nobility nearly as much. They're sometimes built in a copycat style but they need an army of servants to run them. To my mind, ones this size are just about perfect.'

He sounded so enthusiastic Tait and Logan stared at him in surprise.

'I'd really like to go into that house, Father,' Gil said. 'It looks as if it's smiling at us, doesn't it?'

Ellis stared at it again and laughed. 'You're right. It does.'

'I'd not mind a look round as well. I've never been inside it.' Logan grinned and added, 'Proper nosy parkers, aren't we, Tait? We won't do any harm, though.'

'I never thought you would or I'd not have brought you here. Can you get the place open without my help, Logan lad? I'll stay with my pony, let her have a little rest and give her a drink. There's a garden tap round the other side.'

They pulled up at one corner of the paved area in front of the house and Logan jumped down from the back of the cart. As he strode towards the right-hand side of the building, Ellis got down as well and waited for his son to join him.

Tait smiled at them from the driving bench and eased his way down from it more slowly. 'I always enjoy this view, Mr Quinn, so once I've got Dolly here a drink I'll sit here happily for as long as you like. It's nice to feel the sun on your face after all that rain the other day, isn't it?'

'It is indeed. Though we won't be feeling it indoors, will we?'

Logan went round the side of the house to the broken pane and it was as easy as Tait had said to slip your hand through it and unfasten the rather primitive catch on the inside. He did that, then opened that whole half of the window, which had three hinges attached at one of the long sides.

He turned to smile at the others as they joined him. 'Shall I go in first, Ellis, then help you two through the gap? I think I'm a bit nimbler than you.'

'Fine by me because you are definitely more nimble as well as stronger physically. It's one of the things I intend to improve about myself now that I've stopped doing so much office work and don't have to sit through interminable business meetings. I'm going to be a lot more active and therefore will gradually get stronger – well, I hope I will. You don't get physically strong by sitting and fiddling around with accounts, or sitting talking to other business owners, even if you are doing excellent financial deals with them. I've proved that already.'

Logan was tall enough to have got in with little difficulty but he found an old chunk of branch to use as a step and used that to clamber easily over the windowsill into the room, leaving it in place to help the others. Gil looked enquiringly at his father, who gestured to him to climb inside next.

Ellis stood near enough to help if the lad looked like falling, but that wasn't necessary. In fact, Gil was far more agile than he was, so he simply followed his son inside without commenting, trying not to appear too clumsy in comparison.

Logan was holding Gil by the shoulder as if to stop him moving forward across the room, so Ellis remained next to the window as well and began looking round to see what was keeping Logan standing there. 'Is something wrong?'

'No. But I've been studying the floor, Ellis. Look! It's dusty enough to show any footprints from the past few years surprisingly clearly. I can see what I think must be the footprints of the three lads who broke in.' He pointed and they both stared at the marks. 'I can't see signs of any other people coming inside since those marks were made, though. Can you?'

Ellis looked round, studying the floor and shaking his head. Like his friend, he was amazed that the footprints were still showing so clearly. 'No, I can't.' He gestured to some lumpy objects stacked in one of the corners. They were as tall as his shoulders and were shrouded in old sheets. 'What are those?'

'I'd guess they're old pieces of furniture. Perhaps they're ones that were too big for the old lady who used to live here to take with her to the smaller house. Let's go and have a closer look now that you've seen the footprints. I doubt we need to worry about leaving our own since no one else seems to come here these days.'

Logan moved across to the shrouded lumps and lifted one side of the cover to reveal an old-fashioned settle and matching armchairs. Lifting another side showed some shabby kitchen chairs and what looked like a couple of rolled-up small rugs.

'Old-fashioned pieces, aren't they?'

'Very.'

'They're just being stored here, I'd think,' Ellis said. 'They don't look as if they've been moved for years, perhaps not even been looked at since they were put here, because they're dusty where there are gaps in the covers.'

Logan moved to the inner door of the room, stopping to look out into the hall and check the floor there as well before moving forward a couple of steps and calling, 'Hello? Anyone at home?'

There was no answer.

Ellis was puzzled. 'Did you see something that made you think people were still living here?'

'No, but I did think I saw some faint footprints outside in the garden, so I shouted just in case, because I didn't want anyone to think we were burglars.'

'Those footprints outside may have been made by burglars.'

'If so, they didn't come inside through the front door or the window we used.'

'Hmm. We'll keep our eyes open inside the house and we'll have a check round for footprints elsewhere when we go outside again. How long has the house been unoccupied, do you think?'

Logan stood with his head on one side, trying to work this out. 'About five years, perhaps a little longer. I'm not sure. It wasn't a place I cared about in those days because I was too busy earning enough to feed my family to keep track of what was going on in this part of town.'

'Do you know why the old lady moved out of the house and left it empty if she still owns it?'

'Miss Fairfield was getting old and was too infirm to walk into town and back from out here. She only had one maid and a weekly scrubbing woman for the floors, and was rumoured to be too poor to maintain a groom and a pony any longer. I heard that she had to let most of the garden go untended in the last year she was living here.'

He paused then added, 'Everyone knew she was struggling when she couldn't even afford to heat the house properly during her last winter and spent most of her time in the kitchen. Word went round about it. You can't keep anything secret for long in the valley.'

'Poor thing,' Ellis said softly.

'Then she and her maid were suddenly given the chance to rent a small house in town very cheaply, and it was in a nice area, so she took it. The people from her church helped her move. It's thought that one of the better-off members made the house available out of sheer benevolence, but they didn't tell her that was the reason and we can only guess at who it was.'

'That was very kind of them.'

'Yes, and she's still living there, but she only goes out of the house to church or to the local shops these days, and has to be pushed by her maid in a wheelchair. Look, there's another pile of things in the room that opens off the hall to your left. She must have left a lot of the furniture here.'

They stared through the doorway at another lumpy pile of objects, again covered in what looked like old sheets.

'I wonder why she didn't sell the furniture if she was short of money.'

'The pieces would probably be too big for use in most modern houses, I should think, not to mention being extremely old-fashioned. There aren't many houses as big as this one in the valley. Or perhaps the furniture had sentimental value for her. Who knows?'

He went to look more closely at the objects in another of the rooms which opened off the hall. 'This must have been the dining room. Look at the size of that table.'

Ellis went across and lifted the corner of the cloth to reveal a beautiful but again very dusty tabletop. 'It's made of mahogany, one of my favourite woods.' He couldn't resist brushing the dust off one edge gently to reveal the gleaming wood underneath, then he patted it and pulled the cover back over it, murmuring, 'Such beautiful wood.'

Logan went to the foot of the stairs and studied them. 'I don't think the lads who broke in came far into the house. There are none of their footprints in the dust on these stairs. In fact, there are no footprints going upstairs at all. And the old lady must have had the stairs' carpet rolled up.'

Ellis joined him and Gil followed them, for once too awed by his surroundings to do anything except stay quiet and look round the inside of the house, wide-eyed with surprise at what he saw.

'You're probably right. The good pieces of furniture the owner left behind have been protected, so perhaps she cared about them, but their covers are still dusty so no one else could have touched them. Indeed, no one seems to have come into the place for years.'

'Except for those boys. And they didn't come far inside.'

Ellis looked round again. 'I've never in my whole life seen so much dust sitting on the floors and surfaces inside a house.'

'The fact that the pieces of furniture haven't been touched shows how little trouble we have with burglars round here on the edge of the moors,' Logan said quietly. 'I saw a couple of small stools under one of the sheets that would have been easy to carry away and sell but no one has even disturbed the dust on them.'

'Well, this place is on the outskirts of the town and I'd guess that the sort of people who break into houses wouldn't want to come this far out, especially into a house where there are no people living nowadays, so no small personal possessions or purses to steal. There must be places that are far easier to burgle closer to the town centre. You couldn't walk off with a big dining table like that, could you? It's too big even to fit on to most carts and would probably need four men to carry it.'

Ellis glanced back at the pile of large pieces of furniture in the nearest room. 'I can't think who'd buy all these if she did try to sell them, however cheaply. As you said, they wouldn't fit into a normal house and would also seem very old-fashioned to younger folk setting up homes.'

Logan grinned as another thought occurred to him. 'Also, the local magistrate is a distant relative of the Fairfields and he threatened to jail the lads who broke in if they did it again, and also anyone else who so much as poked a finger inside the place. His threat spread all round town within a couple of days of him making it and everyone knows he always means what he says.'

'Is he still making that threat? Our driver seems to have come here a few times before.'

'Tait doesn't go into the house, though, and I doubt anyone using the nearby road would notice him sitting in his cart in the grounds eating his midday meal, or worry about it if they did. I noticed that he went straight to that big tree and stopped in the shade as if he'd been there before. I bet he chose that place originally to be out of sight of casual passers-by on the road.'

'I see.'

'He's well liked in the valley.'

'I'm not surprised. He's good company. Anyhow, if you don't know your way round the interior of the house, we'll inspect the ground floor in more detail first, shall we?'

'Yes. There will probably be a lot more to see down here anyway.'

Ellis looked round and could see no sign of his son now, so called out, 'Gil? Where are you?'

His son's voice came from somewhere to the rear of the house. 'In the kitchen. It's huge. Come and see.'

Ellis shrugged and went towards the voice, and both men stopped to marvel at the large, old-fashioned kitchen.

Then Ellis beckoned his son across. 'I'd prefer you to stay near us from now on.'

Gil looked up at him rather anxiously. 'Yes, all right, Father.'

Ellis started to move, then stopped and pointed across the room. 'Aren't those the keys to the whole house?'

'They look like they could be.'

A great surge of longing to see everything flooded through Ellis. 'Let's try them out.'

'Really?'

'Yes. I want to see every single part of it.'

23

They went round the other downstairs rooms, inevitably raising clouds of dust, which made each of them sneeze more than once.

Ellis looked at Logan once they'd finished going round the ground floor. 'Let's look upstairs now. Stay behind us, Gil. We don't know what we'll find here.'

His sigh was very loud and the two men exchanged smiles.

There were six bedrooms, two larger ones with small dressing rooms attached, but no sign of a modern bathroom. The attics held more shrouded piles of old furniture and some very small bedrooms, presumably for the servants.

'It's a beautiful house,' Ellis said. 'I can't think why it hasn't been sold.'

'The usual reasons, I suppose. Either they're asking too much or no one wants the trouble of bringing its amenities up to date. People expect a bathroom and an indoor lavatory these days, at the very least.'

'They do make life easier and more pleasant.'

'I shouldn't think this is a fashionable location, either.'

'It has beautiful views from the front. Have you heard how much is being asked for it?'

Logan frowned. 'I haven't the faintest idea. Come to think of it, I've never heard anyone talk about the actual price, which is unusual in a place where rumours can spread like wildfire.'

'Perhaps Miss Fairchild hasn't tried very hard to sell it?'

'Who knows? It'd not be cheap, even in this condition. But I don't think she has any relatives still alive to leave it to, so who knows what's going to happen to it in future?'

Ellis stopped moving to turn round on the spot. 'It's not a grand mansion but it's far bigger than the average house. I like the size of the rooms and the high ceilings with the ornate coving. I don't know why the place feels friendly to me, but it does, even though the rooms are in a dusty mess.'

Gil joined the conversation. 'It feels friendly to me too, Father. It's a pretty house, isn't it? I liked looking at the outside, and I like how it feels inside as well. I think the family who lived here must have loved it very much and been happy here.'

The men stared at him, then exchanged surprised glances. That seemed a funny thing for a lad of his age to say.

'I agree with you, son,' Ellis said. 'Strange how houses can feel good or bad as soon as you go inside them.'

'I don't like the house in London but I do like this one. I hope we can buy a house that feels happy like this does.'

'Actually, I don't much like the London house either, which is why I intend to move out of it as soon as we can. My uncle rented it for us, said he needed me to live close by. And it was convenient, not just for walking to our office but also for getting to the various business meetings I had to attend.'

'You sound like someone looking for a nice house to buy,' Logan murmured, wondering if he was guessing correctly about what Ellis was thinking.

'I am in one sense because I do intend to get out of London and live somewhere in the country. But I only came this far north because I wanted to see the moors and because you were available to show them to me properly.' After a moment's thought, he added, 'I'm really enjoying doing what I want when I want, too. And I like this area a lot more than I'd expected to. I wasn't intending to look for a house here.'

He stopped talking and frowned, murmuring, 'Hmm!' as if something had occurred to him.

'That shouldn't stop you buying a house if you see something you like in an area you find attractive. You're not short of money and, as you say, you can please yourself what you do and where you settle.'

'I suppose I can. And I do like this house. I'm surprised at how much. But surely I ought to look round other parts of the country before I start offering to buy anything? That would be the sensible way to approach my move.'

'You ought to do as you wish. That's the sensible way to do things if you're not short of money. A home is more than just an investment because you spend a large part of your life in it. If you're fortunate enough financially to have the choice, you should like being in a house and also like where it's situated, which are the main reasons to buy it. Well, in my humble opinion, anyway.'

Ellis looked at him thoughtfully. 'You know, you're absolutely right. It hadn't occurred to me before that I'm absolutely free now to do what I want, well, it had sort of, but the idea hadn't sunk in.'

He walked slowly back to the window, where he stood staring out, seeming to have forgotten the others.

Logan and Gil exchanged glances, but he put one finger to his lips and the lad didn't move or speak, only waited for his father.

It was a few moments before Ellis spoke again. 'The moors look very attractive. Well, I like the look of them from here. I don't know what they'll be like when we go up there and walk across them. Maybe we should try that tomorrow, if it's fine?'

Logan joined him by the window. 'It's one of the reasons you came here, isn't it? To walk on the moors. I always think they feel even better than they look when you're out on them. The air always tastes fresher somehow up on the tops, which is what we often call them, for obvious reasons. But foreigners such as you don't usually like this sort of landscape as much as us locals do.'

Ellis shrugged. 'Well, I do like the moors a lot, and far more than I'd expected, I admit. Come on. Let's look round the rest of this house now, including the rest of the upstairs and the attics. It's a fascinating old place.'

'It's a pity there isn't a bathroom, though, not even an old-fashioned one. Whoever buys the house will find plenty of bedrooms, but no easy way of keeping themselves clean.'

'Well, no doubt whoever buys it eventually will put in at least two modern bathrooms, one for the family and one for the servants. Every man and his dog seem to be installing them these days, so there must be people round here who can do it for the purchaser. And we'll take a walk round the outside, too, before we leave.'

'Where do you want to go after we've finished looking at this house and its grounds, Ellis?'

'We'll go and look round the nearby suburbs. It's the sensible thing to do. I've got to get in practice for house hunting, so that I don't choose badly, and I'm definitely not deciding on anything today.'

Was he telling them that or telling himself to be sensible? Logan wondered.

They went outside and walked slowly round to the rear, finding some quite substantial outbuildings.

'I think a groom would have lived here,' Ellis said. He went to try the door with one of the keys from the kitchen, but it was locked and none of the keys would unlock it. 'I'll look in there when – I mean if – I come back.' He turned to his son. 'Mind you stay with us from now on, Gil. We're going to drive round this part of town to find out what it's like.'

Logan didn't say it but he was really puzzled now. That had sounded as if – no, surely Ellis wouldn't really want to move so far north? Only, why had he spent so long looking round a shabby old house and was now about to look round the nearby streets and houses? Was he just being nosy or was he actually considering moving to the north and buying a home like this one?

It was a nice home and his friend could probably afford to buy it quite easily and then modernise it. Ellis never seemed to care about the money side of things, which was usually a sign of having plenty for your own needs and even to indulge your whims and fancies as well.

But surely he'd not buy a place like Fairfield House? It was very run down and old-fashioned, however wonderful its views and outside structure. Though actually, you couldn't take the beautiful views away from a hilly area like this. You could spoil the outlook on flat pieces of land by building a lot of terraces all over it, though. Some mill owners hadn't hesitated to do that in Lancashire in the earlier part of the nineteenth century.

However, as they continued to explore the house, Ellis took his time and he made other positive remarks about the different views to be had. Several times he stopped by a window to take in a new aspect and lingered to comment positively on what he could see. He also asked Logan about buildings he could see in the distance.

It surprised Logan that young Gil was also saying complimentary things about the house and even wondering what it would be like to live here. Lads that age didn't usually take an interest in that sort of thing, or not such a detailed one anyway.

At one point, as he and his father were standing together at a bedroom window, Gil said, 'It's lovely to look out on to green fields instead of grey streets, isn't it, Father? There were a lot of motor cars and delivery vans driving up and down our street in London, as well as the horses pulling carts. I nearly got knocked down by one.'

'I noticed. That was your own fault, though, because you ran out of the house without looking where you were going.'

'I was trying to get away from that horrible tutor.'

'Be that as it may, it's a good thing Logan was there to save your life that day, so don't ever do anything like that again.'

Gil didn't speak again for a while, then he said softly, 'I'm sorry he got hurt. He's a nice man, isn't he?'

They both stared out again then the boy said, 'I'd love to walk across those moors, no, not walk but run as fast as I could. I love running but I don't often get the chance to do it. I sometimes escaped for a while when my tutor took me for walks in the park, and then I ran and ran. But I always had to go back home eventually, and then he caned me.'

'Most likely. I'll go and ask.'

They were lucky. It was a quiet time of day, and they were soon sitting enjoying not only the cheese and buttered barm cakes, but freshly baked scones, again buttered and this time with strawberry jam slathered on them as well, accompanied by a pot of good, strong tea, which an obliging woman topped up with boiling water part way through their feast.

Tait joined them after he'd eaten his sandwiches outside, tempted by the sight of the scones and the thought of a cup of tea.

Ellis watched him find a lad to keep an eye on his cart. There always seemed to be a lad hanging around, hoping to earn a few pence.

Afterwards Tait drove them back to the hotel and they all had what Logan thought of as 'a lovely quiet hour' in the sitting room there, resting and reading the local and national newspapers, which had just come in.

This was undoubtedly the best job he'd ever had. And it wasn't only because of the money. The better he got to know his new friend, the more he liked him.

In the middle of the afternoon, Tait came back and Logan had a quiet word with him. They agreed that neither Ellis nor his son would be capable of doing one of the longer walks on the moors. Logan would need to slow down to their pace, not stride out as he would have done if he'd been on his own.

He was, Logan thought, giving them good value for the money Ellis was paying him. That was important to him in any job he did. What's more, Ellis was getting good information from both him and Tait about all sorts of things that caught his interest.

However, both father and son admitted that they were very tired when they got back at the end of the afternoon, though happily so.

'Why don't you go and visit your family now?' Ellis suggested as they all three finished their evening meal, which had been served at an earlier hour than he was used to, but was all the more welcome for that because he'd worked up a really good appetite for the second time that day.

'Are you sure you won't need me for the rest of the evening?'

'I'm utterly certain. I'm ashamed at how much the day's activities have tired me. Gil and I can sit and read our new books. You go and visit your family.'

'Thank you. I will, then.'

Gil beamed as he got his book out, but both he and his father were yawning within far less than an hour and he made no protest when his father suggested he go up to bed.

'You can read in bed if you can stay awake.'

He looked surprised. 'I can? Ooh, that'll be lovely. I've never been allowed to read in bed before.'

Ellis didn't say anything but the thought of that petty and needless restriction angered him, as had the other so-called rules he was now finding out had been imposed on his son. The only redeeming grace to the tutors' care was that Gil had been kept in good health.

But surely anything that encouraged children to read was worth doing? It was a key to knowledge even if you couldn't afford formal education, as he had found out for himself and his own interest in the world.

'Well, you've never lived with me full-time, have you?' he said to his son. 'I approve of you reading in bed.

I shan't be late coming up to join you myself and I often read in bed as well.'

He admitted to himself that he was badly out of condition physically after the last few hectic months of office work and meetings. And though today had been really enjoyable, and had given him a lot to think about, it had also been surprisingly tiring.

When he gave in to his body's demands for an early night and went up to bed only half an hour after his son, the room was silent with a gas wall light burning near the main bed and a small oil lamp standing next to his son's bed turned down low. He crept across to check Gil, smiling as he found he'd guessed correctly when he'd sent him to bed.

The lad was already sleeping soundly, hadn't stirred when Ellis went into the room. And the precious book was lying open on the floor next to the bed where it looked to have fallen.

Ellis picked it up, straightened out one slightly crumpled page and put it on the little table next to Gil's bed, then blew out the lamp. He felt sad that he hadn't taken more of an interest in how exactly the lad was being treated by the various tutors over the past year or two. Yes, and guilty about it too.

Well, you couldn't have everything and at least he now had enough money to buy them both freedom to lead a more interesting life. He was going to get to know his son, and would make up as best he could for the years of not paying him much attention.

But he didn't intend to get married again. His marriage to Gil's mother had been very limiting because although his wife had been pretty and kind, she hadn't been all that intelligent, or interested in anything except her domestic world. So the early attraction had misled him into an unsatisfying and rather dull family life.

Then he yawned and realised he was extremely sleepy after all the fresh air. It was much earlier than usual for him to try to get to sleep but he was ready for a proper rest.

Another huge yawn made him give into temptation, put down the book he'd not even started reading again and turn off the gas wall light above his bed. He could always pick the book up again and relight the gas lamp if he couldn't get to sleep.

Only he didn't need to do that. He found himself snuggling down comfortably and he somehow knew that he was going to enjoy a sound night's sleep for once.

When Logan returned from the long walk to visit his sister and went upstairs, there was complete silence from the hotel room next to his, which the father and son were sharing. And there was no line of light showing under the door. He smiled at that, guessing what had happened.

It didn't take him long to get to sleep, either, not in such a peaceful place with such comfortable beds.

24

The following morning Livia and Janie met after eating breakfast in their own flats, each making it from her own supplies as they'd arranged the previous evening. By that time it was later than either of them normally got up and they both confessed that they'd enjoyed having a quiet leisurely start to their day. Life hadn't given either of them many of those.

'Mrs Crossley said we should have a restful time and perhaps go out for a stroll during the daylight hours so that we can start getting to know the area,' Janie reminded Livia.

'She's kind, isn't she? I'm glad she'll be supervising our work and helping us settle in. But tomorrow we'll need to find the local shop she told us about and buy a few more provisions. That'll also help its owner to survive in business. It's lovely the way she tries to help all sorts of people.'

'I can manage without shopping for a day or two longer, though.'

Livia shook her head. 'You mustn't even try. You really do have to eat better from now onwards because you're far too thin and rather weak compared to me. You'll need to do a lot of walking in your job as my assistant, remember, so you have to be able to keep up.'

She studied her companion. 'We also have to make sure you've got suitable clothing for working with me. I have a smart uniform to wear when I'm walking round town and you'll need something fairly smart, too, with an insignia on a neat felt hat that shows you're an assistant district nurse. I'll have to find a way to get some of those for you.'

There was a knock on the front door and they found Mrs Crossley outside, with three big bundles of what looked like clothes sitting on the floor beside her. Her first words made it sound as if she'd just heard what they were saying, though of course she hadn't.

'I've brought you two some more pieces of clothing. Janie, the two big bundles are yours.' She fumbled inside the top of one and brought out a neat felt hat. 'And Rachel thought you might need this, which used to belong to Hanny, her assistant and friend. That way, what you're wearing is similar to what Livia wears and shows clearly that you're her nursing assistant.'

She took the hat gratefully, murmuring her thanks and tried it on. 'Oh, it fits really nicely.'

'Good.' Mrs Crossley turned to Livia. 'The other bag is for you. I've brought you some extra items as well because Rachel used to be unable to avoid getting her skirts and aprons soiled when treating some patients, so she always kept several spare aprons and skirts ready to change into or put on top of her smarter clothes, not to mention clean items for the following day. You'll need to take that precaution too. And I have the address of a woman who takes in washing and does a very good job of it too. You won't have time to do your own when you get going properly.'

'You continue to help us and we're so grateful for your kindness,' Livia said.

Janie moved forward, ready to pick up one of the bundles, which was big enough to contain quite a few garments. She caught sight of herself in the hall mirror and realised she was still wearing the hat. It felt strange but looked quite flattering she thought. 'Thank you very much indeed. I'm afraid I won't be able to pay you for these till I've earned a few weeks' wages. Will that be all right?'

'There's no charge. These were given to Walter and me at various times and if I give them to you, they'll be used for a worthwhile purpose that helps people who're not well, which is exactly what the donors wished us to do with them.'

She snapped her fingers as she remembered something. 'I nearly forgot. Pearl sent me an assistant nurse's badge to give to whoever took on the job. Wearing the hat with that pinned on it when you go out will show people that you're a nurse's helper and they'll respect you for that.'

She waited a moment for that to sink in then said, 'We're still in the early days of having district nurses in this area, you see, so you'll have to make it very clear indeed what you're doing here.'

'Oh, that's marvellous!' Janie took the badge from her and Livia helped her to pin it to her hat, which immediately made it look different from a normal felt hat. It made her feel good, too. Respectable.

Flora smiled and stepped back. 'I'll leave you to sort through the rest of these and if I find any other suitable pieces of clothing in our shop, I'll bring those to you as well.'

After she'd left, Janie stared in astonishment at the size of the two bundles that were for her. 'I've never had so many clothes at one time in my whole life,' she said in a half-whisper. 'Never had anything like this many!'

'It's lovely of her, isn't it? But you will need several spare garments in this job. And how kind of her to find us a washerwoman.'

She saw Janie open her mouth to protest and added hastily, 'We won't have the time or energy to do it ourselves once we get known and our work increases. I think our first job today is going to be to sort through these bundles.' Livia smiled at her. 'And what a pleasure that will be. We'll need to check not only that the clothes are the right size for us, but that they allow for some growth in yours.'

Janie looked at her in puzzlement.

'As you eat regularly and grow healthier, you'll gain a little weight and you certainly need to do that.'

'You are so kind employing me like this.'

'I think you'll do well in this job and I'm sure you'll work hard. Well, we'll both be doing that.'

'What exactly will I need to wear for work?' Janie asked. 'If it's so important to look clean and smart I want to do it right.'

'I'll help you pick out your clothes for our first day out getting to know the town. Now, let me take my bundle upstairs then I'll come back and help you sort through yours and see exactly what there is.'

'Will I really be getting that dirty doing this sort of work?'

'We both will and we can't help it. You'll need washable skirts and blouses as well as ones that look like part of a smart uniform, because patients can bleed over you or vomit, or else dirty you in even worse ways when illness makes them helpless. I often put an older garment on as well as an apron over the smarter clothes before I start treating a patient I know might cause problems.'

'Goodness. You don't think of the patients soiling the nurses' clothing, do you?'

'Oh, they do, though not always on purpose of course. But some of them do need teaching how to be truly clean in other ways, big and small, not just in the parts of their bodies that show, but all over their bodies and all over their homes too. So we sometimes need to work with them literally at first to teach them how to get things right, for example by showing them how to scrub floors thoroughly and helping them do it at first.'

Janie looked at her in astonishment. 'Do you mean you do cleaning as well as caring for them?'

'Oh, yes. It's a big part of the job for district nurses, especially in their early days in a new area. It can make a huge difference to the poorer families' health just to teach the woman who's managing the home to keep herself and her children cleaner. Yes, and we often have to make it clear to the husband that he has to keep himself clean too. I'm afraid sometimes the menfolk can be harder to convince that it's necessary for them to be as clean as possible.'

Janie could feel herself flushing. 'I've not always been able to stay clean, but I've always tried to as much as I could because it feels so much nicer.'

'I agree. And I do understand what life can be like for some women.' Livia stepped back and studied her. 'That hat suits you. And for your information, it's been found that when people see district nurses and their assistants neatly dressed and with recognisable uniforms, they have more respect for the women personally and also for the job they're doing. It helps the nurses to make better progress in their work as well as to stay safer.'

She could see that Janie was taking all this in and thinking about it, which was what she'd expected. Hungry for knowledge, her younger companion was, which was a good thing in a nursing assistant, especially one new to the job.

She just knew somehow that Janie would do well in this sort of work, she didn't know why but she felt quite certain of it.

When they got home with their shopping, they found an elderly woman with a bad cut on her hand waiting for them outside the house, leaning wearily against the wall, clutching a dirty bloodstained rag round it and holding a straight piece of branch which she seemed to be using as a walking stick.

'You should have gone to the clinic to get this treated,' Livia told her gently. 'This is our home and we don't have the best bandages and sticking plasters here to deal properly with a cut like this, or the other supplies either.'

'Can't walk . . . that far . . . now.'

'Well, we'll look after you this time as best we can, but only if you promise to spread the word about where to go and also that you'll get help next time for yourself from a friend or relative to go to the right place for treatment, which is the clinic.'

'But this is so much more convenient.'

'It's our home not a clinic, and it doesn't have the right equipment to treat you properly.'

'Oh, sorry. I thought it'd just need a bandage, only I didn't have any rags. And I will spread the word. But can you please help me now? It won't stop bleeding because it keeps getting bumped, and I have no one around to help me today.'

'Just this once.' She turned to Janie. 'We'll have to put a chair in the hall to do this, I think. Can you bring that upright chair from the downstairs flat, please?'

They treated the woman's injury and watched her hobble away afterwards, feeling sorry for her. She moved very slowly, and clearly needed the branch as a substitute for a walking stick but even so, they didn't intend to continue treating patients here.

The trouble was, a man turned up later that day also seeking help, and again for a bad cut sustained in an accident at work.

When Mr Crossley called in later to see if they were all right, Livia was greatly relieved because he had saved her a long walk to his farm to ask his advice about the problem of patients coming here for help.

When she explained to him what had happened, he frowned slightly as he thought about it. 'We do have a clinic where they can get help but for people in this part of Eastby End who're not well, I can see that it would be too far away. Would you be prepared to run a small clinic if I set one up near here, Livia? Maybe working half days or some other arrangement? I'll tell you in confidence that I'm trying to hire another district nurse and assistant, but it's not going to happen for a while and it won't be easy to find another suitable person.'

'Yes, we could run a small clinic. After all, some of our cases who go there would have been asking for us to help them on our rounds so it's not all going to be new patients.' She hesitated then added, 'I hope you find another nurse soon. There's going to be too much work round here for just the two of us to deal with properly.'

'I'll look into both those problems, and see if I can find a suitable room to set up a clinic near here and a way of getting you more help quickly.'

He paused, smiling at them both now. 'To change the subject to something a bit more cheerful, I've come to ask you if you know how to ride a bicycle?'

They stared at him in surprise, then Livia said, 'Well, I've tried riding bicycles, but only other people's and I wasn't very good at it. I've never had one of my own to practise on, you see.'

'I've not even tried to ride a bicycle,' Janie said. 'Is it hard?'

'Not really. Most people find it easy to get around on one after half an hour or even less of practice. And tricycles are even easier to ride, which is what I think would suit your needs better.'

They both stared at him in surprise.

'Flora and I have been discussing it and we thought your life would be a lot easier if you could get around more quickly. If we can get each of you a tricycle, will you be happy to learn to ride them and use them in your work?'

Janie gaped at him, but Livia beamed and said without hesitation, 'Yes, definitely. In fact, I'd love to have one and I think they'd be far more suitable for our job than bicycles. If I can practise properly, I'll soon be all right on it and I'll be happy to help Janie learn to ride one.'

She turned to her assistant. 'It isn't hard, I promise you, and it'll make such a difference to our working lives because there are bigger distances to cover than usual round here.' When Janie still looked worried, she couldn't help saying, 'I can't believe you've never tried to ride any sort of bicycle.'

'I didn't get the chance because no one I knew had a bicycle – unless they'd stolen one and they didn't share those with people, just sold them as quickly as they could.'

'Well, I shall say it again and again till you believe me: it's not hard, Janie.'

Walter let that sink in for a moment then went on explaining. 'It was Flora's suggestion that we get tricycles for you two not bicycles. She thinks that with the metal basket racks in front and behind, you'll be able to carry supplies with you far more easily.'

Livia nodded happily. 'That's such a good idea, Mr Crossley.'

'We'll get you some, then,' Walter said. 'Or rather, a chap called Peter will. He supplies most people in the town with bicycles. His business has grown rapidly even in times like these, because he gives such good service. It was he who suggested to us that it might be better for you to have the use of bicycles to save you having to walk everywhere. And he not only agreed with Flora about tricycles being better still but says he can get hold of two for you. They're second-hand and he's going to let us have them at what they cost him and make sure they're safe as a contribution to your work here.'

Livia beamed at him again. 'That's such a wonderful suggestion!'

'There are some good people in the valley as well as bad ones,' he said. 'I'll tell Peter straight away, then Flora and I will bring the tricycles round to your home tomorrow afternoon. Oh, and she said to tell you that you'll need the shortest skirts you've got to wear on them. You don't want your skirts to catch in the wheels, do you?'

'Or we could wear divided skirts, even,' Livia said thoughtfully. 'They might be better for our jobs too.'

'Good thinking. I'll ask Flora if we have any divided skirts among the clothes in stock at the moment. Dark coloured ones, they'd need to be, like your present skirts. Or we could even get a few made for you. In fact, I'll go and talk to her about that as soon as I've spoken to Peter. It's important to get you two kitted out properly as soon as possible, so that people can see at a glance that you're their new district nurses.'

When he'd left, Janie stared at Livia. 'Is it really not hard to learn to ride a bicycle? I'm not nearly as strong as you.'

'I don't think it's hard at all, and Mr Crossley's right: a tricycle is even easier. Really it is!'

'I hope you're right.'

'It'll take a little practice to build up your riding skills and get used to moving in and out of traffic on the roads in the busier parts of town, but I bet you'll learn quickly. You seem to move very gracefully naturally.'

She gaped. 'I do?'

'Oh, yes. Has no one ever told you that before?'

'No. Never.' She shook her head slightly, trying to hide how much the unexpected compliment pleased her, she'd had so little praise in her life.

She didn't count as compliments the leering comments some men made openly about her appearance. They always felt more like nasty insults because you'd not make such remarks to a woman you considered decent.

Mr Crossley brought the tricycles round the following afternoon on the back of his cart, and gave them their first lesson to check that they could manage them.

Livia did reasonably well, though she still felt rather uncertain about when to start slowing down to turn corners as well as when to signal that she was about to turn.

'I definitely wouldn't like to try going any faster than a sedate speed,' she said. 'As if I'm on foot and hurrying.'

'You'll manage to go more quickly as you grow used to it,' Walter said encouragingly. 'Now, let's see how Janie goes.'

To his relief the younger woman took to riding the tricycle like the proverbial duck to water and Livia watched in envy as Janie was soon riding up and down the street, slowing effortlessly to turn corners and even daring to ride round the block, out of Walter's sight for part of the time.

The bruises on her face had nearly all faded now, the last stage seeming to have happened quickly, and she was looking pretty and healthy, her cheeks rosy with the exercise. Men were starting to stare at her in the street, Livia could see, but hopefully the nurse's uniform would help keep her safe from unwanted attention.

'It's wonderful to move about so fast!' Janie exclaimed as she got off the tricycle once she'd rejoined them. She patted the handlebars, gently shook the metal basket set over the front wheel, then touched the seat and the rack behind it as if it were a pet dog she was stroking.

'You're a natural, Janie!' Mr Crossley said with a smile. 'I don't think I've ever seen anyone learn how to handle one of these this quickly. So, there you are!' He flourished one hand towards it. 'This tricycle belongs to you now.'

She gaped at him. 'Belongs to me! Don't you mean I'm the only one who can use it?'

'No, it belongs to you completely. You and it will become good friends during the next few years, I hope.'

'Oh. Well, thank you. I didn't expect that.'

'And the other one belongs to you, Livia.'

'Thank you so much.'

She didn't sound as enthusiastic as Janie but he didn't comment on that.

'Now, you'll need to decide where you're going to store them so that they're safe from being stolen as well as conveniently placed for use in an emergency. Sadly, there are some people who steal bicycles or tricycles if anyone is careless with them.'

He climbed up on his cart and fumbled in a box under his driving seat. 'You'll also need these for when you're out and about, I'm afraid.' He held out two portable padlocks, new ones with chains big and strong enough to make them difficult to saw through quickly. 'There are thieves these days who target bicycles, particularly ones in good condition, like these.'

Livia stared at him in dismay as she took one of the padlocks. 'I think we'll have to use the cellar to store them in overnight then, which will mean clearing out some of the rubbish to make space. We can come into the house and out every morning and evening through the backyard. Though we could leave them in the hall, I suppose. They'd just about fit, I think. Only it'd make the place look such a mess and it'd be hard to get past them.'

'They'd be more convenient in the hall, though, for starters at least,' Walter pointed out. 'And who cares what it looks like? Getting on your way quickly might save a life.'

Janie looked at Livia, who took over. 'Ah, well. There's another problem. We've still got people turning up here and wanting us to treat them. We've been taking them into the hall to see what's wrong, keeping a chair there, but it isn't very convenient for them to come here and anyway, our equipment is at the clinic on the outskirts of Ollerthwaite. There won't be room for the tricycles as well.'

He frowned and shook his head in irritation. 'Then I'm going to make that my next job, to look for a room nearby after I leave here. There are always places available to rent. If I can find somewhere that seems suitable for you two to use as a small clinic, mainly for folk from Eastby End and beyond it going towards the moors, I'll come back and fetch you both to see whether you approve of it.'

An hour later he was back again, looking triumphant. 'I think I've found a suitable place to rent and it's even better than I'd expected. It's actually the whole ground floor of a house rather like the one you're living in now, but not in such good repair.'

'Oh, good. We don't mind whether it looks pretty, as long as it's waterproof.'

'It's only a few streets away from here, so you'll be able to cycle to work very quickly from home and there's a small piece of ground behind a low wall in the front where you can chain the tricycles in case you want to use them quickly. I'll have a bar fixed to the house wall for you to attach them to.'

'It sound very convenient.'

'I think it is.'

'Who will be living upstairs?'

'No one at the moment because there are a few minor leaks in the roof that need repairing.'

He rolled his eyes. 'Some landlords don't do a good job of looking after their properties. I shall have to nag this owner into sorting it out. The trouble is, I gather it's an old lady and she's not very well. Hmm. I'd better do something about the worst of the leaks myself. Or maybe I could buy it from her.'

As they followed him outside, he was still talking, sounding as excited as any young man.

'This house is on the opposite side of Eastby End from the bigger clinic, which is another good thing, because it will spread the clinics out more evenly across the valley. I expect patients will naturally choose to patronise the one nearest to where they live. Sadly, some folk are never really well and I could already name a few who live near there who'll become regulars.'

He frowned again. 'Hmm. If I rent or buy this place, I shall have to find a caretaker to be there at night particularly. I don't want people trying to break in to steal the clinic's supplies.'

'That'd be wise if this place is near Eastby End,' Livia said. 'We may have to take things that might get stolen home with us, which I suppose we could do on the tricycles.'

Janie hesitated, then said, 'I think Ted might make a good permanent caretaker, Mr Crossley, the young man who helped Joss deal with the intruder here. And I bet he won't mind sleeping on the floor in one of the bedrooms or even in the clinic at first, because his family are crammed into two rooms at the moment.'

'Who is this Ted? What's his surname?'

'Miller.'

They explained about how Ted had helped Joss and how trustworthy he'd felt, not to mention him being a strong chap and needing work. Walter nodded. 'I think I've met the family. It's good to see that you're getting to know people. But we're getting ahead of ourselves. Do you both have time to come and see this house straight away? If you don't approve of it, I'll have to go on looking, but it really is in a perfect position for our purpose.'

'Happy to.'

They left their tricycles in the hall, locked up the house carefully then got up on the front bench of Mr Crossley's cart.

'I'll spread the word not to come to your home for treatment,' he said as they drove along. 'People will soon get used to using the new clinic if this place is as suitable as I think. And Flora has promised to sort out a basic set of supplies and dressings, and to collect your weekly order for restocking when she collects the things needed for the other clinic. At the moment she's getting some supplies and small pieces of equipment together for you.'

'Mrs Crossley is very efficient,' Livia said.

'She certainly is, gets more work done in a day than any other person does in three days, I often think.'

The two women exchanged quick smiles. His voice had gone softer, as it did whenever he spoke about his wife. It was lovely to see how they felt for one another.

Janie was thoughtful afterwards. She was meeting men who loved their wives and treated them well, something she hadn't had any experience of before Livia saved her.

That seemed wonderful to her. If she ever got married, she hoped it'd be to someone like Mr Crossley.

Only she didn't think she'd dare to get married. She didn't want to risk being tied to any man again, not ever. She shuddered at the mere memory of the last time.

25

Ellis fell asleep easily but at two o'clock in the morning he woke up suddenly, padded along the corridor to use the bathroom and then snuggled down in his comfortable bed.

But sleep eluded him and instead his mind took him for walks round the interior of the house they'd seen yesterday. He'd liked Fairfield House as much in his dream visits as he had done in real life, and remembered it very clearly.

And he still continued thinking about it because it could be such a beautiful place to live! It was in a perfect setting, as far as he was concerned, one with delightful views already waiting to be enjoyed, and a decent-sized garden. He'd been determined to have these features in his new home. You couldn't build views like that, you had to find them. Just as you had to find a house with a big garden.

Thoughts tossed around in his mind like restless waves and as the faint grey light of dawn began to colour the world outside, he looked at his watch and saw that it was half past four. At that precise moment he realised suddenly, but very clearly, that he wanted to live in that particular house and raise his son here in this particular valley, a place which produced people like Logan and Tait, and kids who'd knock a football around gently with a strange lad who had never tried doing that before.

And since he could probably afford to buy it quite easily, there was nothing to prevent him doing so – nothing except his own hesitation. Well, there wouldn't be as long as it was still for sale and at a realistic price.

On that happy thought he fell rapidly asleep again and didn't wake until his son and Logan came into his bedroom at nearly seven o'clock, and Logan shook him gently. That was late for him to get up because he'd always been an inveterate early riser.

'Are you all right, Ellis?'

'Yes. Just had a wakeful night and making up for it a little.'

Logan gave him a wry smile. 'Well, your son will be reassured by that.'

Gil came closer. 'I was worried about you, Father. I didn't like to wake you up earlier. You're usually up first. When I got up, I asked Logan what to do and he said to give you till seven o'clock. That's a whole hour after our usual time. He said we could wake you then and it's five past seven now, and I'm nearly dying of hunger! All I've had is one piece of toast and a drink of milk to put me on.'

He waited, jigging about from one foot to the other, and when Ellis tried to gather his thoughts together, Gil added in a pleading tone, 'If you don't want to get up yet, can Logan please take me down to the hotel dining room and get us both a proper breakfast? I bet he's famished too.'

Ellis laughed and pulled his son towards him for a hug, grinning at his friend over Gil's tousled hair. 'I not only had some wakeful hours in the middle of the night, I took some important decisions.'

'Want to talk about it?'

He was about to say no, because he was so used to keeping his plans and thoughts to himself. Then it occurred to him that Logan would be an excellent person to discuss the idea with and afterwards to help him with modernising the house if everything worked out as he now hoped, no, more than hoped, intended. He had not, he realised, changed his mind in the brighter light of the morning.

So, he brought his idea right out into the open. 'I'm thinking of buying Fairfield House.'

Gil let out such a loud cheer that both men turned to stare at him in surprise.

'It'd be the best ever place to live,' his son said, then paused and gave him a worried glance. 'You did mean it, didn't you, Father? Grown-ups don't always mean what they say.'

He looked so worried now that for some reason it reinforced Ellis's decision. 'I usually mean what I say, son. I wasn't sure you'd be happy about that, but if you're so eager to live there, it's good to know and will help me feel even more sure of my decision.'

Logan was still looking surprised. 'What made you come to that conclusion so soon after seeing it?'

'Something very simple: I liked it – or I liked what it could become. It will need a lot of work doing on it to bring everything up to scratch and modernise it, but I'll probably enjoy making it into something that suits me in every detail. I insist on having modern bathrooms in my new home for a start. Would there be any problem about getting at least two of them fitted? There will be plumbers in the valley who can do that, won't there? And I wouldn't have to wait for too long to get their help with that aspect, would I?'

'Yes, there are good plumbers. And since there's not been a lot of work on fancy bathrooms for big houses, just cheap bathrooms for ordinary people in smaller houses, I think they'll probably jump at the chance to put two fancy bathrooms into the house for you. If you do buy the house, that is.'

'I shall definitely buy it.'

Logan stared at Ellis, studying his face as if he could read his mind. 'You mean it, don't you?'

'Yes, of course I do. I wouldn't say it if I didn't. Will you continue to work for me? I'll pay you weekly and you could help me move to the valley and then take over finding local people to work on the house and supervising them as they do it. How would that be?' He stopped abruptly and it was his turn to look anxious.

Logan beamed at him. 'I'll do that with great pleasure. I can think of nothing I'd like more than to come back to live here permanently. To find work like that into the bargain, work that I'd enjoy and that pays a decent wage, well, that would be marvellous.'

'And you're quite sure I'll be able to find enough skilled tradesmen in other areas to turn it into a beautiful modern home? There will be a lot of things that will need updating or renovating. I want the interior to be thoroughly modern, even though the exterior will still look Georgian.'

'Of course you'll find good tradesmen. And the work you create will help raise the standard of living here in the valley for quite a few families, making the difference between proper eating and scanty meals. It'll mean new jobs in the future too, including the ongoing need for maintenance, not to mention servants will be needed, or at least help in the house, and you and your household will be making regular purchases of food and other items at local shops.'

'I didn't even think of that side of things, but I really like the idea of my coming here helping other people in future as well as pleasing myself. So, how do I find out whether Fairfield House is still for sale?'

'I think it'd be best for you to talk to Mr Crossley. I'm sure he'll be glad to encourage you to move here and help you to do it. And I can chat to one or two friends of mine and ask them about Miss Fairfield and whether she's still wanting to sell.'

'Let's get some breakfast then, but before we start eating it, perhaps you can send a lad with a message to Mr Crossley, to ask if I can go and see him so that I can ask his advice.'

Gil let out a loud, aggrieved sigh at this further delay in getting his breakfast, but it was ignored by the two men and after looking at their expressions he didn't dare protest any more about it to either of them.

Ellis hurried along to the guests' sitting room where there was some notepaper. By the time he had scribbled a message to Mr Crossley, Logan had found a lad hanging about in the street who would be happy to deliver it, especially when he found that he'd be allowed to borrow Ellis's new tricycle to go to the other side of the valley, on condition that he came straight back on it with the answer and drove very carefully.

While they waited for him to return, they all enjoyed a hearty breakfast. In Gil's case, an extremely hearty breakfast.

By the time they'd finished eating, the lad had returned with a message from Mr Crossley saying he and his wife had to come into town that afternoon and could call in at the hotel to see Mr Quinn around one o'clock to chat to him, if that was convenient.

To make arranging this easier for them all, if he didn't receive a reply, he and his wife would simply assume it was convenient and turn up at the time specified.

'Thank goodness for an efficient man!' Ellis muttered and tipped the delighted lad an extra threepence for doing the job so quickly.

The Crossleys arrived at just before one o'clock, by which time Ellis, Logan and Gil (newly washed and with his hair neatly brushed for once) were sitting waiting in the sitting room of their hotel. Gil had been told very firmly indeed that he was to sit near the bay window and keep quiet unless spoken to.

He pulled a face at the thought of this, but after a brief lesson in football from some obliging lads of his own age during their lunch break from school, he was even more eager for his father to buy the house so that they could move to the valley. He vowed to himself that he'd do as he was told if it killed him to keep quiet.

When polite greetings had been exchanged and the Crossleys were comfortably seated, Ellis got to the point. 'I'm interested in buying Fairfield House and settling in the valley. I thought you two might be able to give me more information about the best way to do all this and find out anything else I need to know.'

'You're already sure about settling here?' Walter asked in surprise.

'Oh, yes. I fell in love with the house on sight – and so did my son, and people here have been so kind and helpful that it only adds to my desire to live here.'

Gil opened his mouth to join in and Logan put one finger to his lips so the boy didn't say anything, only nodded vigorous approval.

'Have you been inside the house and looked round?'

'I confess we have – unofficially though. Someone had broken a pane of glass a while ago so we were able to open that window without doing any more damage.'

'Are you quite sure you want to live there? It's very old-fashioned, completely lacking in modern amenities like bathrooms.'

'It could still be made into a lovely home, though,' Mrs Crossley put in.

'Yes, I could see that from the start,' Ellis said. 'I love that period of architecture and I would enjoy bringing the interior of the house up to modern standards while still keeping the same external style. I love the views as well. Only, no one seems quite sure about what the seller is asking for it – or even whether the house is still for sale.'

Flora leaned forward. 'I think I can help you best there, Mr Quinn, because I occasionally visit the owner. Miss Fairfield is very old and needs help getting around, but she is not lacking in any way mentally, believe me.'

'And she's still wanting to sell the house?'

'Yes. But only to the right person. She loves her old home and will only sell it to someone who'll love it too.'

'I can definitely promise to do that. My son and I both fell in love with it when we first saw the outside and we liked it even more when we went inside. It felt right, somehow, as if it was meant to be our home. Do you think she'd consider selling it to me?'

'How about I go and call on her now and ask her? I visit her occasionally when I'm in town and have time to spare.'

'Will you really do that? I'd be most grateful.'

'How much are you offering?'

'I have no idea. Whatever she and you feel to be a fair price, but bearing in mind that I shall have to spend quite a lot of money on renovating it.'

She stood up. 'Her house isn't far from this hotel, so I can walk along to see her straight away.'

'Do you want me to come with you, Flora?' Walter asked.

'No, dear. I think she'll speak more freely if it's just the two of us.'

'Perhaps you'd like to have a drink of tea with me while you're waiting, Mr Crossley,' Ellis suggested.

'That would be very pleasant.'

Ellis walked to the door of the hotel with Mrs Crossley then went back to wait with Logan, Gil and Walter, ordering a tea tray on the way.

As time passed and the remaining tea in the pot grew lukewarm, Ellis saw that Mrs Crossley had been gone for over half an hour, and didn't know whether to feel optimistic or worried about that.

He tried to settle into a discussion about the history of the valley. Its population had apparently once been much bigger but had declined greatly in the decades when mills grew so large that they needed more space to accommodate their buildings, as well as to build terraces of houses for their workers.

They were just finishing a second pot of tea when Mrs Crossley came back. All four people in the room stopped chatting and waited for her to speak.

'Is there any tea left in that pot?' she asked.

'We might just squeeze a cup out and there is a clean cup, but it's probably only lukewarm by now,' Ellis said.

'Doesn't matter. It'll still quench my thirst.'

They waited for her to take a mouthful or two and sigh gratefully.

'And?' her husband prompted as she finished drinking and put the cup down.

She looked across at Ellis. 'Miss Fairfield does indeed wish to sell, but she's adamant that she'll only do so to someone she thinks will look after and love her family home. So I said if the price she's asking didn't deter you, I'd take you and Gil round to meet her shortly, because both you and your son had indeed fallen in love with the house.'

'Goodness, that's quick!'

'She's an astute woman who knows what she wants and doesn't dither about it. Don't think that because she's over eighty she isn't just as shrewd as you are – or as determined.'

On Mrs Crossley's advice, they all went back with her to see Miss Fairfield, including young Gil.

They were received by a very upright old lady who did indeed seem extremely alert and intelligent. She was clearly won over quickly by the obvious love for the house that both Gil and his father displayed, without even realising they were doing it.

After a chat with the lad, she turned back to Ellis. 'Are you prepared to meet my price?'

'Yes, Miss Fairfield. I feel it's a very fair one.'

'Then I'll sell the house to you.'

There was silence and after a couple of moments, he asked gently, 'You're sure?'

'Yes. At my age you don't hesitate when something seems right. I wonder, though . . .'

'Yes?'

'Would you let me come and see it when the renovations are all finished? If I'm still here, that is? I'd love to see how it turns out.'

'I'd be very happy to invite you to tea and show you round, and if you want to come before that, when the work is only partly finished, you'll be very welcome to stroll round and look at what's going on whenever you have the time and feel like doing it.'

'You're a kind young man. I could tell that when I first met you. I'd love to keep an eye on the ongoing changes, if you truly don't mind.'

'I don't mind at all and I'm not just saying that. I'll get my lawyer to contact yours and arrange the details of the sale and the transfer of purchase money from my bank to yours.'

'Excellent.'

She was still very upright but looking a bit tired now, as older people sometimes do by teatime on busy days, so they took their leave.

The Crossleys stopped further along the street and Mrs Crossley said, 'You did well there, Mr Quinn, and treated her kindly. Selling her old home hurts but she knows she can't care for it as it deserves, and anyway, there are no other Fairfields to leave it to now.'

'I'm glad you think I did the right thing.'

'I do. And I'd also like to say that I'm sure you and your son will make a good addition to our valley. Welcome to Ollindale!'

'Thank you. Will Miss Fairfield mind if we go and visit the house again straight away, do you think?'

'I shouldn't think so. Look, I'll nip back and ask her, shall I?'

She came back to join them a few minutes later, smiling and holding out a large, old-fashioned key. 'There you are. No need to climb in through the broken window again. She says to go ahead any time you like and to give the place her love. Would you like us to take you out there in our cart now?'

'Would you mind?'

'Not at all. But you'll have to walk back.'

Logan looked at Ellis tentatively. 'Is it all right if I go and help my mother with that little job now, as we arranged?'

'Of course it is. Gil and I will just be wandering slowly round the house then strolling back to town.'

The Crossleys took Ellis and Gil straight out to the house and stopped under the tree where Tait usually had his lunches to give their pony a rest in the shade, in the same way as he often did.

'All right if we leave the pony here and come inside with you for a quick peek?' Walter asked.

'Fine by me,' Ellis said.

Once again, the house seemed to be smiling at them.

'It always feels very welcoming,' he murmured and turned to the Crossleys. 'Don't tell me it's my imagination. Whatever it is, it feels good.'

'I like it here,' Gil said. 'And it isn't your imagination, Father. I can tell that the house likes us. It has done from the start.' He stared round as if challenging them to contradict this, but no one did.

They all walked round and as they left, Ellis said, 'The minute the sale goes through, we're moving in, even if we have to sleep on the floor.'

Gil let out a loud crow of joy and gave a couple of hops.

Then Ellis stopped. 'Only perhaps we won't need to do that. There's still some furniture left from when Miss Fairfield lived here, isn't there? Would she sell that to me as well, do you think?'

'If you'd be interested in buying it,' Flora said. 'She and I discussed the idea when I spoke to her, but she said to leave it to you whether you wanted it or not, and wait to see whether you broached the idea of buying it.'

'I'd definitely like to buy it, Mrs Crossley. Even if I don't like some of it enough to keep it for ever, it'll be a good help to move in with. How much does she want for it?'

When she told him, he stared. 'Are you sure that's enough?'

'It's what she wants,' Flora told him. 'She says the furniture belongs to the house, not to her nor even to you.'

'That's a lovely thought. I'll take it and please tell her to be sure about the price. If she wants more than that for it, I'll happily pay whatever amount she's comfortable with.'

'She won't want more. I'm quite sure of that.'

'Done deal, then.'

'And she says you can move in as soon as you wish, whether the sale has been legally completed or not. She's already taken away all the things she wants to keep and can't fit any more into her cottage, so you're welcome to anything that's left, like bedding.'

'That's extremely kind of her.'

'She is kind, but it's practical too because it saves her having to pay someone to clear out the house.'

'We'll do that for her, and be grateful for her help generally.'

They smiled at one another, then Ellis thanked the Crossleys for their kindness and said they'd walk back to the hotel later, after which he and his son beamed at one another and went round the house again, this time more slowly, lingering when they wanted to look more carefully at a room.

They decided which bedrooms they'd have and pulled the covers off the piles of old furniture left in various places to see what else they'd be able to use for themselves. They even worked out that the main things they'd need to buy, apart from food supplies, were new flock mattresses for the old-fashioned but elegant bed frames. They would be able to move in quite quickly, because there was bedding in the linen cupboard and crockery in the kitchen, plus all sorts of bits and pieces, like ornaments and even a bookcase full of old books, including one shelf of children's books, which made Gil cry out in delight.

It was getting late now, too late to do much else, but Ellis decided to bring in Logan early the next morning to help him move the big old pieces of furniture around so that they could be used for daily life. He'd bet his friend would know someone who'd like a job as cook-housekeeper and perhaps even a couple of women to do a thorough clean of the whole place.

He stopped and turned round on the way out and beamed at the house. 'Home,' he said quietly.

His son stood close to him and echoed the word, speaking softly for once. 'Yes, a real home. I can't wait to move in.'

There would be so many things he'd enjoy doing here and as they discussed them, Ellis saw that his son was fairly hopping about with excitement and joy as well, which was lovely to see.

26

Livia and Janie enjoyed setting up the small clinic in a simple way, to give them a start, after consultations with Rachel about some practicalities. But they'd noticed that she got tired more quickly these days, so tried not to bother her too often. She was gradually starting to leave more of the work dealing with patients to them.

It made Livia smile seeing her fighting off a desire to sleep, and reminded her of a woman she'd known who fell asleep in the middle of speaking at times towards the end of her pregnancy. That made Janie stare.

Josh winked at them sometimes and took his wife home to rest when he could leave any patients to them for an hour or two. It was lovely to see how careful he was with her.

'You came here just in the nick of time,' he whispered once. 'She does get tired more quickly these days. Flora says some women do when they're expecting.'

They felt the Crossleys must have spread the word about patients not going to see them at home, because to their relief no one had disturbed them there, though one or two turned up at the partly finished clinic.

Towards the end of the first week they paused to have a quick break, drawing the curtains across the front windows and sitting as far out of sight as they could get in the clinic's waiting room to enjoy the pot of tea they'd brewed.

Livia locked the front door and changed the sign inside one of the windowpanes, which took up most of its top half, to CLOSED.

'It won't stop anyone in desperate need of help from hammering on the door for attention,' she said ruefully, 'but maybe people who haven't got an urgent problem will go away and come back tomorrow or go to the other clinic for help so that we can get some rest.'

'I've been talking to a few people and you're right about one thing,' Janie said. 'What we really need is a doctor in this part of town. Mr Crossley said he'd been looking for someone.'

Livia sighed. 'He has been looking and he did hint that he might have found two doctors, but they couldn't start straight away because they had to finish their other jobs.'

'Is either of them a woman?' Janie asked.

'Unfortunately not and when I suggested that we were really going to need a female doctor soon to replace Dr Coxton when she retires, he said he and his wife had tried to find one but hadn't managed it. And even the doctors they had found were coming from America so it would be a while before even they arrived.'

She sighed and stared into space for a few moments, adding, 'He said some members of the council would vote against paying a female doctor anyway, and sadly they had a slight majority, so he and one or two other forward-thinking people would have to pay her salary.'

'Are these councillors really that bad?' Janie asked. 'I'd have thought the younger men on the council would make a difference.'

'There aren't enough of them, so the older ones who don't approve of female doctors are blocking any extra efforts being made to find one. The sad thing is that Mr Crossley says he does have some money to pay a female doctor, but even he can't find one. Such a pity.'

'He and his wife are delightful people, aren't they?'

'Yes.'

When the two women had drunk their tea and cleared up they attended to a couple more patients, then decided that as no one else was waiting they'd done enough for the day.

'I'm really tired now,' Janie admitted, 'and we've still got to ride home. Those tricycles are much better than walking but when you're exhausted, doing anything so active is an effort.'

'You're doing a lot better lately. You're not looking so drawn and you've got a better colour. And you're eating better so you'll soon start to put on a little much-needed weight.'

'I can't remember ever eating so well for day after day, not for years, if ever,' Janie admitted. 'I'm feeling a lot better as well. And it's all thanks to you for giving me this job.'

'It's worth it. You're a good worker, learn new things quickly and get on well with the patients.'

They exchanged smiles, finished clearing up then went out the back way, loading their tricycles for the next morning's work and starting off home.

As they were passing through Eastby End, however, three men moved suddenly out into the middle of the street, barring their way.

'Get off those tricycles and move away from them if you don't want us to throw you off!' one of them yelled.

Both women immediately began screaming for help. At the same time they reached into their baskets for the

coshes Janie had insisted they carry with them for protection. Livia hadn't really thought them necessary but she
was glad of them now. She wasn't going to give in without
a fight, even if she didn't think they had much chance of
driving away three burly men.

'Get off!' one man roared.

By that time he had put his hand on her handlebar,
so she smashed her cosh down on it, taking him by surprise and causing him to swear and let out a yell of pain.

There was another curse as the same thing happened
to the man trying to grab Janie's tricycle. Both attackers jerked back for a moment, seeming surprised to meet
resistance from two females.

The two women continued screaming for help at the
tops of their voices while holding the coshes at the ready
for using again.

'Shut up, damn you!' one of them shouted. 'No one
will come to help you at this hour and we're three against
two.'

In response they both screamed even more loudly.

Walter and Flora heard their first calls from down a
nearby side street and stopped dead for a moment.

'What's going on?'

There was another scream.

'Someone needs help,' Flora said. 'Those are women's
voices. Come on!'

He hesitated, not wanting to put his wife in danger,
but she had already set off running and he had no choice
but to follow her.

Logan and Ellis were further along the street at the
other side of the tricycles and the men threatening them,
with Gil trailing behind them. As soon as they heard the

screaming, they started down the street. When he saw what was happening Ellis shouted, 'Gil, we just passed the police station. Run there as quickly as you can and ask them to come and help us.'

The lad didn't argue but ran off and the two men ran in the other direction, towards the district nurse and her helper. They didn't call out and took the two nearest attackers by surprise.

Logan launched himself at the biggest of the three men, jerking him to one side, and Ellis yanked another man away from his intended victim by the collar of his ragged jacket.

Immediately the two women turned the tables on the third man, who might have been tall but was hardly more than a lad. They knocked him down and held on to his squirming body by the simple expedient of Livia sitting on him and Janie grabbing one of his feet and holding it in the air, even though he tried to kick it away from her.

Logan knocked his assailant over and hit him hard enough to make him dizzy, but Ellis was struggling to deal with the second man when the Crossleys ran out of a side alley and he was glad of Walter's help in keeping hold of his opponent.

Then a policeman erupted from further down the street, followed by another man and trailed at a distance by young Gil, who stayed back, watching open-mouthed.

The furore died down, leaving three sullen men, two of whom were now handcuffed and being guarded by the policeman and the member of the public who'd happened to be passing when Gil arrived shouting for help.

Logan took over from the two women and held the third man's arm behind his back in a position which made it agony to struggle.

'Can you ladies come with us to the police station to make a complaint about this attack?' the policeman asked. 'Then I'll find someone to escort you home safely.'

'We need to bring our tricycles,' Livia said.

'Walter and I will bring those,' Flora said. 'You and the men go with the police. We want those chaps locked away as soon as possible.'

At the police station, the men were formally arrested by the sergeant in charge, who'd been dealing with another customer and been unable to go with his constable to help.

They all watched in great satisfaction as the sullen villains were charged.

'Is anyone injured?' the sergeant asked.

'No,' Logan said. 'Pity some people didn't get hurt, though.' He glared at the men.

'You can lock them in the cells now, constable,' the sergeant said and turned back to the two women. 'I presume they were after your tricycles.'

'Yes. They told us to get off them if we didn't want to be hurt.'

Flora and young Gil came inside just then. 'Walter won't be a minute. He's finding a lad to keep an eye on your tricycles,' she said.

Ellis looked at the two younger women in admiration. 'You did well, fighting back like that.'

Livia was still furious. 'I wasn't handing over my new tricycle to idle thieves like them. It's needed to help us care for our patients.'

'Besides,' Janie said, 'we carry coshes to protect ourselves and that's what we did, fought back. I didn't grow up with anyone to fight for me, so I've had to learn a few tricks to defend myself.'

'Nurses don't usually need to defend themselves, though,' Livia said. 'People usually respect them because of what they do. I didn't know I could fight at all, let alone get this angry.'

'People will hear that you're not soft touches, which will be helpful. And I'll get word out to leave you alone or offenders will answer to me,' Walter said quietly. 'And I think other people will not only help you as what you're doing gets better known, but will turn on anyone else who tries to attack you. Only the lowest types would attack nurses, believe me.'

As they left the police station, Flora said, 'Have you two ladies met Mr Quinn and his son Gil properly? They're newcomers to the valley. And this is Logan James, who's helping him settle here.'

'We'll escort the ladies home,' Logan told the policeman, 'and make very sure they're not attacked again.'

'It'll take a while for you and your work to be known about here so please be particularly careful after dark and don't go out without an escort,' the sergeant said.

'We'll be very careful indeed.' Livia shuddered.

When they'd gone, Flora turned to her husband. 'We need to get those two young nurses better known. How about we take one of the market stalls and introduce them next Friday?'

'Good idea. And let's do it properly, make a big display of it.'

Her eyes sparkled. 'Oh, I shall enjoy arranging that. We'll get the baker to make us a big batch of small biscuits and give them away to people. That always draws attention.'

'And I'll get a big sign done – something like "Meet Ollerthwaite's New Nurses". What do you think?'

'I think we've only just started making changes here. It won't hurt for the local Member of Parliament to be complained to by women from good families. He's not paying enough attention to security. We're hoping to have new doctors coming here as well and we don't want them to face attacks, do we?'

'They won't attack men as they've attacked these women,' Flora said bitterly. 'However, I know the member's wife is getting tired of his poor attitude and so are the wives of a couple of councillors. I'll get them on our side.'

She frowned for a moment then added firmly, 'I'm going to make it one of my next jobs to take an interest in security at night. We need more policemen and if necessary the council must hire them and watchmen as well.'

'Just let me know it there's anything I can do to help.'

'Don't worry. I will.'

When the Crossleys got home, there was even better news waiting for them, a telegram from America had been delivered to the farm saying the valley's two new doctors had settled all their business, were on their way across the Atlantic and would be in contact when they arrived.

'I only wish they could fly like the seagulls do,' Flora fretted. 'Or that we could have found some doctors here in England. It's taking so long to get settled again.'

'At least they're on their way now.'

She sat down next to her husband cradling a cup of cocoa in her hands but kept staring into space rather than sipping it or chatting.

'I'm quite sure from the look on your face that you're fired up for rebellion.' He chuckled. 'I'm glad I'm on your side, my dear, you're a fearsome opponent. And if there's anything I can do to help, you have only to ask.'

'I shall be asking, don't worry. We really do need to find a woman doctor. I think you and I are going to have to pay the salary and costs for that. But what better use for some of our charity money?'

'You really think it'll make that much difference?' he asked, surprised at how emphatic she sounded.

'To some women patients, yes. And to the general understanding of women's problems as well. People take more notice of what doctors say about such things.'

She sighed. 'What a pity we only have more male doctors coming.'

'Better than none. You can't solve all the problems of our town at once, Flora dear.'

'I can try.'

The following market day the huge sign over one of the stalls caused a sensation. The free biscuits were small but highly popular, drawing people to the stall, and best of all many folk were able to meet the new district nurse and her assistant for the first time and would recognise them in future.

Both women were smartly turned out in their uniforms, and the hats with the official badges. This was much commented on by the women of the valley and drew sour glances from those men whom Flora was now speaking about openly as 'the dinosaurs'.

She scolded Evan Tidby and another councillor publicly for leading the voting against most of the recent efforts to modernise their services by the more modern-minded council members. And she made sure she spoke more loudly than usual as she did it so that all the people nearby heard her.

'There's a lot of whispering going on among the women of the valley,' Walter murmured to his wife. 'You've stirred them up nicely lately and today's effort won't hurt.'

'Give me time,' Flora whispered to her husband. 'There will be more than whispering going on; there will be changes made. You'll see.'

'I'm at your service if there's ever anything I can do to stop those fools blocking progress.'

'I'm relying on that.' She winked at him then turned round and stared at one of the men concerned. 'Remember, we're nearly into the twentieth century now, and we treat our women more equally,' she called to him.

He flushed and hurried away.

As he passed them, two or three women nearby, including his own sister, called out agreement with Mrs Crossley, and he flushed an even deeper red.

In fact, rebellion was brewing among quite a few of the women of the valley.

'You're really stirring them up,' Walter said with a chuckle a few days later.

'It's not enough. It's all taking too long.'

27

When the ship docked, Ernest went to visit a relative he hadn't seen for a long time and whose family had sent him a telegram just before he left America to say that Graham was seriously ill.

He arranged to leave their trunks and all but one suitcase each in the luggage office. They'd pick them up the following evening ready for a journey north the day after that.

Then he summoned a cab and asked to be taken to send a telegram to the man he'd been going to visit, saying he'd be late. After that he'd need to catch a local train to his relative's village.

The cab driver looked at them in dismay. 'Didn't you hear?'

'Hear what?'

'There's been a fire further along the line and it's affected one stretch of the telegraph poles, so that the lines to that chap you're wanting to send a telegram to are down. You won't be able to get through to him for a day or two.'

'Oh dear. But my cousin is dying. I must let them know I'm going to see him first.'

'You could write a postcard and I could send a lad to post that for you. It should get there in time to explain why you're late at least.'

So Ernest scribbled a postcard and the cab driver found a lad to buy a stamp and post it for them and sent him rushing off to the nearest post office, after which he took his passengers and their hand luggage to the local train at a nearby terminal.

They arrived at the cousin's house and were swept inside to say a final farewell and the next day went back to resume their journey.

Walter went to meet the train in Ollerthwaite and to his dismay the doctors weren't on it, nor was there any sign of the luggage you'd expect to have been sent from the liner.

Where was Ernest Stanton, not to mention the other doctor they were expecting?

Had they missed the train? But if so, why hadn't they sent a message? That was the trouble with living in a remote valley. You didn't always get information in a timely manner.

Unfortunately people were expecting the new doctors who really needed their services.

A man who'd got off the train hesitated then came across to them. 'Were you expecting someone, Walter lad?'

'Yes, I was. The new doctors.'

'I didn't see any strangers on the train.'

'Oh, dear.' Walter hesitated then waited for the heavy luggage to be brought from the luggage van, but there was nothing belonging to strangers among it.

'Surely they'd not let us down at this late stage?' he said to Flora. 'Or at least not without letting us know.'

'We'll have to meet the relevant train tomorrow and see if they're on it. Perhaps they missed this one. It happens sometimes.'

But there was no sign of strangers the following day either and the mail had been delayed, due to the fire.

By this time word had spread that the new doctors hadn't arrived and people kept stopping Walter and his wife to ask if there was any news.

'I don't know if it's worth meeting another train,' Walter said that evening. 'You should stay at home, Flora, and not waste another day.'

'I'm coming with you. I'll not only be able to keep you company, I may be able to help with something.'

'If there are no doctors, there's nothing to help with. How can this all have gone so wrong?'

The next day they drove into town and were delayed on the way by a young man flagging them down and begging Flora, whom he'd recognised, to come and help his wife, who had started having her baby early.

She looked at Walter. 'I can't refuse to do that. You go and meet that train.'

'Is it worth me bothering?'

'Well, if they have arrived and you're not there to meet them, no one else will know what to do with them.'

'Well, we can't go on meeting trains every day. New ships don't come into port every day, after all.'

'People always say third time lucky,' she said with her usual cheerfulness. 'Try it today, at least.'

'You're more optimistic than I am. I'll call at the farm on the way back to see if the baby has been born and if so, I can take you home again.'

She nodded, but her mind was already on her sudden patient and she didn't wait to see her husband drive away.

* * *

When Walter arrived in Ollerthwaite he was a little late and the train had already arrived.

There was a pile of luggage and two people waiting near it on the platform, a youngish woman and an older man, but not two men who looked like doctors.

He sighed and was about to turn round and walk away when the porter waved at him and called, 'There you are, Mr Crossley! These people are waiting for you.'

He stopped dead and stared in shock then moved towards the two strangers.

'Mr Crossley?' the man said.

'Yes.'

'I'm Dr Stanton and this is my granddaughter, who is another Dr Stanton.'

Walter gaped at the woman. 'You're a doctor as well?'

She gave him a resigned smile. 'Yes.'

The man bristled, seeming angry at his expression. 'You seem surprised, so let me assure you that my niece is as fully qualified as I am.'

Walter held up one hand to stop him. 'No, no! You've got it wrong. I think it's wonderful that she's a doctor, absolutely wonderful.'

'You're sure you don't mind? Because some people don't treat female doctors with the respect they deserve and if she's not going to be fully accepted here, we shall not be staying, believe me.'

Walter beamed at him. 'She'll be more than respected; she'll be welcomed with open arms. We didn't realise that the Alex you wrote about was female, that's all I'm surprised about. The doctor who is about to retire, because of old age, is a woman and has made a good name for herself in a quiet way so your granddaughter will be well received, I'm sure.'

Just then a pony cart came clattering into the station and Flora got down from it and hurried across to join her husband. 'False alarm! Bad case of indigestion. That baby won't be arriving for another couple of weeks, in my opinion.'

She looked questioningly from Walter to the two newcomers and he pulled her forward to join them. 'One of your big dreams has just come true, my dear.'

The newcomers looked at them in puzzlement.

'Let me introduce you to our new doctors – my wife, Flora – meet Doctors Stanton and Stanton.'

She stared at him then at them. 'You're both doctors?'

The man answered rather stiffly. 'Yes, madam.'

'But that's wonderful!' She clasped the woman's hand but that wasn't enough. She pulled the surprised newcomer into a big hug. 'My dear, we really need another woman doctor. You could not be more welcome anywhere in the country.'

The older man relaxed a little. His granddaughter smiled and gave Flora a big hug in return.

'We're putting you up at our farm for the first few days, till you can look at the houses that are available and choose the one you want to live and work in.'

She gave a quick smile and nod to the male doctor and put her arm round his granddaughter's shoulder again. 'Wait till I send out word that you're here! This is the best news we've received in ages.'

'And the nicest welcome I've ever received during the whole time I've been training as a doctor,' she said.

Her grandfather relaxed and smiled at Walter. 'And to think I was worried at how you'd receive a woman doctor, so I deliberately kept it a secret.'

'I won't pretend that every single person will welcome a female doctor. There are a few people who won't be pleased, but only a few. Most of the women will be delighted about it. Now, let's follow the ladies and when we get back, you two can have a restful evening, because it's my guess that as soon as you open your surgery it'll be filled with patients.'

'Well, my Alex is raring to go.' He stopped to gaze round. 'It's a very pretty valley, Mr Crossley. I've been longing for a sight of the moors for months. I wanted to come home to England and spend my final years somewhere like this, like the place I grew up in.'

He couldn't have said anything which pleased his companion more.

In fact there would be a lot of happy people in the valley that evening, Walter thought, especially the women. But he was smiling too as he drove their visitors back to the farm.

This was one of the nicest secrets he'd heard of for a long time and he couldn't wait to tell everyone.

CONTACT ANNA

Anna is always delighted to hear from readers and can be contacted via the Internet.

Anna has her own web page, with details of her books, some behind-the-scenes information that is available nowhere else and the first chapters of her books to try out, as well as a picture gallery.

Anna can be contacted by email at
anna@annajacobs.com

You can also find Anna on Facebook at
www.facebook.com/AnnaJacobsBooks

If you'd like to receive an email newsletter about Anna and her books every month or two, you are cordially invited to join her announcements list. Just email her and ask to be added to the list, or follow the link from her web page.

www.annajacobs.com

An invitation from the publisher

Join us at www.hodder.co.uk, or follow us
on Twitter @hodderbooks to be a part of
our community of people who love the very
best in books and reading.

Whether you want to discover more about a book
or an author, watch trailers and interviews, have the
chance to win early limited editions, or simply browse
our expert readers' selection of the very best books,
we think you'll find what you're looking for.

And if you don't, that's the place to tell us what's missing.

We love what we do, and we'd love you to be a part of it.

www.hodder.co.uk

@hodderbooks

HodderBooks

HodderBooks